ROYAL REBEL

GAIL GERNAT

ANDREA*James*

PUBLISHING

LERA'S SORROW - (Darkliete Book 1)

Lera and her cousin have completed their long childhood and their training as healers. Sent to their grandparents back in Madean, they must negotiate the strange new world, and attain their werwinstans. Fate intervenes in the shape of handsome young Ian, very human and very poisonous to the elven. Trying out her independence for the first time in her life, what will Lera decide? Where will she discover her loyalty to lay, with love or with duty?

ILLERA'S DARKLIETE - (Darkliete Book 2)

When the messengers from Frain arrive to secure the hand of
Princess Illera for their cruel, selfish heir to the throne, Torul,
she hides. Forced by circumstances and her own father, Illera
and her three companions journey to the cold, dark north.
Fighting against her fate, Illera plunges the quartet into danger.
But when she accedes to the demands of cruel destiny they must
fight against a ravening evil that knows no restraint. Using her
mixed blood heritage, can this innocent child learn and mature
fast enough to control both herself and the forces ripping her
world apart? Can she negotiate the political intrigues and defeat
the hordes of Shul, the pirates of Carnuvon and the hatreds
of Frain?

SHIPWRECK

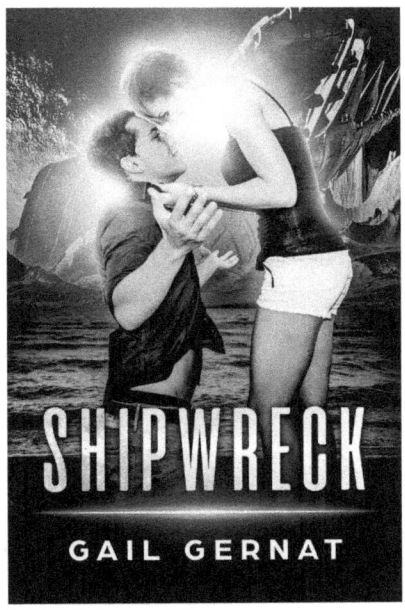

Fiery-haired Bridgit has a temper as hot as her hair, so when the colony transport gets into trouble in deep space she must work with the only other person awake; the man she most despises. Despite their best efforts, the ship crashes on an unknown planet. Bridgit is forced into impossible situations in order to survive and protect the remaining colonists.

Dedication

Dedicated to all brave women who travel uncharted paths to make the world a better place.

Editorial Review

Lady Death will grab your heart and wring it out before giving it back to you. This futuristic look at humanity spread across the galaxy resonates with the same problems we face in the real world today. Ms. Gernat places real characters in the most fantastic situations with incredible tools and abilities but they ring true and genuine and we end up falling in love with them.

-Andrea James Publishing

Prologue

The Melian people owned the planet, but humans had hidden a hermetically sealed dome in the uninhabited hills of the most populous continent. Its round brown shape blended perfectly into the background vegetation of brownish-green and purple.

Inside the sterile white corridors, the ever-present howling of the wind was silent. The chemical reek of disinfectant was pervasive in the tightly sealed space. The gleaming, pristine walls, white rubber floors, and ceiling-to-floor arrays of scientific apparatus defined the life of the sole occupant of this research facility. Doomed by her abilities, young Lady Kirbyson was immured until she completed the task set before her by her professors.

The fourteen-year-old genetic research prodigy sat hunched over her electron microscope. She flipped a switch. The overhead screen displaying the genetic material she was studying displayed swarms of multicolored double helix strands that were unzipping themselves. She smiled a tiny smile of triumph.

Carefully taking a white rat, she passed it through the mini airlock and exposed it to the viral material enclosed behind the partition. Within minutes, the rat started sneezing. In an hour, it was dead.

"Thats the first half," she muttered to herself. "And I have a window of an hour."

She disposed of it in a hermetically sealed biohazard container. Sent to the trash heap for removal from the planet, she expected it to be hurled into the sun, thereby preventing any chance of infection.

The young girl labored on and short weeks later had a second compound. Displaying this on a split screen, she watched the left DNA unzipping itself, and on the right, it was zipping up again.

Again, she exposed a white rat to the first compound. She introduced a small change on a viral vector. Quickly, using waldos, she injected the rodent with the second compound. Three days later, the live rat had turned chocolate brown, without a single white hair in memory of its former self.

Far away, the ever-watching university aristocrats were impressed. Secure in her victory, the young girl slept on a cot in the corner of the lab, as agents of the university snuck into the compound, and rummaged through the trash. They stole the dead, infected rat sealed in its protective container. Removing it, they dropped the hazardous rat in the middle of the largest city on the continent. The slender, fierce, bird-like people who inhabited that continent started sneezing within hours. Within days, the infection spread planet-wide. In a week, all animal life on that world was gone, leaving only tall trees and purple grass waving in the breeze.

The proctors hauled the girl from her sealed research habitat and showed her the desolation. A grieving silence descended on her. Council sentenced her to another project. These strange, furry little people lived in tall trees. They were barely sentient, not even noticing the odd metal mushroom that bloomed on their forest floor overnight. Inside the identical lab on this new planet, young Radhya Kirbyson worked in lonely isolation, mapping the genome of the planetary population. When she could alter the genes at will, the proctors again retrieved her from the science station and showed her a dead world. She spoke not a word.

On the third world, the Chandran home, Radhya refused to work without the presence of her longtime bodyguard, Geo. As her excuse, she used the fact that the Chandrans of the mountains and plains were vicious and warlike, eating their own children with no compunction. The university balked at first, but agreed, for they had no one else to do the work they wanted. These were the last nonhuman species in explored space. She did not plan on being fooled again. Radhya and Geo endured their imprisonment without ever seeing the surface of the world. Pre-programmed remote mechanicals brought her samples. It was the same sterile, bleak white world for Radhya, the same place and routine that she had lived with for the last three years. Not alone this time and with her experience, the work went faster. At the usual conclusion, she was ready. She retrieved certain records and materials, sealing them securely in a pack. The professors never came to bring her out. They firebombed it.

The brown metal and plastic collapsed in seconds. A plume of fire lofted three hundred meters into the sky. She survived the initial blast, but the reek of chemicals and solvents choked and blinded her. The glass partition exploded, and a section of the lab wall pinned her to the melting rubber flooring. The pack of materials blew from her outstretched hand. The hot breath of the flames seared the soles of her feet. Geo crashed through the burning rubble. Using his back, he lifted the beam that was crushing Radhya. She squirmed free. Geo grabbed her arm, pulling her towards the open air. She slipped free, retrieving the pack. They dashed for cooler air.

Panting and gasping, they reached the shores of an ocean. The turquoise waves lapped in quiet cadence against the pebbly golden beach. With the onshore wind blowing the chemical stink away, sparing them from choking on the fumes, Geo fell gasping to one knee. He hadn't been a young man in a very long time. Toppling to the sand, Radhya gazed at the peaceful sea. It was a shocking contrast to the blazing inferno two hundred meters behind them.

"Geo," she stated firmly, "You must get away with this." She handed him the singed pack.

"Milady," he whispered, "I cant leave you. They will kill you."

"You must. If you don't get away and carry out our plan, they'll kill me for sure or maybe even worse!"

"Milady?"

"Enough! Geo, if you love me or care for me, leave now, and as fast as you can!"

Taking a last look at her, he ran swiftly down the sand. Radhya listened to the hollow beat of his footsteps fading into the distance. Tossing pebbles into the water, she listened, waiting, every splash a time mark. Her ears caught a faint, mechanical whisper on the breeze. The electric whine of a hover intensified, growing to an annoying din. Gradually it drowned out the roar of the flames behind her.

Golden sunlight glinted from the silver oval approaching from the opposite direction from which Geo had fled. Radhya smiled her tiny smile, rose and dusted the particles from her hands. The hover swirled to a stop in a cloud of beach sand. It settled to its skirt, the whine of the generators falling in pitch and power.

As the door opened, seven white clad proctors leapt down. Pointing tazers at her, they advanced over the sand. Reaching her, they wrenched her arms behind her back and frog-marched her to the hover. Radhya made no protest.

A week later, in front of the council, she was not so compliant. Standing belligerently before the judges, she drew a breath to speak. The dark wooden walls and high dark rail around the tribunal seemed to suck the oxygen from the windowless room.

"SILENCE!" Boomed the center man.

He was an evil looking oriental, with tiny slanted rat eyes. His narrow face was pinched and pocked, his lips nonexistent. Yet he had a politicians smile. His gaze focused behind where she was standing, on a box, in chains. The small gallery was jammed with people, eager to listen to this sensational case, to see Lady Death. The judge was speaking to the crowd.

"Your crimes have become such as we can no longer pardon them. Your age no longer excuses you from culpability. As is our custom, any freedman or aristocrat caught committing crime is punishable by removal of status, to the point of sentencing you to slavery. I would definitely think that destroying all animal life on three planets should merit the later sentence. However, because you are an aristocrat, or used to be one, should I say, you are entitled to defend yourself, for the record. You may begin."

The judge once again assessed the reaction of the audience. Lifting her oval chin, Radhya looked the middle judge straight in the eye.

"My Lord Judges, if I had indeed destroyed the sentient life of three worlds, I would judge myself worthy of death, not just slavery. However, I can prove beyond any doubt, that certain university aristocrats, who as of this moment I refuse to name, sent men to steal my research. They then used my work to commit these heinous crimes. No one can be held accountable for a use to which his, or her, stolen work is put."

"Oh, poppycock!" Snorted the left-hand judge, a withered desiccated man of considerable years. "Pass sentence and get this farce of a trial over. Some of us have important things to do."

"Excuse me, Judge," Radhya held forth a metal disk. "Here is my proof. If you think to ignore it; I would like you to know that over one hundred copies were sent to high-status aristocrats, including the king and all his plutocracy. Now, you can ignore this, sentence me to slavery, and the king and many others can start inquiries you may not care for, or you can dismiss the charges and give me due compensation for the indignities I have been forced to suffer. Oh, and I want my degree from this esteemed establishment."

The gallery behind her moaned and shifted at her comments. The corpulent right hand judge sat bolt upright, suddenly paying attention to the proceedings. After a whispered consultation between judges, a small boy with blond curls shyly approached her and took the disk from her hand. Bringing it to the judges, he then scampered away. The tribunal kept glancing at Radhya as the message played for their eyes alone. The gallery was absolutely still and silent. The odd person stretched his neck in an attempt to see what was on the personal screen that occupied the judges' attention, but it was impossible.

"Very well," the middle judge croaked, "What do you consider fair compensation?"

His complexion reddened as if he too found the air suddenly lacking in oxygen. The fat judge was gasping like a stranded fish, while the withered judge sunk further into himself, his eyes burning like coals into Radhya's. "As I said, I want my degree, with honors. I have earned that. I also want sole possession of the three dead planets I was accused of killing. If my research destroyed them, it is only fitting that I am responsible for them."

The middle judge opened and closed his mouth several times.

"Of course, this proves the charges are all false. But what of the other copies you have distributed so widely?" Radhya smiled broadly, "Your honors, I have but to give the word and an electronically activated biomaterial will eat, or should I say invalidate any information on them."

"Very well. It is the judgment of this council that Lady Radhya Kirbyson is not guilty of any charges leveled against her. They are dismissed. And in due and fair compensation for any mental or physical suffering, and work stoppage resulting in lost income, and for all her help for the human race in this sector of the galaxy, Lady Kirbyson is granted sole custody of the Chandran planet, the Kartoos planet, and the Melian planet. She is free to rename any she chooses, and any income generated by these planets belongs solely to her." The gavel banged fiercely on the wooden railing. Radhya resolved her determination for the fight ahead.

Chapter One

The white-hot sun hammered down on the most enormous slave market of Jabin's World, itself known as the greatest exporter of slaves in the Commonwealth. It seared the naked flesh of the merchandise like steak being cooked medium rare. Every breath drawn felt like fire scorching their lungs. Their manacled legs quivered and shook with exhaustion. Many pawed the metal dog collars they wore; trying to get relief from the devices that insured their obedience while it barbecued the flesh beneath. Each slave was fearful of the prick of the needle inside the collar that could bring unendurable pain or even death. The moans of the weak and the sick had to be stifled in case they offended a dealer or a passing aristocrat. A slave collapsed. The others edged away, fearful of blame. The tropical sun, however, was still the greatest danger, sucking energy, moisture, life, and color from everything. The once brilliant colors of the vendors pavilions were dusty and their potted plants had become shriveled sticks. A haze of heat, dust, and sweat obscured the distances. Buyers and sellers moved through a miasma of dread and pain in a weird slow motion.

Through the heat shimmer strode a young woman, clothed and hooded in black, her gray eyes roving the merchandise with practiced glance, annoyance visible in every step she took. Since the commonwealth ban on hydrocarbon usage on planets, traveling across the city consumed far too much time. She hurried. She must get to the quarry before the officials could figure out her plan. The gray uniformed slave who followed at her left shoulder had pilots wings and space pilots shooting star tabs on his high-buttoned collar. The sharp peak of a visored cap shadowed his lean face and just visible beneath the hat, gray streaks accented his brown hair.

Stepping around a pile of three corpses, the woman wrinkled her straight, short nose at the stench. The darkness that lived within her threatened to rouse. Muttering inaudible curses under her breath, she paused in front of a faded blue, green and white striped pavilion, one of dozens that lined both sides of the narrow dirt street. The slave at her shoulder stepped forward and lifted the burning hot latch of the wrought iron gate. She proceeded and he shut it behind them. The coolness under the tent was almost shocking. A shiver ran through her body as the dark tried to rear its ugly head. She forced it firmly down while in the distance, a bell tinkled to announce the presence of customers. The proprietor waddled over.

"Seellia," the woman called commandingly to a fat black man with a huge handlebar moustache.

Gravy stains marred the front of his blue, green and white-stripped robe. He moved quickly toward her with startling suddenness for one so large. The whites of his eyes became very prominent as he recognized his customer.

"M-m-m-m-milady," he croaked, how may this humble slave dealer serve you?

"Seellia," she replied, you know me. "My requirements are just small and I am easily pleased."

Seellia shivered in the heat and his eyes grew more terrified still.

"All I require this time are four male slaves and two female ones, and possibly a boy for training by me. Now, I need an accountant. That shouldn't be too hard. They are always caught for fraud or double books or something. I also want someone with either engineering or construction skills. That might be rather hard, but I would even be willing to accept a final year student. The same with a physician. I know they are rare, so a final year student will be just fine. Then, I also want a gardener or landscape architect. The females will be easier. I want a cook or a chef. She must be able to do gourmet fare. Lastly, I want a housekeeper. She must be well trained, clean, and young. A born slave would be fine for that position."

Seellia licked his lips greedily. "Milady, sit down in my chair. May my body servant bring you cool water or fresh fruit? We received a shipment just this morning from the offshore islands. The porple fruit is very nice this season."

The woman shook her head as she seated herself in the slave traders grubby, wicker chair.

"Now, when do you think you can get the merchandise for me?"

"I cant give you an exact time milady, perhaps one day, perhaps seven. The market is large and so am I. If I don't have what you require in my own stock, it will take some legwork on my part. Some items you request are rare. I know that in my own stock, I have an accountant, who although not young, is very qualified. He has a wife who ran a catering business. She served even the royalty of Galatia. They have a ten-year-old boy. I know you, milady, you like complete families if possible. So uncharacteristically charitable of you. Let me fetch them and you can see if you like them."

At the woman's nod, he lumbered out into the sweating ranks of human flesh standing row behind row, until vision failed in the distance.

The lady rose and followed Seellia. Her bodyguard followed her, grimacing at the bitter sight and sour smell of people offered for sale. Short steps from the tent, the woman stopped at a row of men. Seven of the men were not yet as burnt or severely blistered as most of the slaves around them. Fresh red bands of numbers, still swollen and not yet hardened into scar tissue marked this group. She checked the numbers on the arms of three of them against a list in her wrist comp. As the numbers were a match, she glanced at the bodyguard and nodded.

The first one she indicated was second in line. Over two meters tall, with raven black hair, he was very handsome in the aristocratic sense of the word. Dark blue eyes fringed with exceptionally long lashes glared at her from the perfect oval face of the royals and a soft, almost feminine mouth. The nose, however, made him very male, a strong, arched, narrow beak of a nose that dominated all his other features. Wide shoulders and strong bone development indicated that he had benefited from good nutrition during his childhood. Long legged and well muscled for one who was so thin, with a curling mat of dark hair covering his chest, he was slightly darker than the others around him were, but still beginning to burn, especially around the obedience collar he wore. Unslave like, he met her eyes with a belligerent stare and his body language was anything but humble.

Number three was also on her list. Suffering the most of any in his line because he was very fair skinned, with blonde hair and light blue eyes with a downward slant; she could see the beginning of serious blistering on his narrow back. He was two meters tall, slender, with long legs, long thin fingers and toes. His face however, was round and childish looking. He had a short up-turned nose, and full pouty lips. He carefully kept his eyes on the ground, sneaking a brief glance when he thought she wasn't looking.

Number five in the line of seven was her third target. Around the same height, as starved as he was, he was burly looking. Very broad in the shoulder and narrow at the hips he looked as though he should be a wrestler. In a square-jawed face, his huge eyes were a velvety golden brown, fringed with even longer lashes than the first mans were. His nose was long, straight and masculine and the lips were thin, but well shaped. Dimples indented both cheeks, even though he was not smiling. An abundance of brown hair covered his head and most parts of his body. He gazed at her, trying to see her face under the hood. It was a look that implored.

In common, all three looked starved. With ribs and spines were prominent, they all had hollowed cheeks with dark circles under their eyes. The Lady steeled herself against a black tide of emotions as she inspected them.

"Seellia," she called.

The slave master halted. "Milady, you should not be in the slave pickets. Please, I implore you, return to the pavilion."

"Seellia," she replied impatiently ignoring him, "Are these not exactly what I require?"

She pointed to the three men. Seellia blustered about consulting his wrist comp. "I don't know. This is a new ship-ment. I just received it this morning. It is not yet approaching noon. I have had no time to process them. They are fresh from training school. Can't you smell the disinfectant on them?"

"I can indeed," she replied. Turning to the pilot she snapped, "Are those not the correct numbers, Rory?"

"Yes, milady." These three are the ones you want.

"I've done my homework, Seellia. I have no patience that you haven't done yours."

The three men stared at the numbers branded into their upper arms.

"Seellia, fetch your accountant and chef, but unchain these for Rory. I will check them out at your pavilion."

"This is my own merchandise. What if they bolt milady…"

She turned a gray, steel-eyed stare on him. Seellia faded to an ashy gray color.

"Yes, milady. At once, I will fetch the others."

Seellia unchained the three she wanted, and handed a tazer prod to Rory.

"I could use the collar," he explained beseechingly, "But that leaves them useless for days afterward."

He shambled off between the slave pickets as the woman strode back under the shade of the pavilion and seated herself in the owners chair. She tossed back her hood and for the first time her face was fully revealed.

It was the perfect oval shape of the aristocrat; small, full of confidence and intelligence, but with a shadow of sorrow about the mouth and eyes. Her skin was perfect, pale porcelain, lips slender, rosy and well shaped. She had very large eyes, gray with dark rings about the irises and the midnight lashes brushed her cheekbones when she blinked her eyes. Her nose was small and straight. Her raven black hair spun indigo and violet highlights, even in the shade of the pavilion. It fell bluntly to her collarbone. Although reaching only to the slaves armpits, she carried an aura of power about her. The bulky robes she wore revealed nothing of the body beneath. At first sight, slave number two gasped and pulled back. She smiled a tiny smile, a mere quirk of the outside of the lips.

"Do you know me?" she asked the man with the sun-bleached hair.

"No milady, I thought you were someone else." he replied staring desperately at the floor.

"Who did you think I was?"

"I prefer not to answer, milady."

"You are a slave, and I prefer to know who you thought I was. Am I clear?"

"Yes maam." He hesitated, clearing his throat. "I thought you were the royal they call Lady Death."

A wide smile of pure delight spread across the woman's face. The slave hung his head, shivering. The other two looked alarmed.

"Look at me!" she commanded. "Do you have a name?"

"We have no more names, milady, only numbers," he replied extending his branded left arm.

"I am not good with numbers. Tell me your name before you were a number. Just a first name will do."

His voice trembled as he replied, "William."

"Very well, I shall call you Willy or Will. If you prefer I could use Billy."

"Will would be fine."

"Will, do you know why I am called Lady Death?"

"Because you wiped all animal life off three worlds, two of which had sentient beings."

"That is correct, except all three worlds had sentients on them. A fine lesson to keep always on my good side. I am now restoring the third world. The other two are once again thriving ecosystems, which I own, of course, but good living worlds nonetheless. I am repairing the third. Therefore, you see, I correct my mistakes."

"But what about the people that died?" he questioned, greatly daring.

She frowned, the great black tide tugging at her mind and replied, "Two were extremely warlike. I saved their genetic material and can recreate them, without the warlike tendencies. They will work for me one day. However, I want to talk about your medical training. How far did you go before they took you for unpaid bills?"

Will answered Lady Death and the interview continued. Then she interviewed the engineer with the beautiful eyes and the aristocratic looking black-haired gardener. Seellia came puffing up just as she had finished.

"Consider these three sold Seellia."

"But I haven't even put them up for auction yet; maybe I can get more for them."

"Seellia, do I have to sneeze on you?" she asked in a voice like the steel in her eyes. "Besides, when did I ever cheat you?"

Seellia dropped to his knees. "No, no milady. Just as you say, just as you say. Take them as a gift. Just please don't do that to me."

"Thank you Seellia, I accept your generous gift. I trust you will pad the bill for the others sufficiently that you wont go out of business. Now I want clothes for them. They are scorched enough. Find clothes for all I am buying as well. Moreover, the clothing had better be free too. I will interview these two."

Lady Death turned her attention to the three Seellia had brought her. The man looked to be in his fifties, small and shrunken and so thin every joint was a lump joining twigs. The woman was taller than he was by a little, in her middle thirties, brown-haired and dried up. Her breasts sagged like empty plastic sacks, matching the bags under her hazel eyes. Her mouth was determined and somehow proud. Behind her was an emaciated boy, thinner even than his father was. He looked hardly able to stand.

The lady asked a few perfunctory questions which the couple answered. She knew it didn't matter what the answers were, she was going to buy them. She knew that the minute she saw the child.

Damn Seellia, she thought as she asked the woman, "Is this your only child?"

"It is now milady. I had a daughter, five years old when we were arrested; two years ago now. They raped and murdered her before our eyes. Even serving you, Lady Death, is preferable to watching my son starve to death. Please, I beg you, buy us from this hellhole!"

The woman had fallen to her bony knees and her face was in the dirt. The man had his hand on her arm to restrain her.

"Your name is Kaarl and your wife's name is Aninya and I'll call your son Dani. I don't like to use numbers for my slaves, even if it is the custom."

Aninya burst into tears, a downpour of relief and hope.

Seellia came puffing up with some ragged canvas shorts and

six much abused tee shirts, so old that their colors were obscure. At Lady Deaths nod, he tossed them at the slaves.

"This family will be adequate Seellia. How about the housekeeper?"

Seellia jerked his head and his body servant prodded three young women into the pavilion. One, a redhead, was so blistered that her back was nothing but suppurating flesh, crawling with maggots. The smell of rotting flesh was worse than the slaughter yard. Flies buzzed around them.

"Oh, Seellia, how dare you!" whispered the Lady. "You presume on my mercy and compassion to buy your ruined merchandise. I don't want your sick and enfeebled. Give me the bill of sale for these six. You will get no more from me today."

Hurriedly jostling the three girls out, Seellia implored favor, but to no avail. The Lady transferred the funds, took the receipts and collar codes in hard copy, and stormed from the tent chased by the past. Rory followed with the prod aimed at the new slaves.

Lady Death rushed down the aisles and left the slave markets swiftly behind. She needed desperately to put the sight, sounds, and smells of the foul place behind her.

Milady, you should not go so fast in this heat. Your cloak will be unable to compensate. Nor can these slaves, in their weakened condition keep up with you! called the uniformed slave.

She slowed and allowed her slaves to catch up to her.

"Thank you Rory," the Lady said looking closely at her purchases. "I had to get out of there. Those girls... she gagged, but I think these are in need of feeding. Noon is approaching rapidly as well."

Slave market at her back, she led her entourage into the labyrinth of the city. Streets twisted away on every side, enclosed by two and three story buildings, usually adobe, but a few of the more well to do could afford brick. Not a blade of grass or tree existed anywhere in the city's poor section. Piles of steaming dung were scattered up and down the streets, left by the altered dromedaries, used as beasts of burden on the planet. Slaves pulled masters in rickshaws at their best speed in the heat, while the freedmen and slaves bustled through every open space. The bawling of the animals and clang of the bicycles as the freedmen traveled on their business made talking nearly impossible.

She turned aside to an inn that catered to both owners and slaves. Stopping just inside the door, the slaves behind her surreptitiously wiped the sweat from their brows. The inn was immaculately clean and tidy, with wholesome odors of cooking food that were mouth-watering. She could smell savory soup and a roast of some sort as well as baking bread. The babble of voices and the clink of silverware ceased as the patrons turned to stare at her. She flipped back her hood, smiling at the looks of fear on the faces of the freedmen who were dining on the main floor. A fat innkeeper came bustling up to her, wiping his hands on his spotless apron.

"Let me escort you to the royals section milady," the innkeeper murmured anxiously.

"First, I wish to arrange for my slaves, six, and a boy as you see. I want good soup; I doubt their stomachs will take anything heavy. No gruel. Rory, you check it out before I pay for it. I want many vegetables and plenty of meat in it. One bowl for each and a heel of fresh bread. Then fresh milk, one glass each, two for the child."

The eyes of the slaves, except Rory, widened at her generous order. It was more than any of them had eaten at one meal since their enslavement. Aninya began to cry again. The innkeeper nodded and gestured to a serving girl to take the slaves to the back, but Rory hesitated.

"Milady, you'll have no bodyguard." He glanced meaningfully around the room.

She regarded him mildly, and then sighed.

"You're right, but I want them all to be fed and I want you to oversee so they don't get cheated."

The black-haired man spoke up in a cultured voice, "I can wait until the others have finished."

"What either great courage or great foolishness you have," replied the Lady. "Rory has privileges that others do not enjoy."

Her eyes glinted in warning and the man bowed low in apology.

"Nevertheless," she continued, "it is a good idea. Rory, see them started while he comes with me. Then trade places with him."

"Yes, milady."

Rory and the other slaves followed the serving girl, while Lady Death and her temporary bodyguard followed the innkeeper to the stairs. Up two flights to a windowed chamber looking over the city, the tables nestled beside cool sparking fountains, divided from each other by walls of flowering greenery. She sat down beside a vigorously blooming clematis vine. The snow-white blossoms contrasted beautifully with the black marble table at which she sat.

Sighing, she stared across the city, not seeing the dingy squalor, fighting once again against the darkness that threatened to claim her mind. Silence descended on the city gradually as the inhabitants began siesta. The white-hot sky intensified until all vision was lost in the glare, the pale buildings in the distance fading into the shimmer.

The innkeeper coughed slightly. With a start, she returned her focus.

"I'll have a green salad and some of your famous wine," the Lady said without ever looking at the menu.

Bowing the innkeeper scurried off.

"Your name?" the Lady requested of the new bodyguard, her eyes still fixed on the city.

"My name was Padr. And I was once one of the aristocracy,

as you are. I lost my life, my real life, for fighting against slavery. All the conditioning in the galaxy isn't going to turn me into a slave!"

Lady Death looked at him, one eyebrow raised.

"I know, she said quietly. Thats why I had to buy you today. Any other master would kill you immediately, put you to the blood sports or torture you to death. So just for me, will you try to pretend that the conditioning worked, for now? I can only cover for you so much. Okay?"

Padr swallowed and looked at this woman who had been represented as the epitome of evil. He slowly inclined his head.

Just then, following the innkeeper, Rory appeared, anxiety clearly wrinkled across his features. He hurried to the Lady's side. Padr followed the innkeepers steps back down to the stuffy slaves section.

"We might have trouble with that one. Keep an eye on him especially, Rory."

"Yes, milady," replied Rory, taking his stand behind her chair.

When all had eaten, after the slight fading of the noons glare, Lady Death took them through a series of narrow alley-ways to a tailor. It was a shabby adobe building two stories tall. The faded lettering on the front door had at one time been red, and it creaked complainingly as Rory opened it.

Inside were two large worktables, strewn with different fabrics in a rainbow of colors. The two sidewalls had shelving from floor to ceiling, all jammed untidily with bolts of fabrics and boxes of notions. Through the heavy red velvet curtain at the rear came a three-meter tall, skeletally thin man with golden brown skin pleated over his bones. His face was wreathed in smiles, showing his toothless gums, as he greeted her effusively.

"So, Jemediah, here I am again, to stave off bankruptcy from your door."

"Oh, milady, milady Kirbyson, you are too late, he proclaimed mournfully. Just this last month I had to sell my oldest daughter, Jemelina, to the creditors. She will just now be returning from training."

Lady Death looked at him with horror. "Oh Jemediah! How could you?"

"Milady, you well know how prolific my wife is. Eight, eight children in fifteen years! They cost so much to feed and clothe and educate. And my business isn't much anymore. The aristocracy mostly goes to Kemmira's World for clothes anymore, or their slaves wear whatever the stores carry. There is no pride in a slaves appearance anymore. So few are like you who care about fit and quality, especially on their slaves."

Lady Death looked at him with sorrow. "Yes, Jemediah, I see. I will do what I can. Rory, find which dealer has Jemelina, if she is here and available, buy her."

Rory at once got busy on his wrist comp as Lady Death conducted her business with Jemediah.

"Each one is to have a dress uniform in my new house colors. Each of them is to have two sets of work clothes and these three are to have bodyguards clothes as well." She indicated the three younger men.

Rory lifted his hand and nodded at her.

"I will return in one hour for the slaves, when will the uniforms be ready?" she asked.

"Two days milady," the proprietor replied.

Lady Death swept from the room with Rory her faithful tail.

"Lady Death has a name?" inquired Padr.

"Yes, indeed," replied Jemediah, "the Kirbysons have been coming to my family for clothing for over fifty years. I remember Lady Kirbyson as a plump little girl, climbing over my shelves, into everything, always asking questions that one. That family has kept me in business all this time, he answered as he measured an arm."

"But what is her name?" Padr persisted. "What is Lady Deaths full name?"

"Radhya, Radhya Kirbyson. Lady Death is only what they call her to make her feel bad," was the tailors reply.

Outside the tailor shop, a hot wind blew up, flapping the hood around Radhya's face and obscuring her vision. The stench of the dirty clay street offended her.

She turned to Rory and asked, "were you able to locate her?"

"Milady," Rory answered, "she is set for dawn auction, at Gullentras, a quarter of the way around the world. It begins in thirty minutes. Theres no way one of us could make it on time."

"Contact Zantis, the Greek. Ask him to be my agent in this specific purchase. I authorize ten minas for his fee and a further one mina for every one hundred he saves me from the average price of female slaves at the auction. This should provide an interesting diversion for them, don't you think. Go."

Rory nodded and slipped to the vrphone on the corner. Rory entered the coffin-sized space constructed of transparent beige plastic, and inside the narrow aperture took the copper helmet attached to the booth by a wrist thick cord from a peg which was supporting it. Slipping the metal helmet over his head, he made the call. Minutes later, returning the helmet to its peg, he wriggled out of the narrow opening in the front.

"He will do his best, and if he doesn't cheat your planets from under you, his best is very good," Rory said nodding.

"Thank you, Rory. It is a good thing I turned down the housekeeper at Seellias. The royals would have been suspicious of such mercy, anyway. This insistence on such an unusual housekeeper will hopefully give them a red herring to chase. I will pass it off as acquiring a slave of whom I know the reputation. We have to be very careful right now."

"Yes, milady, you must be more cautious than a cat. You are our last hope now Lord Kent is gone."

"Well, not entirely gone," smiled Lady Kirbyson.

In an hour, Radhya returned for her slaves. After a short

walk through the dusty streets, she took Will, Padr, and the other slave called Max, into a seven story, steel, windowless building. Rory waited in the streets with the other three. He was pacing in circles with the sweat trickling in rivulets down his back, dripping off his cheekbones and running into his eyes.

Radhya and her trio entered as far as the black metal bars at the end of the entry.

Name and rank? demanded an invisible source.

"Radhya Kirbyson, owner of Radhya's World, owner of Kirbyson's World, owner of Pleasant, co-owner of Petra's World, co-owner of Stephan's World, co-owner of Sparky's World and member of the aristocracy status number 676. I have three male slaves for bodyguard training," she spoke.

The bars sank into the floor. A very slender, short man with silver hair and liquid brown eyes stepped around the corner. His enormously curved drooping nose ruined his otherwise handsome oval face. The lips were thin and pulled down at the corners and he had a large chin for a royal with a circular dimple in the middle. He was dressed in red from head to toe, a body-hugging uniform, complete with high red boots. His wrist comp was a large size and he carried a whip in his right hand.

"Well, well, my little Radhya. Finally, taking my advice and getting yourself some protection?"

He lifted her chin with his whip.

"You especially cant be too careful. Many people are afraid of you, and thats always dangerous."

"Indeed, my Lord Barone. I haven't been able to get our last conversation from my mind. So, I had to buy some more men in order to still your voice warning me of danger."

"Good. But why these three?" Lord Barone asked inspecting the slaves. The men stared at the dull metal floor, shuffling their feet uneasily.

"They are all tall, and don't appear to have suffered too much starvation. They should bulk up well in your machines.

Moreover, see, I chose those two on the width of the shoulders as you told me to."

Barone nodded looking pleased. "I see you were listening to me after all. I didn't think you were at the time. Super deluxe training course?"

"If thats your recommendation, milord."

"It is. Too many of us skimp on that now. They take just the basic. Even the deluxe course isn't as effective as the super deluxe. All my own guards have it. However, it's three weeks instead of two. Any objections? he asked watching her closely."

"Not at all milord. I have brief business on Kentucky. Then I will return for them before I go home." Lady Kirbyson replied.

"Good."

Lord Barone escorted his customers through a maze of metal corridors to a series of cubicles the size of coffins. There each man stripped and was hooked to the machine, their bodies entirely obscured by wires.

Catheters were inserted and an I.V. line put into their arms as a form-fitting metal helmet covered each face in turn and they were pushed backwards into their sarcophagus. A metal door descended and the training was begun.

"Now I just have to get your holographic image for the indoctrination sequence."

"I want a three week auto-destruct on that sequence. You'll not be selling my image to my enemies so they can zero in on me," Radhya said.

"Very good," replied Lord Noel Barone. You have been learning, haven't you? What about a little fun sequence, just you and me?" he asked as he slipped his hand suggestively beneath her arm, caressing her breast on the way.

Radhya stopped dead. "Noel, I do business with you, business, not *fun*. I don't appreciate your proposition."

He removed his unwelcome hand.

He said stiffly, "I warn you Radhya; people are talking about you. If you want the distaff side thats fine, but when you want neither, people talk, and people don't like different. I try and I try to be your friend, but if you keep rejecting me, you are making trouble for yourself. Jabin himself mentioned you to me the other day."

Blood running icy cold, Radhya said in a conciliatory tone of voice, "Noel, I appreciated your friendship, I really do, but I cant concentrate on relationships, even just for sex, right now. Once I finish building my worlds, then I'll be able to think of other things. Then Im going to retire, have fun, have a family. Why do you think I called my last world Pleasant? But for now, all I can think of is my work."

"Just my luck to be attracted to a workaholic," muttered Lord Barone. "Okay, lets get this over."

Safely back on the street, Radhya looked at Rory.

"That man gets oilier and sleazier every time I meet him. I feel unclean. Did Zantis procure Jemelina?"

Rory nodded.

She continued, "They are there for three weeks so well go to Kentucky and get our stock and pick the men up on the way home. First though, well get Jemelina."

Radhya shuddered at the thought of re-entering the training building in three weeks.

Steam was drifting slowly from the body of the dual ship *Arrow*, making lazy patterns in the air. The sleek double delta-winged spacecraft settled like a crouching tiger between the larger ships in the spaceport. Descending the metal stair, Radhya, Rory at her left shoulder, hurried across the steaming asphalt of the spaceport.

Turning right, they passed the tall metal gates into the city of Gullentra. She shook her head in weariness. Rory unobtrusively touched her elbow. She shook her head again.

Zantis, a very tall robust man with a full dark beard, strode forward out of the mist leading two naked, terrified slaves by chains attached to the collars around their necks. The girl was seventeen, slender but with a stunning figure. She had waist-length auburn hair; cornflower blue eyes and full red lips. Her oval face was dismayed and she appeared totally stunned and disoriented. Behind her followed a bulky man, very big, close to two and a half meters tall. With his brown hair, skin and eyes he was as repulsively ugly as the girl was beautiful. His nose had obviously been broken several times and never properly set. One ear was a ruined mess on the side of his head, and his face was asymmetrical with an odd shape, rounded on one side and flat on the other. He stared at the ground in proper slave fashion.

Radhya looked questioningly at Zantis, the slave trader.

"I am sorry, milady. Corvo was selling them only as a pair. There was no way I could purchase the girl without her husband. I did save you five hundred minas off the average price for husband and wife couples, mostly because of his ugliness."

Radhya sighed. "Well done Zantis. You have earned your bonus. I guess I can always use another bodyguard."

Rory escorted the Lady and two new purchases through the spaceport gates and back to the Arrow.

"Back to Jabin's city Rory, please."

Night had fallen as Radhya, Rory, and the new slave, Dave, approached the tall steel building for the second time that day. Once again, she entered and faced the bars. This time Lord Barone appeared instantly.

"What is this? Two visits in one day. You must have reconsidered my offer," he muttered, a smarmy smile plastered his face.

"Lord Barone I have another candidate for your excellent training. It seems Zantis, the Greek, double-crossed me to double his fee, the snake. I ordered this girl as a housekeeper. I knew her from before as a hard working, trustworthy creature. When I showed up to get her, why, here is this hulk with her.

Oh, they were selling them as husband and wife. Now Im stuck with this. Can you do anything with it?"

Lord Barone looked at the huge young man with narrowed eyes.

"Yes, Ill train him up the same as the others. You can go. I already have your image."

"Thank you milord Barone," said Radhya bowing low.

Chapter Two

Three weeks later, Lady Radhya Kirbyson and Rory stood again outside the recessed entrance to the Bodyguard Training Center. Arms weighted with four large bundles, he moved briskly along behind Radhya. This early in the morning, no other aristocrats were out, just a few freedmen hurrying to their employment. She hesitated, drawing deep calming breaths, forcing down the tide of fear that rose at the thought of entrapment in the training facility. A dromedary bawled behind them, and Radhya jumped. "Milady, we must do this quickly. Seellia's lot went to the auction an hour ago. When certain aristocrats check the manifests..." Rory trailed off apprehensively.

He uneasily shifted the bundles he carried. The Lady nodded and strode swiftly up to the barred gates, the soft crunch of her boots changing to clanging steps on the metal. As the sound changed, her chin rose haughtily, and her stance became more arrogant.

"Name and rank," the gate demanded.

"Radhya Kirbyson, owner of Radhya's World, owner of Kirbyson's World, owner of Pleasant, co-owner of Petra's

World, co-owner of Stephan's World, co-owner of Sparky's World and member of the aristocracy status number 676."

The stunners following her progress retracted, and the bars sank into the floor with a soft ring.

"You are an hour early," anxious, my pet? inquired Lord Barone stepping around the corner.

"Only for a glimpse of you milord," replied Radhya sarcastically bowing just her head. Laughing, Noel escorted them into the bowels of the building.

Barone said, "Well, I guess they will regain balance on the walk to the star-port. I am especially pleased at how well this last group turned out. I hear around about that you are investing in my favorite, well, second favorite sport."

"Indeed, milord," smiled Radhya enthusiastically; "I picked up three whose breeding I commissioned and twelve broodmares. I also bought two stallions. They are not outstanding racers, but as studs, I think they will outshine even Coryov's stable. My track on Pleasant will be done by now, and I plan the opening race for about six months time. It is my hope you will enter. I hear good things about your racers."

Barone beamed, "My dear Lady Death, you sound almost human. I was hoping to receive an invitation."

"Absolutely, you are first on my invitation list. I can't wait to beat you."

Radhya grinned up at him as they walked the narrow hallways, steps ringing loudly on the metal floor.

Lord Barone stopped before a large door and swished his hand before the glowing yellow plate. The door whooshed aside revealing a room the size of a gymnasium and all white; walls and floor well padded. Fifteen naked men shook and stumbled their way around the room. The reek of the disinfectant made Radhya take a step backward, wrinkling her nose. The staggering slaves muted their grunts and curses as they took note of the open door. Some tried to come to attention, but were simply not yet capable of standing up straight.

"Nice looking batch, this last one. Excellent muscular development don't you think?" Noel inquired of her.

"If you say so, milord," Radhya replied evenly.

"Don't tell me you don't even enjoy looking?" smirked Noel with an evil grin.

"Only at you," replied Radhya so sarcastically that Lord Barone laughed aloud. "Touché!" he said.

Privately Radhya was amazed at the transformation wrought on the bodies of her slaves. They looked sleek, fit and well muscled. If the training were as good as the physical result, the high price would almost be worth it. Rory glanced at the Lady, anxiously signalling her with a look of alarm.

"Pass them their uniforms," she commanded snapping her fingers.

As Rory wove his way through the clumsy mob, he passed uniforms to her four new guards, assisting each into his clothing. As bodyguards, they had heatproof, chemical proof, knife and bullet resistant cloth engineered to protect them from every conceivable danger so they could protect their mistress. Rory hurried.

Barone sneered, Most unusual. Most customers take the slaves home naked, and then dress them, if they wish to bother. "Does a naked male upset you so much then?"

"No, not at all," Radhya replied in a cool voice. "I have my dignity to consider, and to me, it lacks dignity to have four naked men trotting behind me, whereas in uniforms they make me appear important and perhaps slightly superior to the other aristocrats with naked slaves. Have you ever known the king, for example, to have naked slaves around him? It's an etiquette situation with me, like matching dishes and silverware at a banquet."

Noel looked at her thoughtfully; "I have never known you to short etiquette."

Radhya bowed her head. "I trust the necessary debits have been made?"

"Of course. Even for you, I give nothing free."

Rory herded the four stumbling men to the door where Radhya was waiting. As she stepped out, Lord Barone restrained her. Dave and Will tumbled to the floor with startled cries.

"Whats this?" he asked eyeing the men.

"What do you mean?" asked Radhya raising her voice for a battle.

"You've changed your house colors," he said pointing to the men.

"I was sick of gray and black which were, after all, my father's house colors. The forest green and royal purple are very distinguished, and they are duly registered. It is my right to choose colors for myself. I trust you'll not hold me up further. I have important stock to get home and settle."

Noel released her arm, and Radhya swept frostily from the door. The four slaves staggered after her, Rory bringing up the rear, assisting the lurchers. She moved out of the building and down the hot dirty street on as direct a route to the spaceport as was possible. Moving as fast as they could without drawing more attention from the bustling crowds than they had to, with four large men having trouble with their coordination and balance, she threaded her way through the jammed streets to the spaceport. The bicycle traffic was especially heavy right now, and Rory leapt aside from by a rickshaw carrying a screaming royal. Padr, Will, Max, and Dave rapidly regained use of their limbs as they went along; Rory pushing them from behind to keep up.

The instant they were through the gates of the spaceport and around the corner from the tall control tower, Radhya broke into a swift sprint. The men reeled after her. She whispered into her wrist comp as she ran. Ahead, the Arrow lowered its companionway as the navigation lights and engines came to life. She dashed up the metal stairs, her feet clanging loudly. She spun left into the phosphorescent lit cockpit with dials and gauges surrounding them on three sides. A slight young man sat in the farther of the two gimballed chairs that filled the area.

"Stane," Radhya gasped, "clearance from the tower?"

"Five minutes go, a ten-minute window," the auxiliary pilot replied.

Behind her, Rory darted in and threw himself into his seat. As Lady Kirbyson left the cockpit, Kaarl came up. She squeezed past him and headed down the twelve meters to the hatch. Through it was the warm tan passenger compartment with its six rows of seats, each with three caramel colored reclining chairs. The smooth walls curved up and formed a convex ceiling over their heads. A slight gap between walls and hatch indicated a gimballed floor. A large, presently blank screen faced the seats, intercom grills above and below. To the rear, a black door in the middle of the wall led to Radhya's small cabin while the other led to the hold below and the one on the right to the head.

"You should be buckled in for liftoff," Radhya frowned at her accountant.

"Milady, you had a message from Pleasant, most urgent," babbled Kaarl following her. "Someone called Singha is kitting. I don't understand; perhaps I didn't get it correct?"

Radhya smiled a brilliant smile that illuminated her face and made her eyes sparkle like clear water on a sunny day. "Praise the creator who made us all! Perhaps we can yet pull this off."

She thrust Kaarl into the nearest chair and fell into the next one, beside Padr. The thrust came before she could get the straps around herself. Arrow lurched forward and left, then violently right. Tossed roughly forward, then sideways onto Padr's lap, her head brutally struck his face. Strong hands from behind grabbed her and thrust her firmly into her seat. Big, bulky fingers nimbly did up her straps. She glanced up to see Dave holding her down and maintaining his balance against the shifting stresses of acceleration. She nodded her thanks.

Padr's nose was pouring blood, and both eyes were swelling and purpling. Radhya extended a hand toward him as the craft shifted and spun.

Rory's voice came from the intercom. "Milady, Patrol is

calling for us to go null and be boarded. They've given us a bowshot; a real one is next. Arrow doesn't have the armoring to withstand a direct hit from this distance."

"Go null Rory. I'll meet the commander at the lock."

Radhya unstrapped, floating free in the weightlessness. A few drops of the floating blood adhered to her sleeve. She stared at Padr enigmatically for a few seconds as she glided to the lock. Within a minute, two troopers appeared, then the commander.

Dressed in the white padded shock suits of the Commonwealth Patrol, gold braid on the shoulders of his uniform distinguished the commander.

"What is the meaning of this?" demanded Lady Kirbyson at her most imperious, with an angry glint in her eye.

"I am sorry; milady Kirbyson, but I have an inquiry for a slave you purchased. There is some irregularity, and you were trying to escape the planet in great hurry."

"I have purchased eight new slaves recently. To which one do you refer?"

" 769 462 777," the commander replied respectfully, "It seems at one time he was a royal, and there is some question of how you obtained him and whether you are too soft to master an ex-royal. Jabin usually reserves them for himself. We also need to know why you are running from Lord Jabin's World?"

"I have receipts, in my wrist comp," she answered fiercely, showing him the information, "and I have hard copy too if you require that. As to why I purchase what I do, that is my own personal business. Do you think I do background checks on every slave I purchase? I buy skills not people. In addition, commander, I am not running from Jabin's World. I have an emergency. My lynx cat is whelping on Pleasant. Each kit is worth a quarter of this planets yearly income. I don't consider your holding me up as good business practice, for I will charge the Patrol for every kit that does not survive its birth."

The commander paled. "Still, I must check on this slave, he replied stubbornly."

Radhya soared gracefully back down the tunnel to the seating section. The troopers followed her. She positioned herself upside down in relation to the seated slaves. The commander's eyes took in the crimson drops suspended in the air. Padr's nose was still slowly leaking blood, which floated about the cabin. Radhya flipped and anchored herself with one foot hooked under the footrest of the chair in which she had been sitting. Her gaze traveled over the ranks of her slaves as if she had never seen them before.

"Which of you is 769 462 777?" demanded Radhya.

Padr raised his bloody hand. She glared at him as if all this was his fault. She flipped upside down again to speak to the commander.

"This man was trained as my personal bodyguard at Barone's school. His uniform, such as it is now, was hand tailored by Jemediah. So, you tell Jabin, excuse me, Lord Jabin, if he wants to have him, he is for sale. I want double my purchase price, double my training fees, and double my clothing costs. If any of my stock becomes injured in this free fall, he can pay for that too. I believe I already mentioned my kits."

The commander whispered into his wrist unit. "How did this slave come to be injured?" he asked.

Radhya gave him a steel-eyed stare. "I have no obligation to explain my treatment of my slaves."

The commander whispered again then listened to the reply. "Please, milady," he entreated. "It would considerably speed things up if you could tell Lord Jabin. First, when did the Commonwealth Patrol become the personal army of Lord Jabin?"

The commander flushed red with embarrassment.

"Milady the king himself signed the orders assigning me to Lord Jabin's World. If I have to serve him in my service of the king, then that is what I have to do. So if you would please just give me the information I require we can both get back to our real jobs."

"Very well," she replied, "he spoke without being spoken to, so I used the prod full in his face."

"But that doesn't account for all this blood"; the commander returned suspiciously eyeing Padr.

Radhya's eyes flashed, "When he cried out, I hit him with the butt. Maybe a broken nose will teach him his place. You call me soft, but I am good to my slaves so they can work harder. A strong body works harder than a weak one. I call it being smart, and I tolerate no disrespect."

The commander whispered into his wrist comp again. "I am sorry to have kept you milady Kirbyson."

Radhya floated down the corridor behind the retreating commander and his troopers. "Inform your ruler I will charge him if any of my stock on board is injured and if any kits die hell get the dead one or ones. This is a new species, and I have orders from here to Andromeda for them. I protest this harassment," she snarled as the lock opened before them. The commander bowed respectfully and closed the hatch.

Radhya floated back to her seat, buckled in and told Rory to continue with as much speed as possible. The Arrow leapt forward. Radhya released a long breath with a groan. As soon as they were beyond the suns gravity-well, the ship jumped into overlight drive. Gravity returned blanketing everything with droplets of blood.

"Jemelina, Aninya clean this up," called Radhya. "Padr, you are the luckiest man I have ever met in my life," she said looking at him.

"I am afraid to say anything for fear you will do what you told the commander you did," replied Padr.

Exasperated she answered him, "If you hadn't been bleeding and banged up your life would have been short indeed. Three of the aristocracy, besides yourself, were sentenced on trumped-up charges for speaking out against the slave trade. They all ended up as Jabin's amusements, in his palace. As you know, he fancies himself a Caesar, and he loves his gladiatorial games. That's where you were destined to go until I bullied Seellia into selling you. To your advantage, he's more afraid of ending up as a pile of goo, than facing a lion. Your training was a big gamble, a very expensive big gamble, but the increase in your legitimate value now puts your price a little higher than Jabin wants to pay for animal food. Thank the creator Singha decided to give birth now. What you heard about the kits was true. I also have valid need for a landscape architect for my pleasure world. I know Lord Kent was an outstanding one. Still, he might have kept you by saying I couldn't master you, but our little accident makes you a man blessed by serendipity."

Aninya gently washed Padr's bloody face. Even with the blood wiped off, he was a mess. Both eyes were blackened and swollen. His nose puffed out on both sides as well. Radhya inspected it. She called Will forward to check out the damage. Padr stared at her seriously.

"You seem to know a great deal about me, and I know nothing about you," he said.

"His nose is not broken," interjected Will.

"Good. Your nose will be fine in an hour or so. It would be a shame to mar those good looks," she smiled.

Padr snorted then winced at the discomfort.

"You want to know about me?" she asked.

Staring at her Padr nodded.

"Interesting, if little-known fact; my parents once sent the proposition of a contract between us to your parents. I come from generations of genetic engineers and we, you and I, are the most advantageous match among the entire aristocracy, or should I say were."

"I never heard about it," puzzled Padr.

"No, your parents flatly rejected the idea. It seems someone of a 600 status is nowhere good enough for someone of a 400 status. A pity Lord Barone does not share such sentiments."

"Is that why you bought me? To humiliate me because my parents rejected you?" Padr asked.

Radhya looked at him in astonishment. Hurt spread across her face like a spill in the water. Shaking her head, she dashed to her compartment at the rear. At her call, Will followed. Seconds later, he returned to Padr with a tube. He squeezed some of the white sticky substance into his hand. Gently he applied it to Padr's bruised nose and swollen eyes. Within minutes, the swelling began to recede, and his face gradually shifted back to normal. He sighed in relief.

"You're really a fool," hissed Will. "The Lady saves your life repeatedly, at the risk of her own freedom, and you accuse her of wanting vengeance. Either you are stupid, or you have a death wish. Maybe you are just too arrogant to see beyond the end of your own nose."

Will returned to his seat in the rear and positioned it so he wouldn't have to look at the back of Padr's head.

Chapter Three

For three days, the Arrow streaked through the void. Entering Pleasant's solar system, she dropped to sublight drive. Every creature aboard felt the jolt. The slaves had been restricted to the passenger compartment for the entire time, while Radhya confined herself to her cabin and only Aninya saw her briefly to deliver her prepackaged meals. Avoiding conversation, the slaves avoided even looking at each other for the most part.

After the jolt, the Lady floated from her cabin. More pale than usual with dark circles beneath her eyes, she smiled wanly at the slaves.

"We should be home in an hour," she informed them. "Now I want to tell you; there is a short ride from the port and then a walk of four klicks to my home. Each of you will be taking two of the horses. Have any of you ever led a horse before?"

"I had a pony for several years as a child," said Max.

"And I am sure you know I used to be an accomplished show jumper," replied Padr sarcastically.

"I know," Lady Kirbyson nodded. "You can bring one stallion. I'll bring the other. The other six of you each take two mares. Stane and Rory will bring the racers. All you have to do is hold the lead ropes and walk ahead. Dave, when we get home, you will be in charge of security for this planet. Right now I want you to concentrate on the port, track, and my home."

Dave looked at her, mouth open, eyebrows raised.

"You are the only one I can spare, and you have had the super deluxe training," she explained.

"But everybody thinks I'm dumb," he protested.

"Looks can be deceiving. I think you are a lot brighter than you like to let on. If the aristocracy want to think I have a dumb security agent in charge of the planet, all the better."

Dave looked at his boots. A slight smile tugged at his misshapen lips.

"You and Jemelina will have your own house. At the entrance to my private acreage, there is a gatehouse. That will be yours, although you will have to travel around a great deal."

Dave's jaw dropped. "Thank you milady, thank you. This is really too much. Since I was born, I have lived in slave quarters, with not enough floor space to lie down on. My own house is unbelievable."

He grabbed the Lady's hand and kissed it. Radhya flushed scarlet.

"Little enough. You have a great responsibility down there. My life will literally be in your hands at all times. You will need good quarters to plan and figure out your strategy. Besides, those slave quarters were never sanitary enough for me."

Stane floated into the hatchway. "You should know that most of milady's slaves live better than freedmen."

"Stane!" Radhya warned.

"Sorry milady. Could everyone strap down? We'll be landing in a minute," he laughed as he glided back into the corridor.

Everyone hurried into their chairs and did up their harness. The Arrow slid through the atmosphere, burning a flash of red across the sky. It swung in a lazy curve and aimed for a barrier of mountains, shot between a pair of ridges and coasted to a smooth stop.

On Pleasant, Radhya hustled everyone from the ship. Sharp-peaked mountains completely enclosed them, the tops frosted with snow. The floor of the large valley was paved and smooth. South, an asphalt road curved beyond view while to the north was a tall control tower, its large ring of windows reflecting the golden morning sun. Assorted metal buildings, big and small, backed against the naked rock of the mountains. The slaves working around them were miniaturized.

The belly of the ship inched open with a whirring noise, the hydraulic ramp lowering. Rory and Stane walked from the interior of the ship, hands crisscrossed with reins. Prancing and sidestepping, the horses jittered behind them. The loud clatter of many hooves echoed back from the mountains. Snorting loudly, one reared and whinnied as he danced into the daylight. Radhya apportioned the animals.

One colt was a beautiful grey with a black mane and tail. He was not that big, but perfectly proportioned. The other colt was a huge, fiery chestnut with a single strip down his nose. He too was perfectly proportioned. The filly was average looking, but tense, like a bow waiting to release its arrow; a blood bay with a star on her forehead and one white sock.

"Tango Dancer, Son-O-War, and Secretary," Radhya said as she handed them back to Rory. "The hope of the North Wind Stables."

A small and a large horsebox pulled up. Rory and Stane led their charges to the smaller van. Its electric purr faded quickly into the distance.

"You are allowed motorized vehicles?" asked Max in surprise.

"I know the laws, but the commonwealth makes exceptions for horses. Funny isn't it, people walk and horses ride. However, that road only goes so far. We'll all walk from the track."

Radhya closed and sealed the spaceship. An equipment

moving alarm hooted from the tower as the cables attached by the spaceport workers pulled the Arrow to its hanger. The horses reared and flailed the air with their legs.

Aninya and Jemelina screamed and covered their heads, dropping the reins; running to the van. Padr and Max caught the animals and helped Radhya in calming them while Will and Kaarl watched. Dave, after watching Padr closely, came to assist. After many shouted orders and much confusion, they loaded the stallions and mares. The slaves squeezed in around the animals. Radhya got a boost and stretched out on the back of the largest stallion.

Setting off on the winding road that hugged the cliff, they enjoyed a brief trip through the mountains that brought them to a section of the road with a tranquil blue-green ocean on the right. They traveled high above the waves next to a rugged rock face, peering through the slats to see their new world.

"That's the Ocean of Delight, and the Mountains of Mist," murmured Radhya from her perch. "We have an unusual day. The mountains are most often covered in mist, although the ocean is usually very nice. My track is on a low plateau, beneath the mountains, overlooking the ocean." She stared at Padr. "It's going to be your first job to landscape the track. I want it to outshine your work on Junction, if that's possible. The setting here is different, but I think it gives you a lot to work with. It must impress the aristocracy."

"I don't know how the work of a slave can compete with the work of a member of the aristocracy," drawled Padr bitterly.

Radhya sat upright banging her head on the roof. The horse under her shifted and snorted.

"Padr! This is important. You have to make it so spectacular they want to come, just to see it. Every royal has had to see Junction. It's still a rite of passage for teens. You must; you absolutely must do even better here."

Padr looked at her, startled by the alarm in her voice.

She continued urgently, "I have risked the plan, risked everything, to get you, because you're the best. I spent a planet's price on the bunch of you, mainly just to get you. I need to trust you to do your best work yet."

Warily Padr replied, "I'll do the best for you that I am able to do."

Radhya slid from the horse. She patted his hand, where it rested on the horse's neck. Then she hid her face in the horse's mane.

A few minutes later, they approached the track. Three dirt ovals framed by white fencing dominated the forefront, while the grandstands behind were dwarfed by the splendor of the upthrust mountains. The stables were just visible beyond, curving around the foot of the massif. Everything was on a generous scale in keeping with the snow-clad giant behind. The absence of grass or trees seemed an absurd oversight. To the right, an enormous building was under construction on a tongue of land jutting out over the water. The clang of tools, buzz of equipment and yelling slaves excited the horses; they began to shift about.

The vehicle stopped just before entering the grounds for the track. The slaves and Radhya gratefully spilled out. A narrow gravel trail split off to the left, disappearing between a pair of tall pines in the near distance. The churned up earth on either side of the path did not encourage straying too far.

As the slaves divided the horses and started up the trail, Radhya threw a tiny saddle to Padr and told him to saddle the stallions. When they were ready, she swung up on the tallest, a bright chestnut with a blaze and four white socks. Padr mounted a big bay that snorted and pawed at the ground. They caught up with the others on the verge of the forest. Many tall, slender pines comprised the bulk of the trees, but scattered among them were white-barked birches and short thicker spruce. The undergrowth was thick and thorny, the bushes laced together in random patterns. On the path, the scattering of gravel gradually changed to a firm, rubbery surface. Curious, Max picked at it. A small chunk came up, roots attached. He looked at the Lady, a question on his face.

"A small creation of mine. It started out as a type of fungus. Now it absorbs fallen leaves, droppings, just about anything organic really. That keeps it clean. It grows slowly, and it loves to be walked on. The only maintenance is a trimming every ten years or so."

The slaves leading the horses stopped suddenly. They paused before a dozen small black creatures with broad white stripes down their backs. Their large fluffy tails lofted upward in a somewhat menacing attitude. The largest one was making a chittering noise.

Radhya dismounted and tossed the reins to Padr, shoving at the horses ahead of her to get through.

"My sweet little pets," she called as she went down on her knees.

The little animals swarmed around her, kissing her with their noses. Radhya murmured to them and stroked them.

"Dave," she called softly, "give your horses to Will and Max and meet the gang. These are my first line of defense. On earth, they called them skunks, and they have powerful spray at their disposal. They have to get to know you."

Dave also got down on his knees and gingerly touched the coarse-haired creatures.

"They don't bite, but they will spray trespassers. It burns the eyes too. Let them smell you. Once you're accepted, they will never forget your scent. If you leave the path, you might meet my other pets that are not so friendly. Giant red deer, very bad tempered and territorial patrol the woods. Then there are the dire wolves. You don't want to meet them."

Radhya nodded significantly to the people. She introduced all the slaves to the creatures one by one. After stroking them a while longer, Radhya rose. Her furry friends vanished into the brush.

"We'll go ahead and open the gates for you. Just stay on the path, and you can't get lost," the Lady said.

Dave gave her a leg up. She chirped to her mount, and they were off at a swift trot. In minutes, Radhya and Padr were in front of a double set of metal gates, three stories tall. The hinges sank deep into granite pillars decorated on the front face with flowers, birds, and insects. The columns were carved from the mountain. The shoulders soared steeply to either side of the trail.

"Never touch the gates. They are randomly electrified," she told Padr.

Bending down, she rapidly stroked the patterns in a series of moves, then whispered into a com box hidden in a flower on the side of the right-hand pillar. The gates swung open as she straightened, her mount prancing skittishly inside.

To the right was a red brick bungalow with a forest green metallic roof. The front sported a veranda and large windows that continued down each side. It was set back in a pleasantly green fuzzy lawn bordered with array of brilliantly colored flowers, filling the air with perfume. A myriad of birds twittered in the hedges.

Left of the gate, a stream bounced down the mountainside and curved to flow beside the fungus path. The creek was also framed with multicolored blossoms and many flowering shrubs that clung tenaciously to the rock, cascading down to the path.

Padr pulled his stallion to a walk in order to take in the beauty of the surroundings. Radhya however, spurred straight down the path at a gallop. He kicked his mount to follow. Coming around a bend, the valley opened up, and he saw the stable, partially hidden by a clump of dark, large boled trees. It was white with green trim, new, and obviously the best quality. A series of lush paddocks were visible to the root of the mountain. Radhya was dismounting in the yard, so he quickened the animal's steps to join her.

A small oriental boy of fourteen was holding the horse

Radhya had just ridden. She stood beside him staring up at the rider.

"This is Won. He will take your horse and care for it, this time. His father, Li, is in charge of the stables. He has an older brother, Tan, my jockey. He is around here somewhere," informed Radhya looking around.

The double row of loose boxes ended at another bungalow smothered in purple flowers. Plants climbed over the entire surface of the building, except windows and doors. A small oriental woman was standing in the doorway. Her long midnight black hair was pulled back severely into a bun, but her almond eyes were warm and welcoming. Her pointed chin was foxy without being sly. Dressed in medical scrubs, with a striped apron tied in back, she waved her slender, delicate hands at them in universal welcome.

"Milady, milady," she called in a high sweet voice. Radhya and Padr walked toward her. "Six, six babies she had. All doing fine, nursing well."

"Ah Sumi, you no doubt did an excellent job as usual. At the house?" Radhya beamed. "Sumi's my vet," she said aside to Padr.

At Sumi's nod, Radhya set off at a jog, through a little white picket gate, and up another fungus path. The narrow trail joined to a majestically proportioned fungus road. It ringed a grove of grey barked trees with finger-like leaves and sprays of fire dancing above the foliage. As they drew closer, Padr could see the flames were blossoms. The gardenia odor was not quite overpowering. Around the trees, they came upon the mansion. It soared four stories into the sky, grey stone backed up against the rugged granite mountain.

"All it needs" murmured Padr, "is a moat and perhaps a fire-breathing dragon. Then I will have stepped into the pages of a crazy fairy tale."

At the muted sound of their running footsteps, the majesti-cally carved panels of the front door swung open. An ancient black man was standing there, dressed in house livery of forest green. Still fit, taller than Padr, but beginning to stoop with age, he showed perfect teeth in a wide smile. Pleasure showed in his velvet brown eyes and all the wrinkles on his face were happy ones. The metal dog collar of a slave was just visible above the top of his round collar.

To Padr's surprise, Radhya hurled herself into the old man's arms. He hugged and kissed her, and she hugged him back.

"Geo, my dearest friend," introduced Radhya to Padr, as she pulled herself from his embrace.

"And her oldest slave," added Geo with a twinkle, in a rich, deep voice.

Radhya grabbed Padr's hand and tried to pull him forward. He pulled back.

"And this is Padr."

"Hmmmmm," mused Geo, "can't see what all the fuss is about."

"Where's Singha?" Radhya asked.

"Impatient as always, you little hoyden. Can't even give an old man a minute of time," fussed the old slave.

Radhya smiled endearingly up at him.

"In the kitchen, where else?" he answered.

Radhya dashed off. As Padr tried to follow, Geo grabbed his arm.

"Listen, you young whelp, if you cause Radhya any problem or hurt her in any way, I'll do for you myself. Old as I am I'll fix you. She is counting on you."

The old man shuffled off as an astonished Padr watched him. There were only bitter old slaves in his experience. He had never met a loyal one before. Radhya had disappeared. Padr walked ahead, looking left and right at hallways panelled in zebra striped wood. Ahead there was an imposing green marble staircase going both up and down, stretching from a floor of green marble, polished to a brilliant shine. A little further on there was another hallway on the right, just in front of the stairs.

There were two doors on the left. He tried the first door. It opened on an ornate washroom. Closing the door, he continued in the main hallway. Opening the second door on the left, he could hear Radhya's voice.

Pushing the door open all the way, he entered a narrow hallway of plain white plaster leading to a brightly lit kitchen. A door with a large window showed greenery outside. The walls were shiny white, and the counters were white marble. The cooking equipment of silver metal placed strategically around the large room filled it with bright reflections. Many counters and islands filled the remaining space and, under one of these was a large box open at the front. Lady Kirbyson was on her knees on the white marble floor in front of it. She was talking to and stroking a very large, feline-type animal.

If it had stood up, it would have been a meter tall with golden brown fur that was barred and striped with dark reddish brown. Clear, cream-colored underparts and enormous ears with long tufts of dark fur at the tips defined its outline. Its eyes were a bright sky blue and had the slit, cat pupil; each one was ringed with black, then white, then black again, like a bull's eye. Black lines descended from the inside corners of its eyes to the flesh colored nose.

"Come and see them," the Lady invited softly.

Padr stepped forward. In the box were six speckled balls of fluff, each about the size of a hand, squeaking in a most unattractive way.

"Aren't they beautiful, so beautiful?" his mistress turned to him.

"Yes milady," replied Padr.

"Oh Padr," she said grinning at him, "at home, there is no formality. That's for when we're among others who are not part of our family here."

"No one here is a part of my family!" answered Padr formally pulling away.

"Maybe not," she replied, "but now you are a part of ours."

Giving Singha a final pat, Radhya rose. Taking Padr by the hand, she led him through the kitchen to a swinging door.

Going through the door, she said, "This is the slave's galley. These stairs lead down to the slave quarters. Special you know, I spoil my slaves. They have plywood beds, raised from the floor and two washrooms with four open showers. There is even a table and a number of chairs. But all that is just for show."

The room they had entered was very plain. A long rough wooden table with matching chairs punctuated the white walls and wooden floors. An unadorned window was on the right. On the back wall was a set of wooden stairs leading down. On the left was a hallway.

Radhya led him out of the slave section and into a hallway that joined with the main hall where he had entered. Geo shuffled out to let in the rest of her new purchases.

"Aninya, back through that hallway is the slave quarters and the kitchen." She pointed the way. "Dining hall above and sleeping quarters below. Every day we get deliveries from the farm in the next valley. Tell them each day what you want the next. Now you, Dani and Kaarl have a house. Out the door in the kitchen, follow the path, and it will take you right to it. Off you go. Return here after supper."

The slave family hurriedly did as they were told.

"Dave and Jemelina," continued Radhya, "the first house we passed is yours. You go and get settled in. Return here after supper. Oh, did you lock the gate? It should respond to your pattern."

"Yes milady, I secured the gate. I can't thank you enough..."

"Just go," said Radhya flapping her hands at them. "Now you three come with me."

She led them to the stairs at the end of the hall. They climbed to the third floor.

"Second floor is bedrooms for visitors," she explained, "the third floor is mine."

At the landing, she turned left down another hallway panelled in glowing cedar wood.

"First door left, washrooms for you," she said. At that, the men exchanged looks of puzzlement. "To the right is the comm room, lab one is next to it, exercise room next to your washroom. Each of you must exercise one hour every day, without fail. Next to the exercise room is lab two. Across the hall is the med lab. You can check it out later Will."

The Lady turned at the end and went back past the stairs.

"On the left is my room. First door right is for you Max."

She opened the door to a large comfortable room decorated in cream and tan, with a feeling of mountains and rocks. A large bed, dresser, desk, and chair furnished the space. Radhya closed the door and moved on.

"Next to Max, I'll have Padr," she said opening his door.

His room was the same size and similarly furnished, but decorated in shades of green, painted like an old growth forest.

"Don't tell me you've been in my bedroom too. This is exactly like my boyhood room at home. How did you know?" he demanded.

Radhya only smiled in answer to his question.

"Will, you're last," she said opening the door to his room.

His room was turquoise, teal, and sea green, like an underwater grotto.

"Thank you milady. It is much like my room at home too, only better quality. My mother did her best, but we never had a lot of money."

"You are welcome Will. These are your quarters, but when I have guests, you will have to rough it in the slave's quarters. Settle in. I'll see you all downstairs, in the slave's galley at suppertime. Ask Padr; he knows where it is."

Chapter Four

After a simple supper in the slave's galley, Radhya met with her new slaves. Geo, Rory, and Stane joined them. A blaze of crimson and lavender shone through the bare outlining the golden setting sun. Singha purred and twisted her way between and around Radhya's feet as she paced before the seated slaves at the table. Her footsteps echoed hollowly on the planks, back and forth, back and forth. She had a frown on her face, and the corners of her mouth were tight.

"I want to outline, briefly, the plan," Radhya began. "Even if you are slaves I am giving you a choice in this because it is too important to our whole society to have even one unwilling participant." She looked hard at Padr. "I don't believe there should be slavery, and I want to eliminate it. However, that is easier said than done, and it has to be done correctly. By our calculations, correctly done, it will take at least a hundred years. That is going about it in the manner most beneficial for slaves."

Padr snorted, disgust in his voice. "That is one way to escape responsibility; put it so far in the future we'll never see it."

"Padr did you ever study history?" she asked. "Ancient history?"

"Of course," he answered curtly.

"Remember the civil war of the United States of America on ancient Earth?"

"I do vaguely," he replied cautiously.

"Three hundred years later and the people descended from slaves were still fighting oppression and prejudice. I want to avoid that. Now in our society, what is the difference between slaves and freedmen?"

Will answered, "Freedmen become slaves for breaking the laws or not paying their bills, but slaves never become freedmen for keeping the laws."

Radhya burst into her brilliant smile, "Very clever Will. However, that was not what I was looking for. Slaves live in terrible conditions; they are not fed, not given medical treatment, not even given clothes in most cases. When they are old, they are abandoned or killed. Often they are tortured for the amusement of their owners. They can be killed for no reason. They have no rights at all. We plan to start this process of eliminating slavery with a bill of rights for slaves."

Her new slaves stared at her in open-mouth amazement.

Radhya continued, pacing faster, "That's just the first step. When the differences between slave and freedmen have been reduced to nil, then the slaves will be freed totally. All level of society need this. The aristocracy is in trouble. Birth rates are so low, except for those who have been illegally 'helped,' that in a hundred years it will be near to vanishing away. A hundred years ago, there were ten thousand in the aristocracy. Now we number slightly more than three thousand. The royals need infusions of new genetic material. Working more slowly like this gives our society a chance to adjust, reducing prejudice by helping slaves and royals. But first, we narrow the distance."

"Yes we have to begin to narrow the distance," Rory put in.

Geo was nodding his head, and Stane looked eagerly at the new ones. Will sat up straight, astonishment plastered on his face, while the others sat in thoughtful silence.

"This is amazing," Will muttered.

"How do you plan to get a bill of rights for slaves?" Max asked, "Every member of the aristocracy who speaks against this sorry institution ends up dead, except Padr of course. And it was a near thing with him," he added.

"I plan to force it if I have too. I have a secret weapon, and I will use it. Publicly, I totally uphold slavery. Behind the scenes, we work against it. Some of the royals are suspicious of me. That is why they were so dead set against my buying Padr. They don't want the two of us working together. We, and I mean all of us here together in this room, have to work hard to allay those suspicions.

In two years and six months, the status review of the aristocracy will be held. I want it held here. Every royal in the Commonwealth must attend. In two years, they will be picking the venue. In six months, my track holds its first races. I need it to be so spectacular that it becomes a must see, like Junction. Then, when my application is sent in to host the status review, I am sure to be invited to hold it here. Eighty percent of the aristocracy is racing mad anyway, so I just have to lure the rest with scenery and other attractions. Actually, luring your job Padr. After three days, the "any other business" question is asked. I will have the ballroom engineered to close up like a prison. Of course, it must be entirely invisible to the most apprehensive of guests. In addition, it must be able to withstand even bombardment from space, should things go that far. That's your part, Max. Moreover, Will, your part will be to take care of them and make sure no one dies. A death would blow the whole plan out of the water. I also need you to devise a method to knock out all the bodyguards at once."

She stopped, faced them and smiled. "I plan to kidnap the entire aristocracy. Anyone want out?"

Jemelina gasped and put her hands to her face. At Radhya's nod, Stane broke an ampoule beneath her nose. As the plastic capsule snapped, yellow vapor hissed into the air. Immediately she slumped unconscious to the floor. Dave dove to her side and gathered her up in his arms.

"I hoped to have the housekeeper on our side," mourned Radhya.

"What's wrong with her?" interrupted Dave anxiously.

"It is just a mild sedative and dismemorizor. When she wakes, probably tomorrow, she won't remember anything past our landing this morning. Don't worry; there is no damage, she'll be fine. Now is anyone else opposed to the plan?"

Will ran his hand back and forth over the rough table, staring at it. Max grinned broadly. Padr sat on the corner looking at her with a sour expression. Dave was very concerned with his unconscious wife. No one answered.

"Now, Padr and Will, anything you need in the line of botanicals or medications, let me know. Even if it doesn't exist, I can probably create it for you. I am a geneticist of some experience. I have been working in the field since I was ten. Max and anyone else who needs other materials see Geo. Anytime I am unavailable, see Geo. He is my quartermaster and right-hand man. Kaarl, my assets must be well hidden and very obscure until the review in two years. I hope to break into the two hundreds by then."

The slaves looked astonished. "Oh yes, I am a very wealthy woman. But I can't get most of what I want for money."

The sudden sorrow and pain on Radhya's face struck them like a blow.

"Okay," broke in Max with a strange look on his face. "I am more than willing to work with your plan, after all, what more can they do to me except kill me. Still, I don't feel very safe with Padr. I think he is trouble. I want to hear his story. How did he become a slave? How do we know that he isn't a spy?"

"NO!" Padr stated emphatically.

"I think you owe it to the rest of us," commented Geo. "We are all trusting you with our lives, especially Lady Kirbyson. I myself rescued her from certain death four times now, and I don't think she should be put in danger for you, so tell."

He shook his head and stubbornly stared at the floor. Dave tenderly lay his wife down and approached Padr menacingly. Will approached from the other side, a large sliver in his hand. Dave grabbed his arm, extending the hand. Will prepared to shove the wood under Padr's fingernail.

"Stop!" exclaimed Radhya. "I will not be as bad as the people I am fighting against. Padr, I know most of your story already, but the others would feel much more comfortable and thus be able to work more efficiently if you could set their minds at rest."

Dave and Will halted immediately. Embarrassed they seated themselves, the sliver discarded in a corner. Padr gazed beseechingly at Radhya. She, however, seated herself across from him and looked straight into his face. Lowering his eyes to the floor, he began to speak.

"I had an older brother who was going to inherit everything, so I set out just to enjoy myself. After University, and Junction, by the way, was my Ph.D. in landscaping, I got heavily into show jumping. One year I beat Prince Phlip so many times it became a joke between us, so at the end of the season, I sent him a colt. It was a full brother to the jumper I was riding. When my birthday rolled around, he sent me a female slave. He and I had discussed many times, at length, what the perfect female was, and anyway, he sent her to me. She was as tall as I am, blonde, slender as a whip, huge brown eyes with lacy white around the pupil, and legs that never quit. I, ah, fell in love with her and I wanted her for a spouse. My parents and brother said a concubine yes, mate no. I fought with all I had to get her manumitted, but no matter what I tried, it didn't work, so I began to work in the political field to abolish slavery. If there were no more slaves, then I could have her. Meanwhile, she got pregnant, and we had a son.

She told me if I didn't 'marry' her and legitimize our son

she would kill him. Of course, I didn't believe her. I tried, creator as my witness, I tried. When he was six months old, she brought him to my room. She asked me again to marry her, and when I said it was impossible just now, she broke his neck in front of me. He died in my arms. She just stood there and watched, no emotions at all. Then she ran screaming from the room, telling everyone I was angry and had murdered her son."

Bowing his head, Padr stopped speaking for a minute; wiping tears from his eyes. Drawing deep, steadying breaths, he continued.

"He was so little. My family was upset, of course, as children are rare among the aristocracy, but it was the word of a slave against mine, so nothing was done. I should have dismissed her then, but she said she was sorry. She begged me to be merciful, and she was so beautiful."

Padr had to stop for some more deep breaths before continuing. "I never mentioned freeing her after that, and she grew very angry. She nagged at me nonstop. Finally, about six months after she murdered our son, I left her at home while I was on a jumping circuit. Usually, we traveled together. Anyway, the night I was due home she set firebombs around the house. As I walked in the yard, it exploded. By the time I reached the front door, it was already burning. I couldn't get in. My father and my mother died in that conflagration, and four hundred and twenty slaves, including my concubine. Fortunately, my older brother was unexpectedly off planet attending to business. Before she died, she sent a letter of confession to the proctors. She sealed my name to it, my signature that she took off one of the love letters I wrote to her while I was away. My brother wouldn't listen to me. He even refused to buy me as a slave from Jabin's World. I think he was hoping I would be tortured to death in the arena. So that's why I am here. How do I go about ever trusting anyone again, especially a woman?"

"Oh Padr, we'll figure it out," sighed Radhya, reaching across the table to cover his hand with her own. "That's the part of your life we could never access. Your brother must have buried it very deep. I'll bet that if you could get the records of that slave girl, she came from Barone via Jabin. Geo see if you can trace her. I know in my bones she was an altered and conditioned plant set to destroy you. What you may not know is that you were part of an experiment before you were born. The aristocracy seems bent on destroying everyone who had anything to do with that study. Your story follows the pattern of the other royals who were made slaves and died. Except, so far, the ending."

"If that is how the other royals were brought down, using slaves, then why do you seek to free the slaves?" asked Will.

Radhya's eyes swerved left and her face twisted into a fleeting look of terror. She controlled herself and answered, "It is not the slaves' fault that they are used like that. They are conditioned, programmed by certain aristocrats. I don't know why yet, except that it had to do with my grandfather and his experiments, but I'll find out."

"Why do you want to free the slaves?" asked Max softly.

"That is a tale for another time," Radhya told him firmly. "I'll only say that atonement is a long and weary road. Now let's sketch in our individual parts in the plan."

Chapter 5

Six Months Later

Lady Radhya Kirbyson woke well before dawn; her body tuned to the long nights and early mornings of the last six months. She slipped into her baggy black exercise clothes and headed to the gym. Guests would be arriving by noon today, so she had to be at the track to greet them. She basked in the quiet of the house, gathering her inner resources for the hectic day ahead. So many strange people challenged her. Will was already pulling weights as she entered the room.

"Can't sleep either?" he inquired.

"I think my body is used to rising at this time and it's getting up whether my mind wants to or not," Radhya laughed back.

She began her circuit running on the treadmill. As she did the rounds of the equipment, first Max, then Padr came in to work out.

"Don't forget you all turn back into slaves and bodyguards today. The bodyguard part is no sinecure, both my parents died in an explosion at a ball; this is for real," she told them.

"That's going to be hard milady," said Padr trying out the

title again. "We have worked so closely these last few months; I feel like we are friends."

"Why Padr," exclaimed Radhya with a smile, "that's the nicest thing you've ever said to me."

She patted his straining bicep on the way out.

"Don't forget bodyguard uniforms, and meet me at 10:30," she called from the doorway.

Returning to her suite to shower, Radhya called Aninya to order fruit and cheese for breakfast in her room. She had just stepped out of the bathing room when the cook knocked at the door.

"Enter; just set it down on the glass table over there please," Radhya instructed. "Now, Aninya, I am having extra help sent from the farm. I hope the royals all stay at the hotel at the track, after all the suites are quite sumptuous; however, I fear some may insist on coming here. So have four bedrooms on the second floor prepared. Have Jemelina clean them, the dining room and parlor particularly well. Also, get some spare clothes and possessions to make the slave quarters look lived in. Move Will's, Max's and Padr's things into them if I tell you we have guests. Don't forget to use the back hallways if anyone is around. As far as meals go, I want gourmet fare, breakfast, lunch, and supper if we end up with these unwanted visitors. Make sure the farms know to send some of their extra here. I need you to oversee the kitchens at the visitor's center as well. Add a little more meat to Singha's diet and that of the two kits. Maybe she will go into heat and drive everyone mad with her yowling. That would be sure to keep unwanted guests away, and it's about time for it anyway. By the way, what is your opinion, should I wear house colors, my usual, or something different?"

Aninya looked carefully at her mistress. "You have a room full of beautiful clothes, and you should wear them. I would like to see you in that shimmering purple-blue, or whatever color robe Jemediah just sent you. And for the ball tonight, you should wear the black-green ball gown you have in your dressing room.

It is close enough to your house colors that it would satisfy the most rule-bound. And wear your hair up, with the emerald choker, bracelet, and tiara."

Eyes large, Radhya looked at her with new respect.

"This is wonderful. I could never stand a body servant, so I just wore black. Sometimes Rory would pick out something for me. The clothing room was just to keep Jemediah going. I never wore any of it. I have no sense for clothes at all. Aninya you are a marvel."

Aninya murmured "Thank you," and left.

Radhya tossed her towel aside and ate slowly. Dressing in the chef's choice of pants and long tunic of glimmering royal blue with lavender where the lights touched it, she slipped on a floor-length sleeveless robe of royal midnight with dancing purple highlights in it, and stamped black leather boots on her feet.

Leaving her room, she clattered down the stairs to the main floor.

"Wow!" exclaimed Max, waiting at the foot of the stairs. "You look sensational. I've never seen you wear anything but black."

"I had an image to uphold. Now it's time to change it. I don't think my own brother or sister would recognize me. I've never worn anything but black for the last fifteen years. This feels very strange," she replied.

Will descended the stairs behind her. "How wonderful you look milady," he practiced. "A beautiful color for a beautiful face."

Radhya blushed and looked at Padr who followed behind Will.

"Doesn't Radhya look wonderful?" Max asked him pointedly.

"Yes lovely," he answered without looking at her.

A brief look of disappointment crossed her face. She spun on her heel and entered the kitchen. Singha and her six-month-old kits, Ringha and Kung, were just finishing large bowls of meat. Radhya called Kung, the male, to her. As she stroked his whiskers, she made the gesture telling Singha and Ringha to patrol. The two females were inseparable since the other kits left for their new homes. Then she left with Kung padding behind her.

She led the way, sparkling in the sunlight, with three body-guards and Kung behind her in perfect formation. The jewel-bright flying lizards were chirping in the trees, and tiny brown birds with red cheeks sang joyously as they walked past. They walked quickly down the fungus path to Dave, waiting at the gatehouse. Passing through, they locked the gates so no one but Dave or Radhya could open them.

It was a lovely, serene walk on a glorious golden day. Coming around the final bend, they heard the whining sound of a generator approaching.

"Somebody always has to be early," snarled Radhya with great irritation. "If I were a betting woman, I'd put my money on Noel. That man is a born pest. The problem is he is intelligent, and suspicious. Everybody stay in character now."

Radhya strode to the track gate as the large horse van pulled up. One of the track slaves was driving as usual. Noel Barone slithered from the passenger's side slapping his whip against his boot.

"I just bet my slaves you'd be the early guest," Lady Kirbyson called.

"And what did you win?" the smirking man inquired.

"Their suppers," she answered with a haughty lift of the lips.

Noel looked at the four men towering behind her and laughed.

"Of my training?" he asked.

"Yes, indeed," she replied, "and a very fine job you did too."

"And you, my dear, look magnificent. I've never seen you in anything but black. You positively take my breath away."

Without warning, Lord Barone slashed at her face with the

whip. Quick as thought, Dave dragged Radhya back while Max and Padr blocked the blow with their arms. Will grabbed Lord Barone's arm to restrain him. Faster than them all, was a blur of golden fur and a vicious growl. Noel screamed a bloodcurdling howl of pain. Kung had both sets of claws embedded on either side of his leg, very near the crotch. The lynxcat's teeth were sunk to the jawbone in the fleshy part of the thigh. Noel sank to the ground, writhing in pain, but Kung did not release his grip.

"In the name of mercy do something Radhya," he howled, "I was only testing the bodyguard's reflexes, to see how the training held up."

"Kung, to me," called Radhya in a firm voice.

Kung at once released his hold on the royal and bounded to her side.

"What a good boy," she cooed as she stroked and fondled him.

"Good boy?" yelled Barone apoplectically, "He's made hamburger of my leg."

Blood stained the red pants he wore and was beginning to puddle on the ground beneath his leg. He gripped above the injury tightly, his face a shocky white.

"Will," she nodded.

Will knelt beside the injured Barone while Dave used his wrist comp. An emergency hover approached on the other side of the track gate. Radhya opened the barrier. Dave scooped up the wounded Lord, then accompanied by Will they got in the hover.

"I'll meet you at the infirmary," called Lady Kirbyson. To the horse van driver, she said, "Take Lord Barone's racers to the stables. See to it that Li oversees getting them settled until Lord Barone can do it. I assume he brought his own stable crew."

"Yes, milady" answered the driver.

At her wave, he drove the vehicle away. Radhya, Padr, and Max with Kung padding behind panting, walked swiftly to the infirmary in the visitor's center. The building was magnificent.

The facade was translucent stone that fractured the light into dancing prisms. Many, large windows decorated the structure that soared six stories into the cerulean sky. It stood on the bluff overlooking the tranquil turquoise ocean. A large fungus court-yard fronted the building, equipped with seven fountains and deep beds of unusual plants. The aroma from the plants was both sweet and spicy. Seven crystal benches nestled in strategic spots, so visitors could sit in a rainbow. The view from the front doors of carved and polished zebrawood was of the track and the grandstands, over-capped by the mountain behind. They entered the enormous foyer and headed to the infirmary, located behind the entry on the main floor.

The large room was gleaming spotless white. Stainless steel appliances and tools were steri-wrapped on stainless trays and shelves. There were four violet steri-lights that covered every corner of the room. Barone lay on an examination table against the far wall.

"Radhya," Noel snapped as soon as she appeared, "I don't want your bodyguard looking after this. Get me a doctor!"

"My dear Lord Barone, Will is a fully qualified doctor. In fact, he is my personal physician. I am doing you a favor in allowing him to treat you. The other closest doctor is at the port, at least half an hour from here. He has only treated slaves, but if you want to wait..."

Noel looked slightly mollified. "I should sue you for this."

"How dare you threaten me?" Radhya snarled in a hard voice. "You attacked me! You might expect restraint from human slaves when a Lord is involved, but Kung is a half-grown kitten who has not even started his formal training yet. Be glad Singha wasn't with me. She would have torn your throat out before I could say a word. Don't you ever attack me again! I should boot your arrogant ass right off my planet."

Lord Barone stared, gaping at her as she shook her finger in the startled man's face, twirled and left the room. Padr, Max, Dave, and Kung followed her.

"Well, I guess she put me in my place. I didn't think she had it in her, always been an ice cube her," said a chagrined Noel to Will, "I suppose I deserve that. Can you repair this?"

"Yes, milord. Milady has developed a series of healing bacteria for her own use. Would their use be acceptable to you?"

"This is her own creation?"

"Yes, milord."

"She uses them on herself?"

"Yes, milord."

"Will it cause any harm to me?"

"I don't believe so milord. If you're reluctant to try them, I can clean and bandage your wounds and let nature take its course."

"How long nature's way?"

"Probably about two weeks, depending on how fast you heal milord."

"And how long your mistress's way?"

"An hour or less, milord."

"Very well. Give me Radhya's treatment. If it is safe why isn't it on the market?"

"I believe milady said she had enough products now and she wants to save this one for a dry spell."

"Ho! The day that woman has a dry spell is the day I give training for free."

Will finished cleaning Lord Barone's leg. Then he poured a blue gel onto the wounds. It immediately began to fizz. Carefully timing it, Will poured a clear liquid over the bubbling blue. It became transparent. Noel watched in amazement as the flesh regrew and the new skin covered the puncture wounds. A single drop of clean blood remained at the site of each hole. Will wiped them away with gauze. Noel inspected his leg, which was now totally uninjured, without even a scar."

"Tell my personal servant, 72, to fetch me another pair of pants," commanded Lord Barone. "He should be with my animals."

Radhya stormed through the guest foyer, her heels pounding back and forth on the travertine. The feathery shuhan trees growing out of it swayed in the wind of her passing. The tiny scarlet meeps that lived and sang in the trees hid silently among the branches. She wove around the carved blackwood furniture and pounded on the white marble check-in counter. The gorgeous view from the glass front held no interest to her. Her eyes snapped lightning, and her brows were black thunder-clouds. Kung nervously followed her. Finally, he began to growl. Radhya subsided into an armchair and took Kung on her lap.

"Poor baby," she soothed him, "you are so special. You pick up my anger? Poor, poor baby. I'll cool it down. It's all right."

She cuddled the kitten against her. Will hurried into the room.

"Lord Barone asked 72 to bring him his pants," he said.

Dave whispered into his wrist comp, and then listened. "72 will bring them right over."

"I used the treatment on Lord Barone," informed Will. "His leg is as good as new."

Radhya hung her head in her hands.

"Oh no," she groaned, "no one was supposed to know about that yet. Why didn't I think to tell you to treat him conventionally?"

"I'm sorry milady. I figured you would have wanted him healed as fast as possible," Will apologized.

"Actually, a crippled Lord Barone would have been such a blessing. Pour Kung got that nasty taste in his mouth, all for nothing." Lord Barone strode into the room. His tunic covered him to the bottom of his hips. He was bare between there and his boots.

"Where are my pants?" he demanded. "Hey you," he waved at Will, "did I not send you to get my pants? What are you standing around here for?"

Radhya rose from her chair spilling Kung from her lap. The lynxcat bristled and growled low in his throat.

"I'll thank you not to speak to my slaves like that. If I want them sent on errands, I'll send them. They take orders from me, not you. I can't see you tolerating it if I sent your guards on errands. Moreover, your pants have been sent for. It's only the speed of your own slave that holds them up." Barone blushed a furious scarlet. He tried vainly to pull the short garment down.

"Milady, I am sorry. I didn't see you there. I thought the slaves were alone."

"Yes and I see everything else," she teased.

Barone blushed more violently and tried vainly to tug his tunic down again.

"You once accused me of not wanting to look, is there now a problem with being looked at milord?" Radhya asked with a tiny smile.

"I only wished to surprise you when we finally set a contract day," replied Barone with all the dignity he could muster.

"Small enough surprise," she answered, much to Barone's mortification. "Come," she called to her bodyguards, "I must greet my other guests. "

The five people and the lynxcat swept from the room, leaving a furious and embarrassed Lord Barone sputtering behind.

"I'm going to pay for that one;" Radhya giggled when they were outside. The men returned her grin.

Chapter 6

The noise of another approach caused the five to hurry to the track gates. A very large horse van stopped beside them, and a large imperious lady leaned out of the opened window. Golden, upswept curls framed a pale face with large blue eyes; a small turned up nose and a cupid's mouth.

"Oh Kirbyson, you may direct me."

Radhya curtsied very low as the men bowed low behind her.

"Follow the road to the right, milady. The first large building is the visitor's center. The driver can just continue down the same road to the stable," Radhya told her respectfully.

The horse van lurched on.

"I never expected her to come," said Radhya wonderingly.

Max whispered, "Was that Princess Felina?"

"Yes, it was indeed. Imagine a single digit status coming for my first race. This is a miracle."

Later, Radhya busied herself greeting one arrival after another. Sixty invitations were sent out and fifty-seven accepted.

"Dave go home. Run all the security checks. Get Aninya to send my clothes for the gala to the owner's suite at the visitor's center. She might have to help the cooks with this mob. We only expected about half this many. Bring Jemelina too; she can help wait on the tables."

Dave hurried on his way.

"The usual turnout is fifty percent. I don't know what happened. Fortunately, I built the visitor's center for the review, so I have more than enough room."

"I think milady didn't take curiosity into account. After all, you've been a recluse for many years. They all want to see what you're about," said Padr.

"You're probably right Padr. You've done me proud, however."

Her eyes roved from the rugged, pristine mountaintops down the hillside covered in masses of bright yellow and royal purple blooms. Bracketing the grandstands were the flame trees, flickering in the wind. In front of the stands was the most spectacular flower show on any planet. Every color and every shape imaginable were encompassed in the beds. Most of the species she had altered or created new according to Padr's vision. Plants and shrubs of total white bordered the burning vibrant colors around the grandstand areas. Beyond this broadband, blooms were pastel, mounded around the paths and shading gradually again, into the rainbow hues around the visitor's center. Cascading down the rocks to the ocean, the plants shifted to blue and green so that the water and land became indistinguishable. Inside the rings of the track, there were no flowers, but an array of fungi species put on a unique display. They appeared as gemstones of unusual shape that were growing from a sheet of solid copper. Everywhere were paths, fountains and flowing water, with benches for visitors to sit and admire the view. Bare patches sported the fuzzy emerald lawn. It was a breathtaking, fascinating kaleidoscope.

Greeting duties over, Radhya returned to the visitor's center. As she entered, Noel grabbed her arm and pulled her to one side. Will seized Kung by the collar as he crouched to launch himself. Max and Padr followed her, watching to see if she needed rescuing.

"Away with you two!" snarled Lord Barone.

He shoved Radhya beside a tree. The meep inhabiting it cheeped in terror, jumped down and scurried across the floor to another shuhan. The lady wiggled her hands to indicate for Max and Padr to stay close. Will joined them, holding tightly to Kung.

"You made a fool of me," hissed Lord Barone.

"Nonsense," replied Radhya squirming in his tight grip.

She drew as far away from him as possible. "You are making a fool of yourself right now."

"How dare you laugh at me in front of slaves?" he continued shoving his face close to her.

"Don't be ridiculous. First, why should you, or any of us care what slaves think? Second, everything that happened is because you attacked me. I could report it to the proctors you know. Third, everyone who matters is looking at us very strangely right now. No one was even here before. Fourth, as if the size of a man's penis should matter to me when I could give him a treatment and have it grow to thirty centimeters in a week. Fifth, you're hurting me, and I will tell that slave to let Kung go it you don't stop."

Noel released her and looked over his shoulder. He noted the curious glances of the aristocracy. He also noticed Kung struggling in Will's arms.

"Do you mean it?" he asked.

"Mean what?" she snapped back.

"About the treatment?"

Radhya raised one eyebrow and looked at him.

"Let me kiss you," Noel suggested. "Everyone will think it was a lover's quarrel. They all know I've spoken of a contract to you."

"On the hand only," said Radhya extending one.

Noel grabbed her and kissed her hard on the mouth.

Releasing her, he swaggered away. Radhya spit and bristled like Kung, eyes like thunderstorms.

"Get me to my suite," she snapped for all the world like a true aristocrat.

Max cleared the way, Padr, and Will on either side with Kung slinking behind. The royals in the foyer exchanged knowing glances. Some of the women tittered behind their hands.

Radhya slapped her hand on the plate of the lift. It whisked her and her companions to her room, which was large and ostentatious. Everything was black, white, or silver. The walls were white, and the flooring was black and white squares. Ornately carved and stuffed blackwood sofa and chairs circled the room. A silver chandelier dangled from the ceiling not far from a large blackwood desk with a built-in comcentre that occupied one corner. The black draperies opened on a view of the ocean. Radhya stood staring at it for some time, distress in the set of her shoulders and the line of her back. Her men stood like statues. This was not the owner they were used to. Only Kung prowled restlessly, investigating the room. A chime shivered in the air.

Without turning her eyes from the waves, Radhya instructed, "If that is Aninya bring her in. If it's Dave tell him to check the crowd and dinner arrangements."

Aninya stepped from the lift carrying many boxes. She stopped short at the tension in the room.

"Milady?" she inquired.

Turning from the window, Radhya shook her head. "You men use the slave's closet over there." She gestured to a door on the far wall. "Prepare for the banquet tonight. Don't, absolutely don't, let that slime-eating piece of hemorrhoid near me tonight, at all! If Barone gets within ten meters of me, I'll puke."

Radhya strode to the large silver bathing room opposite the slave's quarters. She stripped off her dusty clothes tossing them to the silver-streaked marble floor. The facilities were far more than any single mortal needed but Radhya made use of them to the full. The men hurried to do the same in the tiny quarters they were allowed. Two hours later, she emerged, just before they would have been late.

Her men slaves couldn't look away. With raven hair was coiled on top of her head giving her much needed height, a gold and emerald tiara confining it, she looked like a woman from a fantasy. She wore makeup, enhancing her natural beauty, and glowing dark green emeralds hung from her ears, a single strand encircling her delicate neck. A low cut gown of shimmering green-black partially revealed her body, generous breasts threatening to spill from the front, while her waist looked tiny enough to span with one hand. From there the gown flared into a bell and flowed to the floor.

"I don't think I can breathe in this and I certainly can't bend over," Radhya said, "I expect you all to wait on me hand and foot like real slaves."

"Yes milady," they all chorused.

"More than my pleasure," added Max.

"Aninya, I'm sorry, I need you in the kitchen," instructed Radhya extending a hand.

"Yes milady," the cook replied.

"And thank you. You did a splendid job."

Aninya smiled and curtsied. Then she vanished into the lift. Radhya gestured to Kung to rest on the sofa and guard the rooms. She, Padr, Will, and Max followed Aninya into the lift. From the foyer, Radhya and her bodyguards went to the banquet room. The doors to the ballroom were folded back giving a beautiful view of a calm, sleepy ocean; blue and green waves feathered with touches of pink and gold from the setting sun. The ballroom was windowed on three sides, the fourth being the doors from the banquet room. The highly polished zebrawood floors glowed in the soft lighting of a dozen crystal chandeliers. Fully utilized, the banquet room itself would seat three thousand.

Tonight, it was set for a couple hundred guests. Many highly polished tables covered with snowy linens, tall, silver tapers rose from baskets of white flowers that graced the area. Their perfume filled the air.

Radhya threaded her way through the crowd, murmuring polite greetings and inquiries to the other aristocrats. Heads turned as she passed. Whispered discussions followed her trail. One whisper was louder than the rest.

"How come Barone was the only one to notice a piece like that?"

Radhya fixed the speaker with a steely glare. The culprit ducked his head and disappeared behind a slave carrying drinks. The slave offered the tray to her.

"Water only please," she spoke softly.

Will took the glass and tasted it before passing it to her. She absently sipped at it. After an hour of this torture, when the light had faded from the sky, and the stars had yet to appear, the slaves lit the tall silver candles.

"At last," Radhya sighed.

She threaded her way through the crowd to the top of the head table. It was her banquet, and she yielded pride of place to no one, not even the Princess Royal, Felina. The chief steward escorted that lady to the foot. Other stewards escorted the rest of the aristocracy to their assigned places. Soon all seven tables presently in the room filled with guests. Radhya sat down, everyone followed. She could see Dave by the door. He nodded at her. As the serving girls brought around the first course, savory odors wafted through the room.

"I must admit," began Princess Felina, "that my curiosity is piqued. I saw one of your new pet cats at Lady Shansea's house. It was most attractive. I had hoped to see some here, perhaps even buy some."

"I am sorry milady. Kung, who is just a half-grown kitten,

was with me earlier, but he was too excitable, so I left him in my room. Singha, his mother and Ringha, his sister are back at my home."

"What a charming habit you have of naming everything. Perhaps you can sell me one of your half grown kittens," said Lady Felina.

Radhya set down her fork. "I offer sincere apologies, Lady Felina. The lynxcat is much more than a pet. They have as much intelligence as chimpanzees, and they have the hierarchical mind of a dog. That means that at a young age, in their case between six weeks and three months, they bond or imprint on a person or another lynxcat. You cannot change that bonding once it occurs. If you remove them from the people they are bonded to, they will pine away and starve themselves to death."

"Oh pooh. I am sure you could do something about it."

"No milady, I could not. The purchaser of Ringha waited until she was three months old. I could not in good conscience sell her once bonding had begun. So now I have three instead of the two that I intended," answered Radhya calmly.

"But I do so want one of the darling things," cooed Princess Felina.

"Singha should be coming into heat shortly. Six months later, she will kit. I will let you know, and if you wish, you may purchase one. They are very costly, but I will bump you to the head of my list. I already have over two hundred and fifty names."

"My, then they will be very common, won't they?" replied the princess disappointedly.

"I doubt that," returned Radhya. "All the females I sell are sterile, and Singha breeds only twice a year at most. Of course, not everyone can afford the cost either."

Radhya named a price that caused the princess to raise her carefully sculpted brows.

"My, my," replied Lady Felina, "they will be a precious item. You must show me yours."

"When the banquet is over I will bring Kung down briefly. Please tell me about your entries for tomorrow."

Felina giggled. "I am afraid you will need all your lynxcat money when my Silver Bullet cleans out your purse."

The Princess continued bragging about her colt for some minutes. The other royalty joined in the discussion, each pointing out the merits of his or her own stock.

Lord Sutherland asked, "So Radhya, are you entering any of your own races?"

"Indeed I am, milord," she replied. "I have three racers that are good candidates."

"Have we seen them race before?" the stout Lord Pehelalatin inquired.

"No," answered Radhya. "Each one is on his or her maiden race tomorrow."

"Why I never heard of such a thing," exclaimed the pale Lady Amelia, contract spouse of Lord Pehelalatin. "Did you Jimmi, did you ever hear of sponsoring a race to start your own racers on their first run?"

"No, no my dear," he replied patting her hand.

"Ah, but we can always use some novelty, can we not?" spoke up the young blonde Lord Tavi. "Life is just so totally drear and boring, you know."

"Actually, milord, I do not," said Radhya. "I find no time to do all the things I would like to do."

Lord Tavi languidly waved his hand at her. "Ah yes. You are one of those working aristocrats who give the rest of us a bad name. Well please, don't bore us with tales of your wonderful occupation."

"Why milord, I would not dream of it. I do have some plans for further adventure/recreations you might enjoy."

All the Lords and Ladies dropped their languid poses.

"Something new?" inquired Lady Koom.

"Not entirely new, actually very ancient" replied Lady Kirbyson. "You see in my historical reading I came across descriptions of an endurance race. A race of often two or three hundred klicks. One rider, one horse on a prescribed course against maybe twenty or thirty competitors. A real test of skill and hardiness. I thought to see this week if I could interest anyone in such a competition."

"Will there be betting on the outcome?" asked Lady Felina.

"Undoubtedly, there will be wagering as to the mettle of the man and beast," interrupted Lord Sutherland.

"Ah, something to get the juices flowing" replied Lord Tavi, rubbing his hands together.

"A race lasting a couple of days perhaps?" asked Lady Amelia. "That would be perfect. These races tomorrow are over so quickly one has hardly time to enjoy them."

"I'm sure it would be more thrilling than show jumping. That is such a total yawn," Lord Tavi put in.

"I will be surveying the crowd tonight to check on the interest. I take it all of you at the table would be favorable?" questioned Radhya.

Murmurs of assent greeted her last statement. She relaxed back into her chair, smiling.

Finishing the last bite of her dessert she looked at Lady Felina, saying, "If you will excuse me now, I will fetch Kung for you to see."

Radhya rose and glided across the banquet room trailed by her three guards. Returning to her room, she put a new golden collar on Kung and attached a braided gold lead, studded with emeralds. Then they returned to the crowd of aristocrats.

Oh's and Ah's followed their progress across the floor, interrupting the musicians who were just tuning up their instruments in the ballroom. Extra slaves crowded around the tables as they cleared away the remains of the banquet. Radhya led Kung straight to Lady Felina.

"Milady, this is Kung," she introduced, "and I would warn you against trying to pet him. He is not the cuddly type."

She heard a snicker from one of the bodyguards behind her.

"Oh, pooh," said the Princess. She bent over to pet Kung. The lynxcat backed and fluffed his fur, hissing at her. Lady Felina snapped her hand back.

"Well, I never! You were not joking," she said frostily.

"No, milady. You see these have been carefully tailored and bred as bodyguards. Kung guards me...."

"And I wouldn't put his reflexes to the test. I did and paid for the consequences," came the voice of Lord Barone from behind her.

Radhya's men circled her and kept Barone from approaching any closer.

"Oh Noel, what happened?" inquired Felina.

"I was testing the reflexes of her bodyguards, who after all trained at my facility, and this little beast sank his claws and teeth into my leg. Fortunately, the medical facilities here are excellent," said Barone craftily.

"But still, how perfectly dreadful," cooed the Princess. "Is it safe to have him in such a crowd?"

"As long as no one tries to harm me or to pet him I think he will be absolutely safe," answered Radhya glaring at Barone from behind Max.

"Now the first dance is about to start, Radhya," broke in Noel. "I think I should partner you in it."

"Do you now?" snorted Radhya. "I am sorry Lord Barone, but Lord Tavi was to be my partner."

Handing Kung's leash to Max, she held out her hand to the vapid young Lord dressed in pale green. His golden curls bobbed uneasily in response.

"Ah yes, of course, Lady Kirbyson, that is quite the honor. I shall be delighted to lead the dance with you. Ah, with your permission, of course, Noel," he replied glancing uneasily into Lord Barone's raging face.

"You don't need his permission, only mine," stated Radhya emphatically.

She led Lord Tavi to the middle of the gigantic dancing floor and nodded to the musicians. They struck up an ancient tune called a waltz. Many aristocrats and their spouses soon joined them on the floor.

"What a perfect foil," exclaimed Princess Felina, clapping her hands together. "He is so fair and light against her darkness. An absolute picture. Maybe you will have some competition, Noel."

The princess whispered to one of her bodyguards. The woman aimed a holomera at the waltzing pair.

"Princess, since the love of my life has abandoned me, would you console my grieving spirit in the dance?" Lord Barone asked her.

The princess gave him her hand and giggled as he led her into the melee.

Chapter 7

As the orchestra swung into a more modern tune, Lady Kirbyson returned to her guards waiting by the door. Lord Tavi vanished quickly in search of less stressful partners.

"I think trouble is brewing," Radhya told her men. "Felina and Noel are whispering together in a way I don't like."

"Maybe you are a bit jealous of his paying her some attention," murmured Padr.

Radhya gave him a withering look. The conspiring couple soon joined them.

"Oh my dear, oh my dear," began Lady Felina excitedly, "Noel and I have the most perfect plan. You two are to be contracted after the big race tomorrow." She clapped her hands.

"What!" yelled Radhya, "I don't think so!"

"But my dear, he is ever so perfect a match for you. He would advance your status two hundred points. And he loves you dearly."

"Princess for one, Noel Barone loves only a profit. He wants what he can make from me. For two, I can take care of my status myself. For three I am far too busy to take a spouse at this time," spoke Radhya in a tightly controlled voice

Lord Barone stood smirking behind the Princess.

"Oh pooh," she replied, "I am single digit status and if I decide to order you I can, and I shall, or you will lose all status and go down to freedman rank on every world in the Commonwealth. Noel will have your property in compensation. I cannot believe you would be so foolish."

"You would remove my status because I don't wish to contract on your command?" questioned Radhya aghast.

"Why yes. It is our royal wish."

"I could fight this in the courts, with the proctors," argued Radhya. "I will simply ask my father to make it a royal command from the king. No court will deny him. You will lose."

Radhya turned her back and thought furiously for a few minutes. She breathed deeply. Will and Padr were looking at her in alarm. Max, holding Kung's leash, looked almost ready to panic. Radhya touched each man on the arm in turn. She stood looking into Padr's blue eyes.

"Well what is your answer?" demanded Princess Felina.

Radhya answered coolly, "Milady, it is in no way I want to go against your will, but doesn't every woman dream of her contract day as being very special. Even the freedmen make a special celebration for their weddings. You know what we woman want, a fancy gown, cakes, parties, family, flowers, the ceremony itself. Doesn't every little girl dream of that?"

Felina clapped her pudgy hands together. "Yes, yes of course."

"But milady," continued Radhya, "if I contract tomorrow, my family isn't here; there would be no special gown, flowers, cakes, parties or any such wonderful things. I do not want to share my special day with a major horse race either. I would need a decent interval to prepare. Isn't the preparation at least half the fun?"

"Oh yes, yes," cooed Lady Felina. "Noel, you wicked boy,

you told me she wouldn't be sentimental about such things and yet look how dismayed she looks at the thought of not having them."

Barone replied, "Forgive me, Princess, perhaps I don't know Radhya as well as I thought. How romantic to think about getting to know her better. Would a month from now be acceptable?"

Both Radhya and Felina looked at him in horror.

"Oh no. These things take many months to get just right; sometimes even more than a year," said the Princess.

"I know," exclaimed Radhya," I have absolutely the most perfect idea!"

"Do tell!" begged Felina.

"I was planning to apply to host the status review. I am sure your highness could get the status review committee to choose Pleasant as the review site, and if so, I could have a contract day after the review. The entire aristocracy would be there. Why your royal father could escort me to the podium. A fantasy for any girl. And I would be so grateful too if you could help me plan the entire thing, your taste and style is known far and wide."

Princess Felina glowed with pleasure, giving Radhya a suffocating hug.

"How perfect, how absolutely perfect!" she sighed. "Two years is just enough time to plan such a contracting. Moreover, your status can be all settled the day before. Yes, it's perfect."

Radhya interrupted, "that is of course if my status does not exceed Noel's, on my own merits. Then the joining would be of no benefit to me at all."

Everyone laughed. "Of course, my dear. We couldn't have you contracting beneath you, could we? But tomorrow, you must commit and exchange betrothal presents. Yes?" questioned Felina.

"If Lord Barone wishes an unwilling fiancé and if it is your wish milady," answered Radhya.

"I cannot thank you enough Princess," interrupted Lord Barone. "By myself, I could never get her to agree."

Radhya gave him a sour look. "I can't guess what you want for a betrothal present. Perhaps something to make something larger?"

"Delicately put, my Lady. You could give me no greater pleasure, and your pleasure too, no doubt," said Noel.

Bowing to the royals present, Radhya headed for the door. She muttered under her breath as she went up to Dave, who was at the entrance to the foyer.

"Dave, see that everyone is comfortable. They can drink and dance as late as they want. See them all to bed and close things down for me. I have to go home. Don't let anyone follow me, especially that odious Barone."

"Yes, milady."

She strode across the foyer and out into the night. The air was cooling compared to the funk inside. The Milky Way spread a chequered carpet overhead, making it bright enough to walk without a light. Around the track, moonflowers glowed with a cool white radiance adding their offering of light to the night. The Lady went very quickly, and the men had to hurry to keep up. Max slipped the leash from Kung who bounded ahead.

On the trail to the house, it was darker, much darker. The woven branches intercepted the light from the sky overhead. A fair piece down the trail, Kung let out a warbling yowl. A violent snort exploded just ahead as the people halted. A huge shadowy body bounded off the trail.

"Milady," Padr caught her arm.

She touched his hand. "It's okay. Kung scared it away. Giant red deer, very cranky. They don't usually come onto the trail. We are safe from it with Kung, but watch out for dire wolves. They hunt the deer, and I don't control most of them. They would eat Kung in one bite."

They hurried along more quickly, as close to running as

Radhya could get in the long gown. The gates loomed darkly in front of them, sparkling faintly with electricity.

"Padr, I want you to plant moonflowers along the path when this race is over."

Padr nodded at her as she pressed the touchpad and spoke to the gate. Reading her genetic code and voiceprint, it silently glided open. On the other side, she shut and sealed the gate again. They sped on.

At the house, Radhya flew up the stairs, straight to lab two. The bodyguards followed while Kung greeted his mother and sisters.

"Will, assist by going to the archive file and getting Barone's DNA code. Padr mix my unzipping cocktail and reduce it to a tablet. Max, I need the rezipping cocktail, 300 ml. Make it taste very bad."

Geo came in as Radhya got to work. In a hard, tight voice, Radhya outlined the disaster at the ball. Shaking his head, he shuffled off.

Radhya, Padr, Max, and Will worked all night. Just before the sun rose, they examined their efforts, a small white tablet, a very large purple capsule, and a bottle of thick, blue liquid. Radhya packaged them carefully in a colorful box with a red ribbon.

"The first race is at noon. Get some sleep. I'll see you down-stairs at 11:00," Radhya told the men.

As the men all stumbled off to sleep, Radhya used her wrist comp to talk to Geo. She arranged for him to handle the preparation for the race and told him to get Aninya to oversee break-fast at the visitor's center, the light buffet lunch at the track and the final banquet for the evening gala. Then Radhya stumbled off to her own bed for a couple hours of sleep.

Chapter 8

A ll too shortly, Radhya's time sense awakened her. Laid out on her dressing table were beautiful sea green pants, tunic, and hooded robe. The robe had waves embroidered around its hem in shades of green that shimmered and ran like water. Combs for her hair were set on top. They were a solid material resembling water. Under the clothes was a note from Aninya saying she had sent a gown and accessories for tonight's banquet to Radhya's room at the visitor's center. Radhya blessed her as she stumbled into the shower to begin preparations for the day.

She met her bodyguards downstairs, and they retraced their route of the night before. She was soothed on the walk by the songbirds and lizards. Radhya gave the present to Will to carry in Max's new invention, a special stasis pouch on his belt.

At the track, people were milling everywhere. Many more than the participants had obviously arrived this morning. Additional people were thronging through the gate. Radhya checked the boards for the odds on her horses. The distaff mile was the third race, and Secretary was 100 to 1. The fifth race was a mile and a half. Tango Dancer was 87 to 1 in it. The Helix Cup, which was to be a major annual race, was sixth. Son-O-War was 237 to 1.

Radhya smiled and headed for the betting comps. After wagering a small fortune on her horses, she retired to her owner's box. A light buffet was laid out, as per her instructions. She tucked in ravenously.

"Each of you grab something here. Just don't let anyone see you," she told them.

Padr watched as Max and Will gobbled down the sandwiches. As slaves showed up to replenish the trays, they glanced from the corners of their eyes at the slaves eating at the royal's buffet.

"Radhya, my dearest," Noel slid into the box trailed by Princess Felina. "I have a little-written contract for you. Just so our deal is binding."

Princess Felina was wringing her hands.

"I don't think much of you treating your fiancé this way," she scolded.

"But my dear Princess, how could I bear it if after you left, Radhya decided to renege on our verbal agreement?" Noel said condescendingly.

"Oh dear, I suppose you must love her a lot, but it is just not romantic to make her sign a contract to contract with you," Felina whined.

Radhya said, "Oh I don't mind."

Noel looked from under lowered brows.

"As long as my conditions are met I am agreeable to sign this thing. However, if it does not say that if my status, on my own merits, exceeds his, then everything is off," Radhya commented.

"But my dear," replied Felina, "You know the odds of that are astronomical."

"Yes, I know, but I want it in hard copy anyway. After all, the penalty is here in writing. 'If the contractee,' that is me, 'fails to perform by signing the merger contract no later than the day after the status review, she shall be stripped of all status and lands and estates and patents and be relegated to the ranks of freedmen, with no possibility of review.' So I think my clause should be included as well."

"Oh dear, I didn't want Noel to put that in there. It is one thing to say such a thing to persuade a reluctant bride, but another to threaten it in writing. I am so sorry my dear," explained Princess Felina.

"What hold does Barone have on you to make you do this?" inquired Radhya.

Felina's eyes grew wide, and she blushed, shaking her head.

"At least Princess, make my contract day beautiful will you?"

Felina perked up and began to sparkle. "Oh Radhya, I give you my word that your contract day will be the most beautiful one since my mother and father joined. I'll see to it. And this place is so beautiful. Until, yesterday, I never realized how truly unusual and gorgeous this place is. With this, I can do miracles. It is even more spectacular than Junction."

"Thank you milady," said Radhya bowing her head at the compliment.

More high-status aristocrats came by as the time for the first race approached. Without exception, the visitors expressed appreciation for the track and surroundings.

Lord Desmoinnis stayed to watch the first race with them. He was dressed in conservative dove grey, his florid jowls an intrusion in the color pattern for his hair was the same grey as his robe. His colt, Socail, was in the first race. It was 2 to 1 to win. Noel Barone's Killer was at 30 to 1, and Barone sputtered about ignorant idiots.

Lord Barone put his arm possessively around Radhya's shoulders. She shook her head as Max and Padr moved to shift him. As the trumpets sounded for the parade to post, Noel led her to the front of the box. She extracted herself politely. Noel pointed out a big, bony, solid bay. The jockey was dressed in Noel's scarlet red livery.

Socail was a grey with a white star and a white sock. His livery was dove grey and beet red.

"That's my Killer. He should wipe the track with these lesser horses," Noel bragged.

"Socail is no slouch. He'll give your colt a run for his money," Lord Desmoinnis stated.

"My colt running in the fifth, is half-brother to Socail," Radhya said, "and the stud I bought for my breeding farm is a full older brother to Killer. So I will watch this race with great interest."

Barone glared at Desmoinnis, who, engrossed with the animals going into the gates, totally ignored him. Finally, the colts were loaded in the chutes. The bell rang, and they were off.

Socail broke in front and quickly took the rail. A couple of other horses passed him, and he settled third, running well and steady. Killer trailed the pack, bobbing and fighting his jockey. They zoomed past the quarter pole, and the red rider began laying it on with the whip. Killer fought, then at the half, he began to run. The front-runners started to fade, and Socail moved to second place. Killer, moving like a machine placed himself fourth. A failing front-runner boxed him against the rail. At the three-quarter pole, Socail turned on the speed, smoothly springing into first place. Killer fought his way free. He was burning up the track again. Socail spread out and flashed past the finish line, beating Killer by a head.

Lord Desmoinnis flushed redder with pleasure. "Milady it seems I have the honor of being the first winner at your new track. Excuse me, please, to leave for the winner's circle," he requested.

"Certainly milord. Perhaps you will escort Lady Felina. She will be doing the presentations today. Unless she is the winner, and then I suppose I will have to do the honors," Radhya informed him.

"My pleasure" replied Lord Desmoinnis.

He, Princess Felina, and all their guards left the box. Now

their two entourages were alone, the Lady turned to Barone, staring straight into his livid face.

"I don't know what you did to the Princess to get her to force me into this contract farce, but I doubt if you'll get much pleasure from it."

"Bah!" snarled Barone. "I don't talk business when I'm racing. Don't bother me now. Killer should have won."

"He certainly had the speed," agreed Radhya. "He just needs better training and a better jockey."

"Don't tell me how to race horses. I've been racing for twenty-five years. You have not had your first race yet."

"Fine, let's talk about your betrothal present. If it is taken incorrectly, it can kill. Changing your genetic fingerprint is a serious thing. You do realize, don't you, that if you have any genetic locks on anything they will have to all be reprogrammed."

"I told you, I don't talk business at races!" he yelled.

"I heard you. I'll explain how to use it, then, before the banquet, in front of all these Lords and Ladies, who I am sure, are dying for some juicy gossip and your insecurity about the size of your penis will be very titillating I'm sure."

"Sh-sh-sh" whispered Barone, glancing over his shoulder at his slaves and hers. "I guess you are right. Give me the instructions now."

"Excuse me," she snarled back, "I don't talk business at a race."

Lord Barone ground his teeth. "I am sorry my dear, dear Radhya. I should not have spoken like that. I get upset when I lose. Please, let's sit down here and explain all the wonders you have created for me."

He put his arm around her waist. She removed it. Noel put his arm around her again.

"Padr," she called with warning in her voice.

Padr stalked forward. Barone let her go and merely held his

hand toward the comfortable sofa on the back wall. Radhya complied grudgingly.

"Now," he commanded, "tell me all about it."

Arms folded across her chest Radhya glared at him a moment, then smiled a dangerous smile.

"First, it will be very painful. I mean that sincerely. Every experimental subject so far has reported excruciating pain for about two weeks. I hope that in your case it will be three weeks. Then everything returns to normal, except bigger. You have three things, a tablet, a capsule, and a liquid. Timing is essential. Have an attendant standing by with a molecular timing piece, minimum. This is timed to the second. If you are not accurate, it will dry up and fall off. First, get comfortable, you will be very dizzy. Take the tablet. Wait exactly two hours, exactly, right to the second. Then take the capsule. Wait exactly, and again I mean exactly twelve hours and thirteen minutes. Twelve hours and fourteen minutes can kill you. Twelve hours and twelve minutes will not give you your full potential. Therefore, in twelve hours and thirteen minutes you drink the liquid. Get every drop. Rinse the bottle and drink that to make sure you get it all. Now you chug, don't sip. That's about all there is to it. But remember, it is going to hurt."

"How much bigger?" asked Barone.

"At least double maybe a little more. Two centimeters becomes four; four becomes eight, six becomes twelve, you get the idea," she answered. "Oh and don't try to analyze it so you can recreate and sell it. Each one is based on the individual's own DNA. Yours would not work for anyone else. I have had a necessity to become that specific in my work."

"When did you make it then?" he asked. "We only agreed to this last night?"

"The four of us," she said indicating her slaves, "stayed up the whole night making it. And for the record, you forced me into this arrangement. I didn't agree. How about if I give this to you as a free gift and we just forget the contracting. Then we can go back to being friends."

Lord Barone's smile made her blood run cold. She forced back the shadows waiting to pounce, that memory that always hovered, just beneath the surface of her mind.

"Distaff Mile is the next race, and I want to see my horse win," snapped Radhya jumping up from the sofa, fear distilled into anger.

"Very few horses win their maiden race," a smug Noel replied.

Radhya moved to the front of the box. The post parade for the third had started, Secretary in position number one. She pranced tautly; her blood-colored coat gleaming in the sun. She shook her ebony mane and tail fiercely. Radhya's livery colors were light emerald green and dark forest green, a color that glowed against her bay coat.

Lord Barone's entry was Harlot's Heat, a large black filly. To Radhya, his horse appeared to hang over on the front end. The filly stalked along as though alone, to the number three position. The red livery looked gruesome on her darkness.

Lady Love was Princess Felina's entry. She was a pure silvery white, delicate yet athletic. She wore, of course, the royal purple. She minced her way along the track, spurning it with her hooves.

Seven other entries were starting as well. Radhya gripped the ledge at the front of the box until her knuckles whitened.

"You'd best relax milady. You give your suitor too much ammunition," whispered Padr in her ear.

She glanced around to see Lord Barone watching her closely, a superior smile on his narrow lips. Lady Kirbyson relaxed every muscle as much as possible while still maintaining her same pose.

The starting bell caught her off guard. Focusing her attention on the fillies flying around the track, Radhya could see nothing at first, but as they passed the quarter pole, she could just distinguish Barone's filly in the lead. She looked at him, and his eyes were glowing with manic glee, his lips pulled back exposing his teeth like a snarling wolf. Radhya shivered and looked away.

The horses were tearing down the track at a furious speed. Harlot's Heat was still in front, but Lady Love and Secretary were breaking from the pack. Stride by stride they crept closer to the black filly, running together neck by neck. The audience in the grandstands rose roaring to their feet. In a rush, the white and the bay passed the front-runner. In an astounding burst of speed, Lady Love pulled ahead of Secretary and flashed passed the wire a half-length in the lead.

Radhya felt a knife of disappointment course through her. She looked around. Noel was flying thunderclouds again, stamping back and forth across the floor. Radhya quickly grabbed hold of her emotions, deciding never to be a sore loser.

Placing a smile on her face, she said, "Not too bad for a first race is it now?"

Padr gave her a sympathetic look, but Max and Will looked blank.

"Excellent, my dear," sneered Noel. "Excellent for you anyway."

Lady Kirbyson swept from the box and down to the winner's circle. Princess Felina, flushed with success and pleasure, was beaming at the crowd. After the presentation, Radhya stayed to speak to some of the other aristocracy. She was gracious to all, receiving congratulations on a fine start to her racing career. She returned to her box for the fifth because Tango Dancer was a contestant. The box was fortuitously empty when she returned.

"Oh Will," she sighed, "this is going to kill me. I don't seem to handle such excitement very well. Have you got something to help calm me down, keep me cool?"

As Will reached for his kit, Padr pushed him away.

"This is part of living. You've been a recluse so long you don't know how to live anymore. Are you so scared of having an honest emotion that you want to drug it away the first time it appears? If you drug yourself every time you feel anything, you're not the person I thought you were," He stated.

Shocked, Radhya looked at him, her mouth agape. After thinking a minute, she replied, "Thank you. You are correct. I must control myself by myself, not rely on a drug. That would have been a shameful mistake. I am grateful."

Padr bowed his head and turned away. Radhya went to the front of the box to watch Tango Dancer.

Her colt was number seven, a beautiful gleaming grey. He walked the track calmly, ebony mane and tail glistening in the sunlight. He was undoubtedly the most beautiful animal on the track that day. Radhya could see patrons below her pointing to him and consulting their programs.

Just as they were at the starting gate, Noel pranced in.

"Well" he gloated, "did you see my Keddedy Bay win the fourth? My Voyager will clean up this one as well."

The gates flew up, and the horses were off. Fleur-de-Lis and Calcutta Rat took the early lead and fought a seesaw war for first place. First one then the other was leading, throwing clods of dirt backward to the third and fourth place runners. Tango Dancer kept his fourth position until the halfway point. He exploded down the track. Calcutta Rat and Fleur-de-Lis might as well have been standing still. Radhya couldn't breathe with the beauty of Tango's running. Faster and faster he moved, like clouds before a hurricane. Tango Dancer crossed the finish line seven lengths in front and still pulling away. The stands were silent. Then a roar clove the air.

Radhya felt so weak she backed to the sofa and sat down. Noel stared at her, mouth hanging open.

"I never," he sputtered, "I never saw a horse run like that. You bred him?"

"No" murmured Radhya, "I commissioned a breeder on Kentucky to breed him for me. I just selected his parents."

"Amazing," said Noel shaking his head. "When we contract he will belong to me as well."

"Milady," interrupted Padr, "They will need you in the winner's circle."

Radhya rose on shaky legs and left. This time the roles were reversed. Lady Felina presented her with the trophy. Radhya hugged Li and Tan, the jockey.

"A reward for you both. Tell me what you want when we all get home tonight."

She hugged them both again. "Hurry," she cried to her bodyguards, "the main event will be starting soon. I don't want to miss Son-O-War. "

"I hope you don't hope for another race like that. Something like that happens once in a lifetime," commented Padr.

Radhya merely grinned at him and rushed on her way. Back in the box, Lord Barone was waiting. Radhya felt the joy drain from her at the sight of him.

"Now all the premium runners will be out," he explained to her. "There's Lady Felina's Silver Bullet. He's a full brother to Lady Love. Then there's Lady Koom's Exodus; he's a real bugger to beat. Ocean Pearl is a big threat, so is Irritation. Of course, my big black colt, Single Might, is going to be the winner. I am glad though, one of your entries won, and second isn't a bad place for a maiden race either."

"Milord, let's have the Helix Cup run before you hand out the prize to yourself," Lady Kirbyson replied.

The field was very large, twenty-four horses. The post parade seemed endless to Radhya, and she was sure time stood still until the barrier was sprung.

Son-O-War sprang to the lead; his huge body blazing like wildfire down the track. His distance from the other racers grew with every stride. All the mighty racers, the cream of the aristo-cratic stables, were left behind in the dust, like smoke to his flame. He crossed the finish line thirty lengths ahead of Silver Bullet and Single Might who had a photo finish for second place, Single Might's black snout a hair ahead of Lady Felina's favorite.

"Well, it seems I am destined to be second to you, again," snarled Lord Barone. "Today only, you realize."

"Hopefully forever" laughed Radhya as she bounced off to the winner's circle again.

Princess Felina handed her the huge double helix of emeralds, rubies, sapphires, and diamonds. It was a gaudy barbaric thing, exactly as Radhya had commissioned it. As the crowd cheered and applauded, Radhya beamed at everyone. Crowds surrounded her and congratulated her making the guards work hard to get her some breathing room.

When the commotion cleared, Padr spoke quietly to her. "These are animals you picked the parents of, and I am very impressed. I understand you also picked me?"

"No" she replied softly. "I never picked you, that was all my grandfather's doing. I'll try to explain it to you someday."

Chapter 9

In her room, the Lady looked dubiously at the outfit Aninya had left.

"I don't think this exactly fits my image as Lady Death, do you?" she asked her bodyguards, holding up a small gown, shoulderless, very low cut, skin tight to the knees where it flared like a goldfish tail. It was black with red tiger stripes running downward. There were spike-heeled black shoes and red elbow high gloves striped in black.

"Where did she find a monstrosity like that? I can't remember anything of this sort in my clothing room," Radhya puzzled.

"I believe that Dave said Jemelina made it," replied Will. "At least try it on. She probably worked very hard on it to please you."

"No!" stated Radhya emphatically. "I'll go to the banquet in what I am wearing."

"If you do you'll offend every aristocrat there, especially Lady Felina," said Padr.

"Everyone will think it's for Lord Barone," spoke Max in a

tight voice. "And think how hurt Jemelina will be if you don't wear it."

Radhya frowned and wrinkled her nose. "Is there anyone at home who could bring me something else?"

Max tried his wrist comp. "The only one around is Geo. He says wear what you have; he is too old to run over here and be a ladies maid."

"I don't want to look like Lady Sex."

"Unless you want to go naked I don't think you have a lot of choice here," counselled Padr.

Radhya dragged off to prepare herself. Will called her as soon as she had slithered and stuffed herself into the dress.

"Radhya, Aninya sent these up," he told her displaying a necklace and hair band of fire gems and black pearls. "Aninya apologized. She is too busy to see to you herself. The final food preparations are not going well in the kitchen, Dave found something, and they had to redo a lot of dishes."

"I can't breathe in this thing. It is excessively tight. I can't draw any air in," Radhya complained. "How am I supposed to put that stuff on with these?"

She thrust her arms encased in long gloves in the air.

"Let me," chimed in Max.

Max slipped the string of gems around Radhya's throat. Unfortunately, the clasp snarled in her hair. After much tugging and ripping of strands, he got it free and fastened properly.

"I am sorry milady," he apologized.

She brushed her hair smooth again and tried to put the hair band in. Every attempt it went crooked. She approached Max. He couldn't straighten it either. Nor was Will able to get the recalcitrant piece of metal to sit evenly on her hair.

"I paid a fortune for the pack of you, and there is not a decent serving wench among you. Padr give it a try."

From a drawer, Padr extracted his measuring tools. It was to no avail; the hair band would not sit straight. Radhya gave it a tweak.

"If you can't get perfection, then go for randomness," she instructed, the gems glowing lopsidedly in her hair.

"Well," interrupted Padr sarcastically, "You might as well look the part all the way. Lord Barone is going to think you are hot for him. They probably will call you Lady Sex after you parade around in that all night."

"You're the one who said I had to wear it," Radhya snarled back.

"I'm sorry milady. I didn't realize that it was so revealing. It just looks totally out of character for you, more like something you would find in a pleasure house."

"Well, it is certainly no pleasure for me. I can't even breathe. Jemelina had better appreciate my wearing this for her. By the way, don't let her design anything for me ever again."

Radhya and the bodyguards left the safety of the room. As Dave met her at the door of the banquet room, her face was like thunder.

"I am sorry, milady. I told Jemelina to check with you first. She fancies herself an extraordinary fashion designer. I apologize for her. Please, don't punish her, she was only trying to make tonight special."

"Especially embarrassing," snorted Radhya. "Dave, I appreciate her efforts. But the measurement is wrong. I can't walk and can barely breathe and don't, just don't ever let her make me anything again."

Dave bowed his head as every eye in the place fastened itself on Lady Kirbyson. The sound of shock rippled through the room. Noel fairly flew to take her arm.

"My dear," he murmured down at her, "I am horrified. I never suspected you of wanting to be a nightclub singer."

"Why my dear almost fiancé I thought you would be wanting to make all the other men and some of the women jealous of your excellent taste," she snapped. "Maybe you could take a holo for Krin."

Barone stopped dead on the journey across the floor,

flushing a bright scarlet. Radhya tugged him forward, very aware of every eye upon them.

"Shall we get this farce over?"

"I think I prefer you in your basic black," he replied recovering his composure.

"Then I chose well," she smiled thinly.

Radhya and Noel ascended the musician's stage. The attention of everyone in the room remained riveted on the couple.

"At the request of Princess Felina," began Radhya nodding at the Lady, "Lord Noel Barone and I are entering into an agreement to contract together, in two years time, right after our status review, provided my status, on my own merits does not exceed his. If this criterion is met, we will contract on the day after the review. However, if my status is higher, then the whole contracting is off. Therefore, as we sign the agreement, I welcome you to our final banquet. I want to congratulate all who had winners. I want to console all who had losers. I hope you will bring your horses frequently, and race often and well. Please stay as long as you like. Now that the invitational is over, there is still regular race season. Please enjoy yourselves. Noel and I will sign our agreement and exchange tokens. Then everyone can eat."

Polite applause hailed her speech. A slave placed a document on the lectern. Radhya reread it to make sure it was suitably amended. Then she affixed her thumbprint after a struggle with the glove. Noel did the same with less effort.

"Now for your gift," said Radhya coldly.

She nodded to Will who removed the package from its container. He handed it to Lady Kirbyson. She, with great ceremony, bestowed it on Lord Barone.

"A planet's ransom," she stated with a smile, "and a man's whole ego, made large."

Lord Barone accepted eagerly but with equal reverence. Those in the crowd shook their heads in puzzlement. A buzz of confusion rose from the floor. Noel clapped his hands. A bodyguard in Barone's scarlet livery escorted three naked females, with slave collars, across the floor to the podium.

The first was as tall as Padr, slender as a whip. She had short blonde hair and large brown eyes with lacy rings around the pupil. Radhya saw Padr stiffen from the corner of her eye. The second slave was her height. She had blunt-cut black hair to her collarbones. With her large breasts and small waist, Radhya was sure it was as close to her appearance as Noel dared to get, yet her eyes made her look very different from Radhya. The third was a willowy girl with lacy ringed blue eyes and fine, curly brown hair. She didn't resemble anyone Radhya knew, but she heard Will gasp behind her at the sight of the last slave.

"Three slaves for love," Lord Barone was speaking, "one for faithfulness, one for truth, and one for beauty. A gift for my betrothed. All have been trained as guards and body servants as well, to protect and take care of you. Now you can get rid of those inappropriate men."

Lord Barone smiled broadly. A spattering of applause greeted his gift; all the men nodding knowingly. This was a gift they could understand. Radhya's blood ran cold. This was the purpose of the whole betrothal thing, saddling her with spies she could not decently get rid of; who were no doubt going to disrupt her plans, using their sex as a weapon against her closest co-conspirators. She looked coldly at Noel; the noise of the crowd roared in her ears. She felt like vomiting, and was afraid she would mortally embarrass herself. The noise receded, and the world went away.

The Lady crumpled to the floor of the stage. Noel jumped back and quick as thought her three guards surrounded her. Dave came plowing through the crowd like a battleship, shoving servants and royals alike from his prow. Rory appeared like magic from nowhere.

"Get her to her room," the pilot commanded.

Padr cradled her head and gathered her in his arms. They made their way to the lift the other men made a wall around her with their bodies. At the room, Padr laid her on the bed and gently straightened her limbs. Will checked her thoroughly with his equipment.

"No poison, no devices," he diagnosed. "I don't know what is wrong with her."

"Perhaps that ugly dress is too tight?" said Rory.

The men looked at each other perplexed.

"We should call Aninya for help then," ventured Will.

"Oh for pity sakes," said Rory.

The bodyguards turned their backs as Rory stripped off the offending dress and hurled it to the floor. He threw a blanket over her. Radhya drew a deep shuddering breath, then another. A few minutes later, she opened her eyes.

Rory whispered into his wrist unit. He went into the bathroom and disappeared. Padr, Max, Will, and Dave exchanged puzzled looks.

"What happened?" Radhya asked softly.

"I think you fainted," said Will.

"I what?"

"You fainted. I think your dress was too tight and you weren't getting enough oxygen or something like that," he ventured.

"I don't faint," she snorted sitting up. "Are you sure there wasn't some poison on that paper I touched?"

She snatched at the blanket when she noticed she was no longer clothed.

"I'll run the tests again, but they were clean the first time," Will told her.

"Dave, tell them to go ahead for the banquet. I'll return for the dance if I am able. Ask Princess Felina to serve as hostess in my absence."

Dave nodded and disappeared into the lift.

"Somebody get me some clothes I can wear," she demanded.

Rory reappeared from the bathroom. He carried a midnight

blue sequined ball gown, high necked and long sleeved. Radhya looked at him sharply.

"I had to make sure you were all right," he explained. "I thought you had been shot when you collapsed like that in the middle of his betrothal speech. They eliminated Lady Reena just like that in the middle of her betrothal speech." "Rory, I thought the secret..."

"Yes milady, I'm sorry."

"Why couldn't somebody have given me this dress before I went downstairs the first time?"

The lift chimed, and Aninya dashed into the room.

"Milady, milady, I am so sorry. I thought Jemelina's creation too daring, I am so sorry. The child was so excited about her design. She stayed up at night for weeks to have it ready for you. I am so sorry, but you were very beautiful."

"It's enough. I'm not going to punish the girl for a total lack of taste when it comes to clothing. I don't have any myself. But I won't go anywhere again in that sort of outfit," replied Radhya sourly.

Will gave her the all clear and the Lady rose holding the blanket.

"Come and let me help you with this," coaxed Aninya as she shooed the men into the slave's room.

As she fingered the material, Radhya told the older woman, "My grandfather gave me this the year before he died. I've never worn it."

Quickly she was dressed. Aninya fussed with her hair, piling it in curls on her head.

"It's good enough," said Radhya as the guards peeked out of their little room.

"That's much more in keeping with who you are," stated Padr approvingly.

"I feel more myself for sure, not totally, but as close as I can dressed up fancy. I almost feel my Grandfather with me when I wear this."

Padr looked at her strangely.

"It was his gift to me, before he died."

"Oh," Padr nodded. "Who was your grandfather?"

"Lord Kerry, my mother's father," Radhya replied.

Padr looked startled, "I remember him when I was young. He was at our house a lot. I always wanted him to notice me and talk to me. He was so kind. He was even kind to the horses and dogs."

"Grandpa loved every living thing. I've never met another human with as much love as he had. He taught me to treat everyone as well as I could, no matter what his or her status. He believed that a human was a special entity whether slave or aristocrat; any sentient is." Shaking herself and bringing herself back to business she commanded, " I don't want any of you telling what happened."

The slaves bowed their agreement.

"We ignore it," continued Radhya, "except that I dance with the three of you exclusively. I might need to dance with Barone once, but only once. You three after that. It's reasonable if one has had an attempt made on one's life and the royals can wonder about that can't they."

The banquet was over when they returned. Lady Felina rushed over immediately, fussing like a broody hen.

"Oh my poor little girl, are you okay? I've been so worried. Tell me you are all right," she babbled.

"I am fine now. Fortunately, my physician is well trained and very well supplied."

"What happened, was it an assassination attempt?" Felina asked breathlessly.

"I am fine," reiterated Radhya. "Shall we get the dance started? Please accept my most sincere gratitude for taking care of the banquet for me."

"Oh pooh, it was nothing," the princess answered, smiling widely.

"Well, what is the verdict?" Barone asked sidling up. "Was my gift such a shock as all that?"

"Yes, it certainly was. Imagine, Lord Barone, giving training for free. Absolutely unbelievable. But why not just admit what was on the paper I pressed my thumb to?" Radhya insinuated. "If we have an agreement, and you get rid of me, then perhaps you are hoping to inherit all my holdings, and patents ahead of my family. Anywhere close?"

Lady Felina's mouth opened in a round O of surprise. Others, nearby, were stretching their ears closer to listen to the exchange.

"Why my dear Radhya, you know I love you," protested Noel.

"Why such trickery and force getting me to contract with you if you really love me? Is it me you want or just my possessions? Are you financially troubled Noel?"

"I, I, but who...." sputtered Lord Barone.

Barone's eyes shifted from side to side, and his face blazed crimson. His mouth opened and closed several times. Radhya knew she was on to something. Princess Felina had a hand to her mouth, shock written across her normally vapid features.

"What's done is done. No chance of review remember," Radhya said to her.

Barone regained his composure. "Come; let me finish introducing you to your presents."

He led Radhya to the corner where the three naked women were waiting.

"This is D'Bara," he indicated the blonde-haired woman. "This is Rada," he touched the Radhya look alike, "and this is Amlina," he said of the brown haired girl. "I am sure they will all serve you with great loyalty and care. I know how fond you are of names, so I took the liberty."

Barone was almost laughing as he said it. Dave approached at Lady Kirbyson's summoning wave.

"Have them wait outside," she instructed him.

"Yes milady," Dave said as he escorted the three new slaves outside.

Without a word, she took Padr's hand and strode onto the dance floor. The waiting musicians began to play immediately. As they danced, the other royals joined them, many, like Radhya partnered by guards.

"You dance well bodyguard," she told Padr.

"Thank you milady. I only had the finest teachers in the Commonwealth," Padr replied, his eyes following D'Bara as she left. "My mother put great importance on proper dining and dancing for her boys. We had lessons every day for eighteen years."

"What was your concubine's name?" she inquired.

"Debra," he replied.

"Padr, listen to me. This D'Bara is altered. She probably has an implant and communicators in there somewhere."

Padr was not listening. She trod hard on his foot. He glared at her.

"Listen to me," she continued.

"But she has those beautiful brown eyes with the white lace around the iris. You know I thought I could never feel an interest in a woman again. I thought I was crippled, but you taught me to trust, to feel like I could connect with a woman. You can't know how very grateful I am to you."

"Padr don't be so stubborn, listen. The white lace you find so attractive is a marker only found in someone whose genetic structure has been altered after their birth. Once Noel uses his pills his eyes will go like that too."

"Debra had eyes like that," said Padr looking down at her.

"I told you before I thought Debra was an altered. She was made to fit your image of a perfect woman, just as D'Bara has been altered to look like Debra."

"Then why do your eyes have dark grey rings around the light grey? You must be altered. Women don't normally look as beautiful as you do, even if you are not my type."

"Padr both my father and my maternal grandfather were geneticists. They bred for looks. You should see my brother Stephan and my sister Petra. She is so beautiful planets stop spinning in their orbits to stare at her. That's what one royal wrote in a poem to her. It's a pity there is no brain between her ears, to speak of anyway. She's built just like your perfect woman image too. Steph wears a disguise when he goes out. Too many women were walking into walls when he was around and hurting themselves. Believe me when I say I'm the ugly duckling in the family. I was the despair of my mother, and my father wouldn't even look at me."

"You haven't been altered then?" he asked staring at her.

"I have been 'helped' exactly the same way you have."

"What do you mean?" he asked as the music came to a sliding halt.

A new tune started up, and Radhya stayed with Padr on the dance floor. She moved in closer to whisper to him.

"My grandfather conducted experiments. You were one and so was I. Will and Max are both versions of his work as well."

Padr almost stopped dancing. Radhya pulled him ahead. "Don't tell me I'm not human."

"You and I and all the others are totally human. Human DNA. No mutations, no alterations that make us more or less than human. He was simply trying to access the full potential of humanness."

"I don't understand."

"I don't either entirely. I told you that he had picked you for me. That's not completely correct. I was made for you; we were supposed to go together."

"No that's impossible. You are just trying to distract me from D'Bara. We are both slaves now. Before we were master and slave and that's why it didn't work. Just like you and me now. But this D'Bara and I are both slaves. It could really work this time."

"Padr, a plant is a plant, is a plant, is a spy, is a plant. These were sent to bring me down. They knew a male wouldn't work, so they made females for me, to destroy me through you, and Will and Max. Noel has to get his filthy hands on my wealth. Please, Padr, don't jeopardize the plan like this with thoughts of that spy. Think of what this means to every slave in the Commonwealth. Promise me?"

Padr just looked at her. As the song ended, Radhya switched him for Will. Will started to talk before Radhya could ask him anything.

"Amy-Lynn and I shared an apartment together at the university on Prime. We were both going to be the best doctors in the Commonwealth. We never slept together or had sex. We studied, and we shared expenses, and we were very good friends, platonic friends. In fact, I've never had sex with anyone yet. I never had the time to have that kind of a relationship. I always had too much to do. Now it's too late. Her scholarship never fell through, so I imagine she is an excellent freedman doctor by now."

"Thanks, Will. My life is much the same in that respect. Do you realize that those three are plants, spies sent to bring me down?"

"Yes milady, I know. I plan to stay as far away as I can. I think when we were in Barone's training facility that he had some method of reading our memories. That must be where he got the image of Amy-Lynn. I've never talked about her to anyone."

"What can I do about Padr? He will not listen to me."

"I don't know. He was raised very differently from me. I can try talking to him. Maybe he will listen."

"Thanks, Will."

Radhya was laughing when they finished the dance. The next one was very fast, and there was no breath left for talking. When finished, she sat down and had Will bring her a drink. Max was looking outside. Radhya went to talk to him.

"Max, did someone miscalculate in giving me Rada?"

"I'm not sure what you mean;" he replied turning to her.

"You know these three have been given to me to bring me down to the slave level so I can be easily killed."

"Yes milady, I know that."

"It is the same pattern they used for Padr and the other aristocrats who spoke against slavery. One girl resembles Padr's concubine, one girl resembles Will's friend, and one girl resembles me. Is she for you perhaps?"

"That girl is not you, milady, her eyes are blue and have these ugly white rings in them. Her eyes have no soul at all; it is almost like she is already dead. Don't fear my loyalty, I am yours, body and soul. You rescued me from the slave market. I was scared, starving, hurt, and ashamed. The first thing you did was feed me, and you have treated me like a friend ever since. I finished my education, actually better than my education. I have every tool and toy I could ever want. All this is due to you; so yes I appreciate you. If I were a freedman, I still would not be in as good a position as I am now. I actually get to invent things, and that is all I ever wanted to do. No artificial slut is going to get me to betray you. If I betray you, I betray myself."

"Thanks, Max. I appreciate that, but Padr is being a problem. Geo traced his first girl back to Noel. He was set up. Now I am set up. Padr won't believe that."

"Will and I will help him believe. We'll convince him."

"I hope so, or you will be sold, and I will be dead. I couldn't help anyone then. What will happen to all my slaves? Without rights for slaves our society is doomed," she sighed.

The night dragged on and on. Radhya danced with one of three bodyguards often, mostly to keep the nosy aristocracy away. Finally, the night limped to its finish.

Most of the guests were gone, and the musicians were putting their instruments away. The clink and rattle of slaves cleaning up the room was loud. Princess Felina approached Radhya.

"May I speak with you please?" she inquired. "By ourselves without the slaves?"

Telling her guards to wait for her by the door, Radhya led Felina behind a tree in the foyer.

"I feel very ashamed of myself. I had no right to force you into a contract with Barone. You are right. He offered to reveal an indiscretion of mine. However, I had no right to trade my reputation for your happiness. I am so sorry."

"I'm glad that you are sorry princess, but it doesn't make things any better for me. I am still stuck with contracting with that sleaze, if I survive that long."

"What do you mean Radhya, if you survive that long?"

"Princess," Radhya sighed, "I don't know if you are aware that recently six of the aristocracy has been made into slaves. Five of them have died in Jabin's arena. All of them were given presents of slaves just before something was found about them that required they lose their status."

"But one of them didn't die."

"Princess, I bullied the slave dealer who had him into selling him to me before Jabin could buy him at auction. I almost didn't get away with it. Now it is happening to me." The princess went very pale, and her hands started shaking. She clasped them tightly together in front of her.

"Radhya I'm so sorry. If I hadn't forced this on you none of this would be happening. Is there anything, anything at all I can do?"

"No princess, there is nothing anyone can do now. No, wait. You can do something for me. If I am made a slave, it is the same as if I had died. If I create a living will and give certain of my slaves to you, will you get your father to grant them a royal pardon and set them free?"

"I don't know. How many? You know a pardon is rare, and I couldn't do it for a large number."

"Five. The five who are most at risk of being put to death with me, especially Geo."

"Who is Geo?"

"Geo is the bodyguard who raised me. He's the one who

bandaged my scraped knees and found my dolls when I lost them. He is my father in deed if not in body."

Tears leaked from Felina's eyes. "Tell me who else must be freed."

"Rory has been with me for many years. He is a pilot and a spaceship pilot. Padr who was once an aristocrat and they want to kill him as well. Will and Max are too good to be lion food."

Radhya grabbed hold of her hand, "Please princess, if any can be free, see to these five."

"I give you my word as Princess Royal; on my father's name I will take these five slaves and have them set free should anything happen to you."

Radhya hung her head wiping at the tears tracking down her cheeks. "Thank you milady."

They went their separate ways. The Lady composing herself as she joined the waiting guards at the entrance. She had Dave lock the doors, and they left the visitor's center. The three females were waiting outside. With them were Lord Barone and seven of his servants with baggage.

"Well, my betrothed are you not inviting me to stay with you at your home? After all, I understand guest status ends tonight, and any all who stay after have to pay. You wouldn't expect that of me now would you?"

Wearily Radhya just stared at him.

"Have it your own way. You will anyway," she muttered.

She turned and headed for home.

Chapter 10

Radhya enjoyed the smooth feel of the fungus path and the twittering of the night birds in the brush. The odd crashes from it gave her great pleasure as it frightened the unwelcome visitors with her. Lord Barone's troupe stumbled the whole way along the path to the gate. The silence she and her servants kept served only to make the trip seem darker and more sinister. She murmured to her bodyguards at the barrier, had each press his palm to the plate, and speak a phrase to the gate. Lord Barone watched with interest. Radhya assumed he was memorizing the words and sequence. She finally took her turn speaking in a voice so low the locking device had trouble picking it up and she had to repeat it.

After reading her genetic code, the gates majestically parted and the group stumbled through. Dave secured them, and returned to his house with Jemelina. The rest continued straight ahead, bypassing the trail to the stables. At the circular drive, Radhya had a brief conversation with Aninya, regarding tomorrow's arrangements. Then Aninya broke away to the path leading to her house. Radhya continued around the drive to the mansion. Tiny tendrils of fog were creeping up the walls, across the lawns and gardens, shrouding trees and shrubbery alike in a mist of obscurity. Although the night was clear above, vision was diminishing minute by minute as the fog spidered its way higher.

"So you give slaves their own houses?" queried Lord Barone.

"Some milord," she replied formally. "Those who have jobs that need it like Dave or Aninya."

"But doesn't Dave's woman work here? Why let her stay in her own house?"

"If I made her stay here then it would not be punishment, just the ordinary way of things. However, if either displeases me, and I make her stay here, it becomes an effective discipline."

"You don't have to pretend anymore to me you know," sneered Barone.

"Why I wouldn't dream of it Noel," she returned sarcastically.

They ascended the stairs, and Geo opened the door.

"Geo, old friend," greeted Radhya, "we have guests this night. Could you please see Lord Barone and his slaves settled in the rooms I prepared? These three," she said indicating her betrothal gift, "are presents given to me. If you could take three sets of blankets out of storage, I'll show them the slave quarters when I'm finished with them."

Geo stiffened, and Radhya knew he recognized the danger.

"Yes milady," he replied formally. "This way please milord." He escorted Lord Barone into the house. Noel gave her an unreadable look as he followed the old man.

"Will, take these three to the med lab. I want them checked for everything, and I do mean everything. Can't have any diseases being introduced here can I?"

Will left with his three charges. Radhya spoke to Padr and Max.

"The three of you have to return to the slave quarters tonight, however, no fooling around with the spies," she gave Padr a hard look. "I expect you to tell Will. One of you sleeps in front of my door each night until Barone is gone. You can take turns. Now come with me."

The trio went to the third-floor med lab. Will was running Amlina through the scanner. He was not satisfied, so he repeated the test. He looked at Radhya and shook his head. Amlina left from the machine and Rada took her place. Will scanned her twice as well.

"Follow me," the Lady said to the girls. "You three stay here till I return."

Radhya led the women down the stairs, into the kitchen where she stopped to greet Singha, Ringha, and Kung. The lynxcats bristled and snarled at the newcomers, especially D'Bara. Then Radhya led them through the kitchen to the slave's galley, down those stairs to the quarters.

"Padr's, Will's, and Max's," she said pointing out their bunks. "You three choose bunks at the opposite end of the room."

Radhya hung a blanket in between.

"What's the matter milady?" D'Bara asked. "Are you afraid we'll seduce your men away from you?"

"Aren't you a little bold for a slave fresh from training school?" replied Radhya in a hard voice.

"Who says we're fresh from school? Anyway, it wasn't the type you're thinking of."

"Geo laid out nightclothes for you with the blankets," said Radhya choosing to ignore D'Bara.

"I'd much rather sleep and work nude," said D'Bara.

"Well in this house we wear clothes. It adds dignity to a person. Don't push me too far D'Bara, lenient I may be, but I have my limits."

"Oh, you'll never do anything. You never do," sneered the slave.

Radhya, eyebrows furrowed, looked at the tall, bold woman. She left the slave quarters. Geo, coming down the hallway, gestured to her to follow him into his office.

She paced back and forth.

"Radhya, this situation is very serious. Barone grows bolder with every royal he destroys," he told her quietly.

"Barone is betrothed to me now, so maybe he won't try to bring me down."

Radhya sat on the corner of Geo's beautiful hardwood desk swinging her leg.

"You are wrong. I checked his financial history these last few years. He has lost almost everything gambling and on his horses. He is hoping to take everything you own when you die or are busted to a slave."

"But he has to wait until after the review, and we are contracted doesn't he? And that's two years from now."

"No Radhya. According to your lawyer, you both signed a contract to contract, in front of witnesses so if anything happens to you; it is assumed you would want everything to go to your partner, to him."

"That miserable excuse for a horse dropping's worm!" exclaimed Radhya jumping from the desk. "How dare he. Get my lawyer to draw up an ironclad will. I've already discussed this partially with Princess Felina. She is to inherit you, Rory, Padr, Max, and Will. I want all my patents and property to go to Stephan, my brother. All my other slaves go to Sparky."

"Sparky is not very well I'm afraid. He probably wouldn't live to see the slaves arrive. He has no heir but you. That would send them right back to Barone."

"Damn. Then give my money to Padr's brother on the condition that he takes my slaves as well. I've never heard anything but good about the way he treats his people."

"I'll make sure it's a living will as well in case you get sold as a slave and don't die, or Barone only cripples you."

"Thanks, Geo. That's a good thought but if I am a vegetable in his hands I want you to find some way to kill me."

Geo nodded his head. "I've got the security running

constantly. What are you going to do about your boys with those girls down there? Barone was pretty crafty about it."

"Yes. I don't know what else to do. I've talked to them. Max and Will are being intelligent about it, but Padr figures this is his chance to have the girl of his dreams again, a fresh new start. Moreover, of course, it's my entire fault for showing him how trustworthy a woman can really be. He is already in love with D'Bara. She is a bold slut, almost as bad as Petra."

"Yes, I heard her speak to you. There is something so familiar to me about her manner. Who did the work, Stephan or Petra?"

"Too clumsy for Steph. Their eyes were horrible, a real mess. Petra probably wanted a new bauble, or maybe another boy-toy. I don't know what she wanted; it looks like her handiwork."

"Mmmmmmmmm yes. You are probably right. She is a spiteful enough bitch to do it for free if it would inconvenience you."

Radhya laughed, "Geo, that's no way to talk about my sister."

"No, it is the only way. However, I was thinking, what about the fidelity stick you invented years ago when you were a teenager. It's still here somewhere."

"What about it?"

"It is one way to assure that your guards don't get involved with these spies. I don't know why you never put it on the market. You could have made another fortune with it."

"Don't you remember what Grandpa said? I have no right because of my intelligence to create anything that impairs another person's free will. In addition, Geo, the fidelity stick creates a biochemical situation where the other person experiences a physical illness if someone other than the person they shared with becomes physically close. It doesn't control the mind. How could I do that to them?"

"How many slaves are counting on you to make their lives

better? How can the free sexual will of three men for six months count against that?"

Radhya looked at him with dismay. "But doesn't my integrity count for something as well. It is a slippery slope you want me to go on. I'll ask them. If they agree, I'll use it, but it has to be of their free will."

"Radhya, your principles will get you sold as a slave yet," said Geo shaking his head sadly.

Radhya left the room and returned to the med lab. Max was asleep in the chair, his head pillowed on the desk. Padr was half-asleep on the examining table, and Will was agitatedly paced the floor. Radhya perched herself on a corner of the desk.

"Radhya, D'Bara is fitted with a nano device in her liver, very, very tiny. I almost missed it except for the new scar tissue created when it drilled its way in. From the small amount I can glean about it, it is explosive, rigged somehow to the slave collar. That is what Max thinks anyway. Rada has a device, also, but planted in the heart muscle. Either one could kill you in an instant," Will explained.

Padr and Max both woke up and listened. Max handed Radhya the printouts of the three spies.

"Only Krin does work that fine. And she has been in Barone's bed for the last decade," Radhya said looking at the papers.

Will continued, "Amlina is clean of any nanotech I could find, but she has a cancerous brain tumor. It is so big there would be absolutely no way to operate without killing her. I don't know if it's supposed to be contagious or not, but it is fast growing and aggressive."

"I can fix Amlina," Radhya said after looking closely at the sheets. "I just rewrite her genetic code to reject all forms of cancer, and her own body heals itself. But not tonight. I am too tired. I want to ask you three something." Radhya looked each man straight in the eyes, blue, brown and blue again. "I have a product; I called it a fidelity stick. Some of my saliva goes on the outside. You break it open inside your mouth. A biochemical change is triggered that lasts about six months, depending on your metabolism. It, ah, keeps your hormones true to me. Geo wanted me just to use it on you, but I feel you need to have free will concerning your own desires."

Will replied slowly, "If it will help our cause, I don't have the slightest problem with it. I don't plan to be with anyone in any case."

"My loyalty is yours, now and always. It is no concern to me, and if it would help you to sleep better, without worrying, I want to do it," smiled Max.

Radhya looked at Padr. He was staring at the floor.

"Geo told me," said the Lady, "I should consider the cost of three men's sexual liberty for six months against the misery of all the slaves in the Commonwealth."

Padr looked at her with agony in his eyes. Finally, he silently nodded his head. Radhya went to lab two and returned with three slender brown tubes six centimeter's long.

"Who's first?" she asked brightly.

"Let me," said Max, rising and coming toward her.

Radhya licked one tube, and as Max opened his mouth, she broke it. Dark purple vapor rose, and Max inhaled it. His eyes widened. He reached a hand toward the desk and sat down.

Lowering his head, he said, "Dizzy."

"Me next," chirped Will.

Radhya repeated the procedure, licking the tube and breaking it in front of Will's open mouth.

"Ahh," he gagged and sat down abruptly on the floor. "You weren't kidding about the dizzy."

He lowered his head to his hands. Max staggered to his feet and waved a hand in their direction.

"Night, I'm off to the slave quarters."

"How long does this dizzy last?" inquired Will from the floor.

"Only about fifteen minutes," the Lady told him.

"Then I'm going to follow Max. Padr you had better do the guard duty tonight, just to let this stuff settle into your system."

Padr glared at him from the other side of the room. Will lurched to his feet and stumbled after Max. Radhya held up the final cylinder. Padr approached her. She licked the tube, and he opened his mouth. As he inhaled the vapor, he turned away clenching his fists. He fell against the examining table.

"What is the matter with you anyway?" Padr snarled.

"What do you mean?" She asked him.

"Why do you have to do this to me?"

"Padr, I explained all this not ten minutes ago."

"I'm not stupid," his voice rose," I know you didn't do this for the other guards, this is for me. They just went along with it so I wouldn't look like a fool. You don't want me with D'Bara."

"That is right. I don't want you with D'Bara. Remember who brought you to the slave rank you hold now. It was a slave from Barone. Now I have three slaves from Barone. They must really want to bring me down and destroy any hope the slaves might have. This means the lives of millions of people. Can't you get that through your head? It is not about you; it's about them."

"You are just a jealous little bitch. You have wanted me since you bought me and I haven't come on to you, and you are jealous."

"Padr, you are crazy. I like you, yes, but I never tried to get you into bed. That is not my style. This is not about you, and it is not about me, except that my work is to help the slaves have a better life. They are trying to stop me. They don't want any sort of process begun that might end slavery. That is what this is about."

"I had a chance here; I had a real chance to be happy at last. With D'Bara, I could have been happy even as a slave, and you stopped me. Now I can't go near her!"

"Padr will you listen to yourself. Think! What happens to

you if I am busted to a slave? How long before Jabin has you in the arena?"

Shock rippled across Padr's face.

"Exactly," Radhya continued. "If I am brought down you leave here. You and D'Bara would not be together. If I can keep it together and survive, I'll give her to you in six months. This is temporary. If you still want her in six months, and I survive that long, I'll give you a house and D'Bara as a bride. Your only chance is to work with me Padr. I thought you cared about the dilemma of the slaves too."

Padr leapt upright. "You don't know anything about me. All your spies can tell you about my life, but you don't know me. Why don't you just castrate me while you're at it?" He swung his arms wildly clipping her on the jaw. Radhya fell backward. Grabbing a tray of medical tools, he hurled them to the floor. He punched his hand into the wall, then grabbed Radhya up from the floor and thrust her against the wall his arm across her throat.

"You can't control me. I am myself whether I am an aristocrat or a slave. I won't be bribed by you any longer."

Radhya could not answer. Just as her vision was getting dim around the edges, Padr was torn away from her and thrown against the desk.

"Go to your room," snapped Geo, "while I explain things to this young pup."

Radhya pulled her wits together and staggered to her room. Throwing her clothes to the floor, she crawled under her covers naked. There the fears and the tears came.

Chapter 11

Radhya, exhausted, slept late. Aninya woke her with the news that lunch would be served shortly and that Lord Barone was expecting her. Grimacing at that bad news, she tottered to the shower. Coming out, she ignored the lacy pink outfit Aninya had laid out and chose her usual comforting black. She whipped open the door, and there on a pallet was Padr, sleeping. Shadows on his arms and face told her what his conversation with Geo had been like. She stepped gingerly over him, wondering what the outcome would have been if Geo had not intervened. Would Padr have killed her? He seemed angry enough to last night.

Aninya had the goldwood table and chairs burnished to a high gloss, the metallic grain sparkling in the subdued light of the cut crystal chandelier. It contained two settings of Radhya's finest china, a beautiful green with yellow hand painted lilies, set at either end of the long table. D'Bara and Rada, dressed in house livery were waiting behind her chair when she entered the large, elegant dining room.

"Send me Will and Max," she commanded. "You two go clean something."

Barone rose from his seat, bowing low from the waist.

"Radhya, I trust you slept well? I waited for breakfast for you for an hour."

"Noel, I hope you didn't," Radhya replied absently.

She waved her hand at Jemelina who left at once to fetch the meal. Max and Will hurried in and took the place behind her chair. Rada scurried off to the kitchen while D'Bara strutted slowly to Lord Barone, and giving him a seductive look, wriggled her way from the room. Deja vue struck Radhya with a powerful force. The actions of the slave were so familiar her neck hair rose.

"So Noel," she covered, "you've obviously bedded that one a few times."

"A time or two I suppose," he answered offhand.

"Poor way to make a gift. Do you suppose I want your used merchandise?"

"My apologies. I didn't think you leaned that way."

"You don't know anything about me," she snapped. Echoes of last night rang in her head and she gripped the table edges tightly.

Barone continued, "Oh, I've talked to others about you, you're difficult to find out about, but it's not entirely impossible."

"Well who are these wellsprings of my personal information?" She inquired coolly.

"That would be snitching."

"Then how about who did your alteration work? That's a short list. I should know. Stephan, Petra, or me. Now I am not a likely candidate, am I? Steph, well last time I talked with him he still had some integrity left, and he still hated your guts for beating him in the chess tournament in the third grade. Let's tentatively stroke him off. Therefore, we come to my sweet sister Petra, the beautiful, who would cut my throat for a child's marble. Not too hard was it?"

Noel bowed his smirking face. "I bow to your superior intellect and logical reasoning ability. I was hoping to start my treatment after lunch. Do you have any further advice?"

"Only to do what I already told you. Oh, you might want to eat a lot of protein today. Be very careful in your timing and I hope yours hurts an extra amount."

"My we're bad tempered today. I hope becoming a spouse mellows you."

Radhya snorted into the soup before her.

"If I just paid you off, would you cancel the contract to contract, take your slave girls and go? You can even keep and use the gift I gave you."

"Tsk-tsk-tsk. Why how could I leave my Lady Love?" asked Noel ever so sweetly.

Radhya sighed and continued eating.

Noel continued, "Very heavy fog this morning. I was hoping to see your grounds and your stables this morning, but I was honestly afraid to leave the veranda for fear I would be lost."

"Fog blows in from an inlet to the northeast. We have a lot of fog."

"Must be bad for your racetrack."

"No, the same wind blows it clear of fog, except in very still conditions. That's usually in midwinter when the season is over. Besides I like fog. It helps me to think."

"I hope you will take me to this inlet when the weather clears. I really want to get a good assessment of this place."

"Impossible," Radhya replied around a mouthful of food. "I am running an experiment there, biohazardous. It's absolutely impossible to go there."

"How intriguing," pondered Noel, "then perhaps you will give me the grand tour of our house after lunch. Give me something to dwell on while the treatment is on going."

"Noel, if you can think of anything but how much you hurt during the treatment you're not the man I think you are. As far as my home goes, you may have the run of the first and second floor. Use it how you will. Geo's quarters and office are that way; the parlor is behind me. The den and library are those two doors. The kitchen is off the hallway behind you and the slave's quarters are off that. Grand tour finished okay?"

"Radhya, how ungracious. What about the third floor?"

"My rooms and working labs are on the third floor. It is off limits to you or any of your slaves."

"Is that so you can sleep with your bodyguards?"

"Where do you get this drivel? One guard was on duty last night, guarding me from you, outside my room. The others slept in the slave quarters or didn't your little spies tell you?"

"I hear you do medicals on the third floor."

"Yes, I have a med lab there. If your penis falls off, maybe you will see it. Then again, maybe not."

Noel laughed. "I see I'm not going to get any good will from you today."

"No, you will not. I don't like company. Remember that I'm Lady Death, and death is the loneliest estate. Excuse me, I have work to do."

Noel sobered at her words. He rose as she left the table. Radhya returned to lab one and called the three new slaves' medical files to her big comp. After staring at D'Bara's for sometime, she tapped the hard copy with her finger.

"I know this," she murmured.

Setting it aside, she called up the files. She brought up Amlina's code and began working on it. She set Max, Will and Padr working on the unzip and rezip portions of her cure.

Several hours of intense concentration passed when a frantic pounding on the lab door disturbed them. Max interposed himself between Radhya and the door. Padr opened it while Will stood behind him.

Barone's slave, 72, was standing there, his fist raised to pummel the door again. The whites of his eyes bulged and he sported a large, purpling bruise across both his eyes and the bridge of his nose.

"Please," the man croaked, falling to his knees, his hands raised in supplication, "please, come, the master, he is dying. I know he is dying. Please save us."

Radhya gestured the men away as she went to the door.

"Tell me," she commanded.

"He took the pill and exact to the second he took the purple capsule. Now he is swollen, red, there is much pus, and hurt, hurt, hurt. He is screaming like he is dying. Please come."

Radhya looked puzzled. "It sounds like everything is progressing fine."

She could hear bloodcurdling screams from the next level down. Gesturing for the bodyguards, she went to the room where Noel lay in a large four-poster bed on top of a royal blue comforter. Her guards recoiled in sympathetic horror at the sight of the Lord's swollen and pus filled member. Radhya inspected him closely.

"I see no problem here. Will check his readings."

Will ran the portable scanner over Lord Barone. "Everything seems to be progressing well inside normal parameters."

Barone shrieked an ear-piercing scream; twitching and squirming as the waves of pain took him again. He screamed until his oxygen ran out and he had to subside into an agonized panting. His slaves cowered in the corners.

"Is your bunch useless?" asked Radhya annoyed. "Put cold compresses on his head. He has the normal fever," she ordered one of his slaves. "Bring me a basin," she said to a scantily clad female.

When the basin arrived, she showed the woman how to give the squirming man a slight amount of relief by removing the accumulated pus.

"Rinse and disinfect the basin. Every time he gets filled with pus, do that."

Noel looked at her wearily. "Thank you," he whispered, his

voice raw and cracking. "You didn't tell me what agony this would be."

"Yes I did," contradicted Radhya. "You are rewriting your genetic code; do you expect it to feel good? This is just a little taste of what you put your make to order slaves through. Can you imagine how painful it would be to change almost your entire appearance, not just one little part? Imagine what you are going through in every part of your body. That is what you do to those slaves when you rewrite their codes. I wonder how many of them die and you just start over with a fresh body. If nothing else, you will gain a new appreciation for pain. I have to get back to work now; your slaves can take care of you."

"No I don't want you to go."

"I don't care what you want. I am not your servant and I will die before I become your servant," Radhya warned.

Noel started to groan and pant again as another wave of change came over him.

"Now milady?" asked the slave girl.

"No," Radhya explained, "Only when it is full of pus. Probably in about six hours. For now, he just has to put up with the discomfort. See you in a week or so Noel."

She turned to leave the room.

"No, no, no don't leave me. Don't leave me alone like this," Barone howled.

She turned at the door.

"You'll be just fine. Everything is progressing perfectly. You'll probably end up thirty centimeters if I'm not mistaken, and I rarely am. You should be delighted."

"It hurts, dammit it hurts. I can't stand this. It is killing me damn you," screamed Barone at the top of his voice.

Lady Kirbyson strode from the room trailed by her white-faced bodyguards, dashing up the stairs to her lab. Throwing open the door, she came face to face with D'Bara, just rising from the comp screen. Radhya leapt across the floor and smashed D'Bara across the face with the back of her hand.

"How dare you!" screamed D'Bara.

"How dare I? I am your owner, you are my slave. How dare you invade my lab? What are you doing in here? You know this is off limits, I told you myself. Why are you even on the third floor? Where did you learn to read genetic notation? What kind of betrayal is this Petra?"

The woman froze. The three men behind Radhya were rooted to the spot.

"I hate you," screamed Petra. "I hate you and I came to take the man you love away from you. I'm going to bring you to ruin. Noel is going to give me everything you own, everything that should have been mine in the first place. You'll be a slave, for Jabin's amusement. He has quite a few interesting little plans for you. We have it all arranged."

"Why Petra?" Radhya asked in a soft voice shaking her head. "You were the most beautiful woman in the galaxy. You had men falling over their feet for you. Everyone always loved you the most. I was forever second best, if I rated at all, you were given everything. I worked since I was fourteen. I had to earn every mina myself, every single mina. Why did you do this to yourself?"

"To get you. You're so smart, always parading around and showing off. You always sneered at me because I wasn't as smart as you think you are. Remember, "I wonder how Petra keeps her ears apart 'cause she got no brains"? Grandpa always loved you best. He only spent time with you and after Mom and Dad died all we had was Grandpa. Don't forget that you stole half my world and all this stuff besides. Now I will have it."

"I worked for my half of your world, or do you forget all the new fiber bearing animals I created for you so you could have a fashion industry for income when you didn't like genetics. I spent two years working for you. All that other stuff is from when we were little children. Besides, you are a branded, collared slave now. You can't own anything. Who has your property now?"

"Noel promised to reverse everything as soon as you are out of the way. Did you really think a man like that could desire an ugly thing like you? It was all a ruse. And your smart brain turns men off. Noel will never contract with you, but it got me in here. I will find your illegal research then you will be removed and Noel will contract with me."

"You can't reverse a branding. Moreover, the only way back is to get a royal pardon from the king. You should really look into these things before you jump into them. That branding goes right through your genetic code. Do you even know about the explosive nano planted in your liver?"

"It's a communication device, for when I want to contact Noel, when my part is over."

"Wrong. It will blow your head off. What exactly is your part?"

"If I couldn't find anything, I was supposed to plant evidence of tampering with human embryos. Then you would be busted to a slave. But you've caught me, so, I'm going to kill you instead. I'll leave your body to the dire wolves, and no one will suspect a thing sister dear."

"Petra, look at the readout. That is Krin's work. She's the best. In addition, she is also Noel's bed partner and has been for the last ten years. See how the device communicates with your collar. Noel can kill you at any time."

Petra shook her head, "Never, never! Noel loves me. He's told me over and over. Loves me, not you, you black haired freak, nobody could ever love you. Mother and Father never did you know. You were too nosy, too smart, and too ugly. You should be glad I'm killing you."

She lunged at Radhya and caught her by the throat with both hands. She was tall and strong and she began crushing Radhya's windpipe. Padr and Max sprinted across the room. One on each arm they dragged her from Radhya.

"Will, med lab. Third drawer, dismemorizer capsule," croaked Radhya.

Petra was lunging in the guards' hands, screaming and fighting. She kicked at Radhya, snarled and tried to bite Padr. Will came trotting back. At Radhya's nod, he broke the capsule under Petra's nose. The girl collapsed, hanging limply from the hands of the men.

"Take her to the slave quarters and throw her on her bunk. Don't be gentle."

Padr picked her up carefully, giving Radhya a withering look, and carried her out the door. Radhya threw her hand in the air.

"Men!" she cursed, "Let me get this rewrite finished. Absolutely no more distractions. Out, out! Everyone out. Lock the door."

As Max and Will returned to the slave's quarters, Rada pushed back the blanket Radhya had hung. She boldly strutted up to Max, pulled his head down and kissed him.

"Owwwww," he yowled as he pushed her away. His hand grabbed the back of his neck. Rada, hands on her naked hips laughed at him.

"Oh come now, you can have me tonight and pretend it's her. I don't mind. I could give you some orders if that turns you on," Rada tittered at him.

"No, thank you," replied Max backing away. The pains in his stomach made him double over.

"You're a slave," she purred, "and a slave has got to grab what pleasure he or she can when he or she can. I can fulfill your fantasies. I know moves she has never heard of."

Rada grabbed him and drew him closer, fastening her mouth to his with magnetic suction. She reached into his pants and pinched his buttocks hard.

"Noooo!" he yelled as he hurled her to the floor. She laughed up at him.

"Leave me alone. I don't want you near me. Just leave me alone," he snarled.

Rada made a pout as Will hauled her from the floor by one arm and hustled her back to the women's half of the quarters.

"What's the matter handsome, a few little girls bother you?" she said slyly batting her eyelashes at him.

Silent, Will returned to their half of the room restoring the blanket to its place. He found Max something to settle his stomach as he sat on his bunk having the dry heaves.

Chapter 12

Radhya worked with total concentration until Aninya tapped on her door with a supper tray.

"I'm sorry to disturb you milady, but it's after eight and I thought you might be hungry."

Max and Will entered behind her. Radhya raised her head from the screen abstractedly.

"Let me just run this simulation, and I think I've got it."

She tapped a few spots on the smart screen then pushed back from the desk. She stretched until her spine popped. Will was standing behind her chair observing her work.

"Where's Padr?" she asked.

"He ate with the slaves tonight milady," replied Aninya. "Although that D'Bara, can't stand that girl, she was sick and didn't come for supper. Last I saw Padr; he was playing with Kung."

"I guess he is avoiding me. Okay, just put the tray anywhere Aninya and thank you."

Radhya opened her tray, rewarded by the savory smells of gourmet fare. She wrinkled her nose but ate few bites.

"Join in don't be shy," she told Max and Will.

"Don't you like your food?" asked Max.

"Not really. I prefer soup or salad, perhaps a little fruit. I don't care for all this overcooked spiced stuff."

"Can I have what you don't want?" asked Max eagerly.

"Certainly," said Radhya pushing the remains of her tray over, then snatching the fruit off with a grin, "except this."

"Radhya," asked Will, "how do you do those recombines so fast? I would think it would take weeks, if not months to run enough variations to get what you want. I don't know as much as you do about genetics, but I do have the basics. What you do seems impossible at that speed. I noticed it before when you were designing plants for Padr."

"To tell you honestly Will, I don't know. When it comes to genetic code, I am an idiot savant or something. I was very smart in school. I earned my Ph.D. in genetics at fourteen and started working for the university then. I had a lot of trouble. Three worlds were destroyed, using my research. The Melians, that's our name, we couldn't whistle their real name, were wiped out."

"On the second world were these horrid snakelike things. They burrowed up your anus or down your throat while you were sleeping and laid their eggs. The eggs hatched in about twenty-eight hours and the larvae ate their way out. These things had already wiped out most of the animal life larger than an insect, but there were these fuzzy little people who lived high in the trees where the snakes couldn't go. They were sentient, but just barely. And ever so cute, huge violet eyes and pink noses. I was supposed to be working on a way to destroy the snakes and save the little furry people, but I destroyed them all. That planet had very valuable mineral resources. I was fifteen."

"When I was sixteen, they brought me here. It was the most beautiful planet, with the perfect climate; I had ever been on. However, I was locked into the habitat. A sort of wasp or insect was attacking the Ocean Chandrans' children. It carried many diseases, and they were losing about fifty percent of their children to it. I was to remove the disease vector. This time I changed both the virus and the vector. There could have been absolutely no contamination unless it was deliberate. I didn't want another world like the Melians. Yet every bit of animal life on dry land was wiped out. They knew that they were exterminating these people, but they wanted the planet. I made sure the planet was not available to them."

"That was the last of my work for the university. Grandpa set up a small lab for me beside his, and I began working for myself. Then Grandpa died, poison. I had so many patents of my own that my older brother who is in the same field was embarrassed. So my parents threw me out to fend for myself. I have been working ever since to put things right. I had the three worlds as a settlement from the courts. The Melians have been recreated on their world, in secret. They make paper, glass and the finest silk you've ever seen, but if certain aristocrats find out they live there instead of the slaves that are supposed to be working for me, then they will find another way to wipe them out. That's called Radhya's world now."

"My Kirbyson's world, the snake world, was so full of metals I had an idea to make trees that deposit gold, silver, copper, and platinum, whatever in the leaves. Collect the leaves in the fall, and you're rich. Sparky sponsored me, and I gave him trees for his metal-rich planet. He had a congenital defect that had proved impossible to correct surgically. Therefore, I made a cure for him. I made him whole, and he gave me half his world. Pleasant is where the Chandrans lived, Mountain Chandrans, Plains Chandrans, and the Ocean Chandrans. On the plains and in the mountains they were very warlike. Totally evil. They would kill any stranger approaching their villages. They ate their own children when the population went too high. They were so nasty I didn't even mind that they were wiped out. Nevertheless, the Ocean Chandrans were another matter. Anyway, that is my entire life's story. I'm tired of sitting, and I have something I want you to see. If you're done eating come with me."

Radhya rose and left the room. She tiptoed to the first floor, Max and Will followed her. She entered the den.

The den was square and dark with five comfortable chairs around the walls. The walls were panelled in carved rosewood, flowers twining up and down their lengths. There was an old-fashioned wood burning fireplace against the back wall.

Rada watched them walk past from her hiding place behind the kitchen door, sneaking behind them. She opened the den door a tiny crack and watched.

Radhya went to the right back corner and twisted the stamens of a carved moonflower. A split appeared in the paneling. Grasping it, she pulled it open. She stepped into the dark with Max and Will following. Rada watched them disappear and eased across the den floor behind them. As soon as the panel closed a light came on, not too bright, but enough. On the left was a lift, on the right an arsenal. At the rear was another door.

"The lift will take you up to my rooms or down to the subbasement, below the slave quarters and storage," Radhya spoke softly. "Can both of you use a tazer?"

"Of course," they answered in unison.

"Grab a weapon and let's go," she said as she snapped one to her belt.

She led the way through a tunnel, perhaps wide enough and high enough for a horse. It twisted and turned through the grey stone of the mountain for a half a klick. Bulbs came on ahead and turned off as they traveled, like moving in a bubble of light. The passage came to an abrupt end at a blank wall of rock.

Radhya stopped, touching a flat, grey, metal plate on the left. With a rumble, a small section of the barrier slid aside. Radhya, Max and Will scrambled out of the way.

"This way," Radhya said with an absolute sureness. She plunged ahead into the fog.

Fifteen minutes behind them came Rada following the signal

device she carried in her hand. Radhya and her guards traveled swiftly through the fog unaware that they were being tracked.

"It's about five klicks, but we have to watch for wild animals," she told them. "Keep your tazers ready."

Weapon in hand, Radhya stopped under a large pine tree. The fog and darkness made vision useless. She sniffed the air.

"Do you smell it?" she asked.

The men scented the air. On the tang of brine in the breeze was a musty odor, like old, dirty laundry. Max and Will nodded. Radhya stood still, her back to the tree. The fog swirled in patterns and shapes more frightening than any real foe. The smell grew stronger. The shifting curtain parted to release a nightmare.

The size of a small horse, it was brindled in colors of fog and mist. A long coarse mane ran from behind its pointed ears to the base of its tail. The large black twitching nose ended a pointed fanged face and above intense eyes glowed yellow. Other pairs of eyes were intermittently visible in the shifting mist.

"Shurra," cried Radhya with relief. "It's okay. Max, Will, this is Shurra's pack. I raised her from a pup, and she thinks I'm her mother."

The gigantic animal sank to its belly and crawled forward, pulling back its lips to reveal teeth as long as butcher knives. A thin pink tongue was licking in and out.

Radhya greeted Shurra in wolf manner, allowing her to lick her chin, then shaking Shurra roughly by the mane. The wolf rolled over, and Radhya rubbed her belly for five minutes.

"Away," she gestured, and the pack vanished.

Max looked in awe at the smiling Radhya.

"We were lucky," she said. "That's the only pack that I can influence, because I was Shurra's mother. She is the mother of the rest."

"How many other packs?" asked Will.

"Four at least, possibly even five by now."

As they moved from the tree, a commotion ahead caught

their interest. The sounds of growling and snarling floated on the breeze. Radhya veered from their path giving the clearing ahead a wide berth.

"Another pack feeding on a kill," she whispered.

They continued even more swiftly as the trail began to go downhill, steep in places and rocky. Slowing they had to pick their way carefully, weaving around the rocky outcropping that scattered unseen across the body of the hill.

As they circled a large boulder, the hunting scream of a dire wolf played a dirge above them. A huge grey animal hurtled from the top of the rock. Radhya, Max and Will jammed themselves against the stone face, the nightmare creature landed in front of them. It whirled swiftly and slunk to its belly in a hunting crouch, paw lift, pause, step, very slow.

"Tazer the snout. It will leave and take its companion with it," whispered Radhya indicating the trail ahead where another giant wolf was crouched.

The dire wolf sprang in a sudden bound. Three tazers hit it at once, right in the face. It couldn't stop its forward momentum, and it crushed them into the rock. They continued hitting it with their tazers and the enormous beast scrambled to its paws, tucked its tail between its legs and tore up the trail whining like a scolded pup. Its companion glanced nervously at the prey, and then followed at a gallop.

"Is everyone okay?" asked Will.

"I am, bruises aside," said Max.

Radhya said, "I think I sprained my wrist."

Will wrapped his Lady's injury in gauze from his kit. The stronger winds here blew the fog back, so the night became clearer as they continued down the trail. Without further incident, they reached a beach of sand as smooth and white as sugar. The ocean, still hidden by billows and curtains of fog, made its presence known by sound alone. They walked easily for a while then Radhya stopped. She closed her eyes and stood there as the men looked uncertainly at each other.

Out of the ocean, fog materialized three extra large human shapes. They looked human, yet not. The proportions were wrong, too long in the torso, and the legs had much less calf than human legs. The arms, as well, were not human shaped, with the upper arms being longer and the lower arms shorter than in comparison to humans. Instinctively the hair raised on the back of the men's necks.

"Max, Will, meet the Ocean Chandrans."

One shape moved towards each human. Coming close, they enfolded the human in a hug. Overpoweringly tall at two and a half meters each, their bellies were smooth and rubbery, like dolphin skin, and their backs covered with short, dense fur. Max's was golden, Radhya's was brown, and Will's was black. Each Chandran had two enormous eyes in the human fashion, sea green and calm, quiet and deep.

Then they heard the alien's thoughts, low and rumbling, somehow, like waves lapping beneath a boat.

"Radhya, our friend and recreator, how may we serve you?"

Radhya answered aloud, "I want you to know my friends, Max and Will. There is another who could not come."

"Yes, your Padr. Your seliflacn are welcome among us."

"I don't understand your term."

"We see the mutual shadows of bonds growing among you. A bonded group is selifla. You are not that far yet, so you are seliflacn."

Radhya glanced about, confused by the thoughts for a moment.

"I have a problem" she began. Then she proceeded to tell them all that had happened with Lord Barone.

"I must warn you," she finished, "they will try to eradicate you if they get rid of me. You must be ready to hide. Never reveal yourself to humans."

"We will bring your thoughts to the mother. We will all conference. Return in seven moon risings. We will tell you our thoughts then."

"Thank you," replied Radhya.

The big aliens released them, and the humans retreated along the shoreline. Max and Will glanced at each other behind Radhya's back.

"That was somewhat terrifying," ventured Max.

"I was rather intimidated by that hug," said Will.

"They have no vocal cords, and they can't communicate telepathically with us without touching. The Chandrans are the most morally ethical of any creature I have ever met. Any advice they give will show us the way to do the right thing. They have a racial memory that goes back to the beginning."

A sudden scream tore stopped her explanation. Radhya halted, oriented herself and began to run up the steep hillside. The men followed. The scream came again, and it went on and on shredding human will. Radhya plunged on, removing her tazer from her belt. Finally, it ended in a rattling gurgle.

Rounding the boulder where their fight with the dire wolves occurred, the trio came upon the same two animals pulling and snapping at a body, a human female body. Radhya flicked on her tazer as the two men came up to flank her. The wolves snapped their heads around to glare at them. The female wolf growled low in her throat. Radhya hit her with a half charge in her left eye. The wolf whipped away and leapt the corpse. The male followed, slinking on his belly. Radhya kicked over the woman.

"Rada," she snapped in disgust. "Let the wolves have her. It is at least honorable to feed something when you die. Will, take a holo for me would you?"

Silently Will did as she asked. They retreated further up the trail. The brush crashed and shook as the wolves circled back to feed on their kill, and the sound of growling and bones crunching follow them a good way up the trail. Staggering, Max made it to one side of the trail where he threw up repeatedly until he was empty. Groaning he sat on the trail with his head in his hands.

"She wanted him to sleep with her last night," Will explained.

Radhya was instantly alert asking, "Did she touch him anywhere?"

"Oh yes, several anywhere's in fact," replied Will.

"Get him to the med lab and scan him for transmitters the moment we get in. I should have checked the body better. I might have found a receiver."

Will answered seriously, "Yes, milady."

They retraced their way in silence and entered the tunnel from a large boulder. Twisting and turning their way back through the mountain, they trotted steadily in their bubble of light. On reaching the entry, the trio racked their weapons, and Radhya pointed to the lift.

In seconds, they were deposited in Radhya's bedroom. As they stepped from behind an ornate plaster screen, a child's fantasy of a garden intrigued the men who stared around curiously, craning their necks to see it all. Flowers and animals, birds and butterflies were everywhere. It was difficult to tell what furniture was and what was ornament. The bed was a living creature designed to hold and comfort the sleeper, its coverlet a flap of fur. The floor was fuzzy grass. Radhya led the way around another screen at the opposite end of the room, and they exited into a familiar hallway.

At the med lab, a quick scan revealed two transmitters, one in Max's neck, and one in his rear. Will gave him a local freezing and removed the one in his neck with a scalpel. It had burrowed deep.

Max was cursing beneath his breath. "I thought she was only coming on to me. I didn't realize I was having nanos planted. How could I be such a fool? I even have that stupid super deluxe training. I should know better."

"Max," cut in Radhya sharply, "there is no way you could know. I told you to expect seduction, not trickery. Besides, Barone knew what he was going to do. I never suspected him of being stupid. He certainly wouldn't give you any hint of how to protect yourself or me from his schemes. I have been so involved with this D'Bara/Petra thing that I haven't been focused on the whole picture. Anyway now you can educate Will and Padr on the feelings of a nano plant."

"Feels like being pinched hard," Max replied. "But I never felt anything after that."

"You wouldn't," Will said holding up the first one. It was the size of a fruit fly. "It releases an analgesic as it burrows. Only breaking the skin hurts."

Will poured the instant healing compound on Max's neck and started to remove the second. Radhya put the tiny machine in a test tube. The second joined it in a minute.

"What to do?" she mused.

Finally, she placed the tube in the rear of the freezer in lab two. Will was just wiping the blood drop from Max's buttocks as she returned.

"Go to bed," she told Will. "Max you can have guard duty. Tomorrow we cure Amlina."

Chapter 13

The day dawned clear and sunny. The house was quiet. Radhya awakened Max with a light touch on his shoulder. He seized her arm and pulled her down on top of him.

"I'm sorry milady," he apologized scrambling to his feet. "I thought you were an intruder."

He lifted her to her feet. She held up a hand as he started to apologize again.

"After exercise, breakfast in the kitchen. Tell Aninya," she told him.

Fulfilling the requirements of her body, she clattered down the stairs to the second floor. At Noel's room, she tapped softly. 72 opened the door. His face was pinched and bruised with wild and haggard eyes. Noel lay exactly as she had left him, still panting in pain. His larynx was strained from screaming; he could not even speak. He looked at her, eyes dull with misery. She checked out the alteration.

"Very good progress," she commented lightly. "Now you had the liquid exactly on time?"

The slave 72 nodded vigorously.

"Everything should gradually shrink to its permanent size and the pain should lessen. Have any of you slaves ate or slept?" she asked with narrowed eyes.

"Milady, we can't leave milord Barone," 72 replied in a whisper.

"Nonsense. If you collapse, I'll have to care for him and no thank you. Now divide into two shifts. First shift stays here. Second shift follow me."

Three slaves sorted themselves from the bunch and followed Radhya downstairs. She strode straight to the slave's galley and sat at the head of the table. Aninya approached with fruit and cheese which she set in front of Radhya. The slaves looked uncomfortably at each other.

"Thank you," Radhya said to Aninya, and to the slaves, "sit. Are there any eggs Aninya?"

"Yes, milady, over two dozen this morning."

"Cook up a bunch for this crew. They look like they are starving to death."

"Yes milady," Aninya replied. "They are all excessively thin."

She left the room.

One of Barone's slaves summoned courage and spoke. "I'm 97 milady, and if milady pleases, a bowl of gruel for us to share is what we're used to, or sometimes, a bowl of rice. Eggs is too fine for us. Lords and Ladies eat eggs, not slaves."

Padr ascended the stairs in time to hear the slave's final remark.

"Here slaves eat better than most freedmen, but don't let that fool you. Milady Death knows a well-fed, healthy body works longer, harder and faster. Not to mention without disease. Lady Death hates disease," informed Padr.

Will, Amlina, and D'Bara came up the stairs behind Padr, and seated themselves at the table where Radhya was eating.

"I'm not pleased to feed you gruel. Only sick horses get gruel; healthy horses eat better than that. Amlina, I want to see you after lunch, in the med lab. D'Bara help Jemelina with the cleaning," Radhya commanded the slaves.

"What?" shrieked D'Bara. "You want me to clean house?"

"D'Bara, you are my slave. You do as you are told!" stressed Radhya.

"I was told I'd be your personal maid, not some housekeeper."

Radhya smiled sweetly, "I choose where and when you work, not some mysterious person who told you that you would be my personal maid. Since housecleaning is not to your liking, I'll find you another job."

D'Bara smiled arrogantly around the table.

"Padr," continued Radhya, "escort D'Bara to Li. Tell him I said to give her M duty."

"Yes milady," Padr answered.

Aninya came, bringing breakfast for everyone. Max followed right behind, sniffing eagerly at the food.

"Oh, I see Max was the man in your bed last night. I guess you needed to reward him for turning Rada down," sniped D'Bara bitingly.

Radhya slammed her hands on the table and rose.

"When D'Bara finishes her work at suppertime, give her KP. Then she can clean out the litter boxes for Singha, Ringha, and Kung. After that I want her to scrub and disinfect the entire slave's quarters, walls, ceilings, floors, toilets all of it. If she doesn't do it, or is reluctant, use the prod."

Radhya stamped from the room. She went straight to Geo's room where he was just finishing his tray of breakfast.

"Your will is finished, my dear. It needs only your endorsement," he greeted her.

Radhya did that immediately.

Geo continued, "The offshore retreat on Spa Island is complete. It just needs a staff, and I am moving the crew to the big Island, Africa, to start the hunting preserve."

"I completed all the plants and animals for that a month

ago," sighed Radhya. "Do you think it will be necessary now that Princess Felina is speaking up for me to hold the review?"

"For all her influence, Lady Felina, rank 5, still does not have the final say as to where the review is held. She can only influence her mother and father. Stick to the plan," was Geo's advice.

Radhya nodded. "Something Puzzles me. The Chandrans said Will, Max and I were Selflicn or some such word. It means about to be bonded. What do you think that means, Geo?"

"You know much more about the Chandrans than I do Radhya. Are you upset because Padr wasn't there?"

"No, I've given up on Grandpa's dream of a more human race. I'm just curious about this bonding bit."

"The Chandrans are simply confusing you and your friends with their patterns of life. Doesn't every mother have three or four males join with her to make up a family unit? They are mixing up human patterns with their own."

"Thank you, Geo. Your good sense is my most valuable asset. And thank you for the other night. I guess I didn't realize exactly how much Padr resents my authority over him. I think he could have killed me."

"Well," the old man paused, looking embarrassed. "I think you might feel better if I explain. You see, Padr had a bad reaction to the fidelity stick. You, ah, shorted out his brain for a while."

"Geo, what exactly are you telling me?"

"I gave him a good beating. I did it without checking anything. He scared me when he attacked you. I ran the scanner over him when it was over to make sure there was no serious damage, and the reaction showed up. He is allergic to one of the components in the fidelity stick. He was not attacking you; he was reacting to the medication. I reversed it of course, but I left the bruises. I thought they were a good lesson for the arrogant young pup."

"Does he know about this?"

"No, I never told him. I believe he thinks he lost it and almost killed you. It has quieted him down quite a bit."

"But that is not fair. If he wasn't responsible, he should know about it."

"Do you think that he could still fall in love with you?"

"No, old friend, I know very well he only has eyes for Petra, well Petra pretending to be D'Bara pretending to be Debra. I won't stand in the way of what he thinks will make him happy."

"He rejected her the other night."

"What? Tell me about it."

"You know I keep a close eye on the slave quarters when they are all in there. It was when she woke up. He was sitting on his bunk, doing something with string. Over she comes, naked as you please and sits down beside him. He just ignores her at first, but then she's all over him; you know her style. Anyway, she tries to reach in his pants he grabs her wrist and just says "no." He did this flip thing, and she ended on her bare bottom on the female side of the room. Then she spent the rest of the night calling him names and talking dirty. He just ignored her."

"That's just the fidelity stick. He knows it will make him sick."

"Radhya, I had to neutralize that. Padr isn't under that influence anymore. He could do whatever he wished, and there would be no effect."

"If he thinks it's there then it's almost as good as being there."

She smiled broadly. "This doesn't matter anyway. Let's just get the slaves of the Commonwealth on the road to freedom and then I can work on my love life."

Radhya kissed the old man on the forehead and hurried from the room. She returned to lab one, checking the simulation one more time, then she moved to lab two to formulate it. While Padr exercised, Will and Max worked on the DNA unzipper. Padr came in quietly and helped them work on the rezipper.

At lunchtime, Aninya brought them steaming bowls of soup.

"Milady, do you think I could have Amlina for the kitchen, to help me? The girl is a wonder, and she loves working with food," Aninya trailed off.

"Yes, you may, but not until I'm done with her, maybe a week. Then she's all yours."

"Thank you milady," Aninya bowed and left.

When they finished eating, they went to the med lab. Amlina crept timidly up the stairs, and when they caught sight of her, Padr took her arm and escorted her to the lab.

"Amlina," began Will, "you have a serious brain cancer." The girl nodded. "We, well Lady Kirbyson, has created a cure. It will be painful, and it will take about a week. Do you want to try it?"

Amlina looked at them with her large, pale blue eyes. It was as if she couldn't speak. Finally, she nodded assent.

Max was the timer. Amlina took her first pill. Will led her to the gurney in the corner, where she lay down. Shortly she was sweating profusely. Exactly two hours later Amlina took the capsule. She squirmed in pain as her code was rewritten, but she never opened her lips, never uttered a sound.

Radhya, Will, Max, and Padr took turns with her during the long hours that followed. Radhya checked to make sure Noel's slaves changed shifts, and the other shift was fed. The rest of the time, they spent caring for Amlina. Exactly twelve hours and thirteen minutes later, they gave her the rezipper. Her pain subsided, and she fell asleep. Padr approached Radhya when it was her turn to watch.

"I uh, I wanted to say how sorry I was about the other night. I don't know why I went berserk like that. I didn't want to hurt you," he muttered with his head down, feet shifting uncomfortably.

"Don't worry about it. It wasn't your fault," she replied changing the compress on Amlina's head.

"No, I had no right to hit you like that. I've never done

anything even remotely like that in my whole life. I am ashamed."

"Padr," she replied turning to him, "it wasn't your fault. You had a reaction to the medication."

Staring at the floor, he whispered, "I know you are just saying that to make me feel better. You always do that; try to make people feel better."

Radhya went to the comp. Scrolling back through the readings, she found the one Geo had taken.

"See here. That is your histamine level that night. Here is what it is supposed to be normally."

"You mean this proves I had a reaction?"

"Yes, Padr you did. You might not have survived if Geo hadn't reversed it either. I didn't think it was that serious. In addition, yes, you can kiss D'Bara and nothing will happen, you are a free agent in that respect. I just hope you won't."

"Don't worry. I was there when you blew her cover. I do not want anything to do with someone with that much hate and venom in her. Besides, we have to get the slaves on the road to freedom don't we?" he smiled.

She punched him in the arm, "Right you are."

"Radhya, I'm curious about your Grandfather."

She moved to check Amlina again, changing the warm cloth for a cool one.

"What do you want to know?"

"Experimentation on human embryos has been illegal for thousands of years. How did your Grandfather get away with helping us?"

"Grandpa never did experiments on human embryos. He ran comp models to find the optimum combinations. Then he ran eggs and sperm separately through certain processes and allowed them to combine. He worked like that with animals for years. In vitro is illegal, but in the main part, the Proctors look the other way, especially with freedmen. Anyway, Grandpa developed his technique to the point where it could be done in a living body. Mom and Dad drink a potion, engage in sex and presto, the desired child is conceived. That's where we come from. Nice and normal, just like everyone else, except for our potential."

"Can you do the same thing?"

"No. First, I wouldn't do anything right now that could be interpreted wrongly. Second, I don't know how. I told you I was an idiot savant with genetic things. So was Grandpa. I keep very good, detailed notes. He didn't. When he died, the process died with him."

"So what was he trying to accomplish?"

"Humans don't use their full potential. He was trying to help us access more humanness. He noticed that there are good aristocrats and bad ones. Statistically, it goes in the classic Mendelian twenty-five seventy-five split. That led him to think that this trait might be genetic. Caring about people and being altruistic seem to have been his major goals. He surmised it was inborn, not necessarily learned. So here we are. Just as human as anyone else."

"You mean I'm bred to care."

"Yes, I guess that is what it means. Anyway, it's your shift now, and I am going to lie down. Night."

Max was watching Amlina when he noticed something strange. She was crying big, slow tears in her sleep. One would gather at the corner of her eye glittering in the faint light. It rolled down her cheek to the pillow, staining it vermilion. Max woke Will.

Will stared at the strange phenomenon a while and then he caught several tears on a glass slide and scanned them. Immediately he hit the panic button and sealed the lab completely. Radhya and Padr woke with a start.

"Radhya, this is unbelievable, unimaginable! Don't touch Amlina! Padr, Max, Radhya get into contamination suits!"

Will was shrugging into one as the others scrambled to obey. When they were all isolate, Will handed them the printouts.

"The cancer was a screen. They knew you would try to cure her, so they planted nanos so small they don't register on a normal scanner. These are molecular nanos. Touch one, and it will burrow into you and create the same sort of cancer. In six months, we'd all be dead. In addition, it would spread to everyone we touched or who touched us."

"Not me," said Radhya; "I'm immune to cancer. So are the three of you. I used our immunity as a pattern to create Amlina's cure. Nevertheless, we could contaminate everyone else. Can you figure out how to destroy them?"

Will was thoughtful for a moment. Then he started taking inventory in the lab. About an hour later, he held up a concoction. In the meantime, Max worked feverishly modifying some equipment to scan for the minuscule devices.

"I hope this will rid us of them; it should dissolve their connections.

Amlina stopped crying. Max scanned her very carefully.

"Her clothes are crawling with them."

Radhya undressed the semi-conscious girl and wrapped her in a clean, sterile sheet. Max scanned her again. Using microforcepts, he plucked a machine from her ear. After making sure Amlina was clean, they scanned the rest of the room. They were meticulous, scanning the room four times and destroying every device they found. On the fifth pass, they couldn't find anymore. Radhya slipped from her contamination suit. Max scanned her, but she came up clean. Padr and Max unsuited and were likewise clean.

Will, however, had two. One they easily removed, but the other had burrowed. Will stared at the death sentence he carried in his arm.

"Don't despair," said Radhya cheerfully, "you are just going to be very sick."

She unsealed the lab and went quickly to lab two, returning with a bottle containing a liquid, glowing lime green. The label said metal purge.

"Get some basins," she commanded. "Get ready for fire-works. Padr and Max take care of Will. I'll care for Amlina."

Radhya had Will drink the entire bottle. Within two minutes, Will was sicker than he had ever been in his life. He threw up so continuously he could not breathe. At the same time, he had diarrhea without any possibility of control. Sweat poured from him in sheets. When the nano was expelled in the sweat, Max picked it up and destroyed it.

"Got it!" He yelled in triumph.

Radhya produced a hypospray. She injected Will in the arm and slowly his symptoms subsided.

"Go to bed," Radhya told him quietly. "Padr, help him to shower, please, then put him to bed. I guess you are on guard duty again Max. Padr, when you are done with Will, you can sit with Amlina. Oh, have D'Bara clean the med lab and disinfect it in the morning would you?"

Padr turned from helping Will to give her a wicked grin.

Chapter 14

Max was so soundly asleep when Radhya left the next morning to exercise that she had no heart to wake him. Facing the hallway, his lashes making dark shadows on his square face, he looked like a sleeping child. She stepped over him and left. On her return, she again went to step over him. Like lightning, his hand shot out and grabbed her ankle. Radhya tumbled to the floor and Max had his knee in her back.

"Let me up," she commanded him.

The weight on her back lessened but did not vanish.

"Who are you?" He demanded.

"I'm Radhya, in a minute I'll turn into Lady Death if you don't let me up!"

"Radhya is asleep in her room. Who are you?"

"I'm Radhya. You were asleep when I went out, so I didn't wake you."

"Radhya always wakes me."

He removed his knee and pulled her around.

He continued, "You look like Radhya, but how do I know you're not just another look alike come to assassinate her?"

His eyes were hard as stone. Radhya struggled in his grasp, but his strength was superior.

"Max let me go. I'm tired already, and I have a busy day."

"Not until I know who you are."

"Open the door. If I am there, then I'm not me."

Max opened the door of Radhya's room and peered inside. The screen fencing the entry blocked the view. Venturing gingerly inside, he inspected every corner while still holding tightly to Radhya's wrist. She snapped her arm away and headed for the shower.

"Wait! I haven't checked the shower yet or the dressing room."

Radhya waited impatiently as he checked the shower suite.

Finding it and the dressing room empty he said, "Radhya could be in one of the labs, in the kitchen, or even at the stables. I don't know if this is enough proof."

Sighing Radhya asked, "Could you read a genetic code scan?"

Embarrassed Max shook his head.

"I know," she said.

Radhya went into the hall and whistled. Singha, Ringha, and Kung bounded up the stairs in answer. Purring they circled Radhya begging for petting. Radhya obliged.

"Is this good enough proof?" she asked him.

"Yes milady," he replied. "I am sorry. I think there was an invader in a dream I was having. Someone small was digging a hole in my head. I'm sorry I inconvenienced you."

"Wait Max, an invader in your head. Come with me."

Radhya led him to the med lab and shoved him in the scanner. Will was asleep in a chair beside a drowsing Amlina. Radhya was impressed with his dedication after his own bout with sickness the night before, brought to her attention by a dreadful smell was beginning to creep out into the hall. The ping of the scanner caught her attention.

"Come here Max," she whispered. "Do you see that white

spot there? That is a nano, if I isolate the image; I think a viewing and hearing device. Somehow, Barone sent this up the stairs, and it got on you. He has been watching and listening to everything you did since whenever it got on you."

"It wasn't there last night."

"No, it certainly wasn't. He probably put it on you in the middle of the night. I hate the thought of him prowling around up here when I am asleep."

Spraying freezing on the spot, Radhya dug forceps into his forehead and extracted the machine. She put it with the others in the freezer in lab two. Returning to the med lab, she checked on Amlina. She had Max carry Amlina to his old room, across from hers. Radhya then woke Will and sent him to bed.

Amlina was doing well. Her fever was lower, and the scan revealed the tumor was shrinking rapidly.

Radhya descended to the next floor to check on Barone. He was also much improved.

"Well Noel, you are progressing very well. Just my luck you are one of those fast healers. In another day or so, you will be well enough to travel," hinted Radhya.

"Where am I going?" Noel croaked.

"Why, I thought you might feel like going home, to show off or whatever it is that men do," she replied. "I actually have business to conduct on Jabin's World myself. I'm sure you wouldn't want to be here while I'm away."

"Actually my dearest, I would like that very much."

"Well, I wouldn't. If you want to stay on Pleasant you'll move to the visitor's center and pay the going rate," she said in a hard voice.

"Radhya, are you throwing me out?"

"Why of course not Noel, I'm just telling you, you can't stay here."

Radhya turned and left the room fuming at Lord Barone's obstinacy. She pondered his power to arouse her to anger every time she was in his presence. She dashed down the stairs and into the kitchen. Aninya was cooking, Singha and the kits purring around her feet. Radhya slowed and took a deep breath.

"Milady, one of the slave girls, has disappeared. Her name is Rada," Aninya began.

"Yes Aninya, I know. She went, ah, walking in the forest outside the fence, and the dire wolves got her. We found the body, but didn't retrieve it. Will has a holo for proof. Tell all the other girls to stay away from the woods will you, especially at night."

A horrified Aninya stared at her. Radhya walked to the slaves' galley. A number of slaves were having breakfast. 72 rose hurriedly to his feet.

"Sit down," she told him. "Finish your food. This is your territory on which I am intruding. My own slaves don't seem to mind. Your master is improving so rapidly that he will be leaving here in about two days."

A look of severe disappointment crossed the faces of Barone's slaves. Radhya felt stricken at their pain. When the most important thing in life was getting enough food, and it was taken away with one breath, it must be a terribly frightening thing. She closed her eyes at her insensitivity and shook her head.

"I'm sorry," she apologized, "I'm leaving myself, or you could stay longer. I'll have Aninya make you up some care packages, dried fruit, protein bars and a few things like that before you go, okay?"

"Thank you milady," answered 72, "we have just been enjoying your good food, and the fine quarters so much we hate to leave. Such packages would be a blessing to us, but what if my Lord finds them?"

"Since when does Lord Barone ever lift anything? You carry all the gear everywhere, so you just put it in with his stuff, he doesn't notice because he doesn't ever carry it. If he does, tell him it was a present from me. He'll throw it out because he will think it is poisoned. If he doesn't notice, you have a little food for a while."

"We are forever grateful."

"I'm sure Lord Barone will drag you back here as often as he can," she consoled. "See to it please Padr. And after lunch wake Will and meet me in the den. Until then do whatever needs catching up. I'll be with Kaarl and Geo all morning, so you are free. Moreover, don't forget to have D'Bara clean the med lab. Use the prod if she is reluctant. It's good for her to learn a little discipline."

D'Bara glared at Radhya from her seat at the table, hate flickering in her eyes like fire eating through wood. Her hands and arms had prod welts on them from the day before, and her beautiful face had bruises as well. Radhya smiled at her sister, grabbed a piece of fruit from the bowl and left the room.

In Geo's room, she first discussed finances with Kaarl and arranged to buy some more slaves. More than ever, she made sure the full extent of her wealth was hidden. Kaarl left with his instructions.

"Radhya, your brother is supposed to call anytime now. We should go to the comm center," Geo told her.

"Have Padr transfer the call here and lock the comm door," she said.

Minutes later the holophone in the corner lit up. Radhya accepted the call.

"Steph," she smiled, "It's been a long time since I heard from you."

The most handsome man in the known galaxy peered out at her. His hair was as golden as spring sunshine and his eyes an incredible amethyst and blue, with long, long dark lashes. He had a generous full mouth with perfect teeth. Dimples complimented his perfectly shaped oval face. The classic Grecian nose was the final touch. However, he looked very cross.

"Why did you message me to call you?" he asked. "You know I'm too busy to chitchat."

"Steph, we have a serious problem with Petra."

"You know I have no concern for that stupid slut. I don't want to be bothered." He reached to cut the connection.

"Wait! It involves money."

He paused, "There is something else?"

"Steph, she is here in disguise, a genetic makeover as a slave to kill me."

"Radhya what are you babbling about? Where's the money?" Stephan asked with irritation.

Beginning with her forced contract to contract, Radhya told him the whole story, suitably edited to leave out the plan.

"Well little sister, this is a fine mess. You know Barone probably has her assets now, so she is unlikely to be restored to royal status. She is done for as far as that goes. Do you have proof she plans to kill you?"

"Steph, Geo records everything."

"Send me a microburst."

Geo sent a transcript to Stephan. He stared at it off screen for a moment, revealing his stunning profile.

"How is it that she is still pretending to be a slave and trying to kill you after an interview like this?"

Radhya sighed. "I developed a substance I call a dismemorizer. It removes a person's memory for about twelve hours. It's like that time never existed to the person, so Petra doesn't know I broke her cover, and she is carrying on. I made her clean stables yesterday, and today she is cleaning feces and vomit from my med lab."

A delighted smile illuminated Stephan's face, like the sun coming from behind clouds. He chuckled aloud.

"Sister dear, that alone is worth my help. Unfortunately, I'm more mercenary than that; I want your dismemorizor formula."

"I already hold the patent."

"I want permission to duplicate and put it into production."

"If anyone can buy it, it kind of defeats its purpose."

"I still want to produce it. Take my terms or do without my help."

"I want half your earnings then."

"I'll give you one third."

Radhya thought a moment then agreed.

"Another matter Steph."

"What now?"

"If Barone gets me busted to slave, all my property is forfeit. I don't want him to get any of it. I have a living will, and you are to get everything but my slaves. I have made other arrangements for them. But I want you to know Barone intends to take everything I own and I don't want him to have it."

Stephan smiled wolfishly. "Don't worry about that sister. If you have left it to me, rest assured I will get it. I'll get back to you when I check this info out. At the very least, I can contend we should split Petra's property and not allow it exfamilia at least. Take care sister, take very good care."

Stephan cut the connection. Radhya looked at Geo.

"Too bad he isn't at least part human," Geo snorted.

"He's all I have left of family," replied Radhya forlornly.

"Bah. Your mother hated you. Her eyes were only for Petra. Your father ignored you; only Stephan existed for him. Your grandfather was the only one in the whole family with both a heart and a brain. Should be glad to be rid of them," he snorted.

Radhya smiled wanly at the dear old man.

"You have those three young bucks for friends. And just you wait until you fall for some smart young aristocrat and have children. Listen to me, and you won't make such a mess of their lives as your parents did."

"Oh, Geo, you are my parent," cried Radhya hugging him. "What would I ever do without you? You keep me sane."

Geo grinned back at her and hugged her in return. Radhya left, crossing the dining room to the den. Padr was standing just inside the door. Will was sitting in a leather chair munching breakfast.

"Morning," she called to them both, pulling down a map. "Sorry to cut your sleep short again Will, but I want you to see Spa Island."

She pointed to a small island many miles off the coastline, southeast of the track.

"This is my Spa Island. It has every pampering device and technique known to humankind. Plus a few I've invented myself. The older ladies are going to love my bacterial facelift. I need medical checked out in case I have forgotten anything, and I need the whole unit landscaped. So we are going to go and see it in person."

She snapped the map back up. Locking the door to the den, she led them through the back panel to the secret entry. Padr looked surprised.

"Didn't you tell him?" Radhya asked Will.

Will shook his head as Radhya pushed the men into the lift. This time it sank very far down, and they were deposited in a huge cavern. The lights on the far walls appeared misty with the distance. Three hovers bulked to one side.

"Can either of you drive a hover?" Radhya asked.

"I can," Padr replied.

"Good," responded Radhya, "I can, but I'd rather watch the scenery go by. You drive, I'll navigate."

The trio climbed in. It was roomy and comfortable, even while fastened in the safety restraints. Radhya pointed the way, and Padr drove. Will went to sleep in the back, shifting gently with the vector changes.

After ten minutes of slow travel, they burst from the tunnel onto the ocean. The sea lapped grey and green around their vehicle as they sped over the low waves, throwing curtains of water from their base. Radhya adjusted the course, and Padr picked up speed, going faster and faster until the hover was flat out. An involuntary grin of pure pleasure split his features as they raced over the water. Radhya beamed back in response.

All too soon, Radhya tapped his forearm and pointed to the land rising majestically from the sea. Padr reduced speed and brought them around a pair of steep arms that opened on a spacious bay. He eased the hover into the harbor and skillfully landed them on the sloping sand beach. Will woke with the cessation of noise and movement.

It was a semi-tropical paradise, where large trees were waving in the warm breeze. Up the path, gleaming white stone buildings lifted from the sand, like Moore sculptures.

"This is my spa, for those royals who do not crave the excitement of racing nor the thrills of hunting. It contains everything the pampered aristocrat could desire, from hot springs to mud pits," Radhya laughed to the men. "We'll bring Max later but Padr, bring out your sketchbooks. Plan the landscaping. I want it to be as special as your last." She sparkled at him.

"I can't wait to start another project," he beamed back. "I've been feeling useless."

"Never useless Padr, you're never useless, decorative maybe, but never useless," Radhya laughed.

Padr wandered outside the complex of buildings noting dimensions and elevations while Radhya and Will inspected the interiors. When that was accomplished, they sat in the shade on the sand and discussed the plan. Gradually the sky grew darker, and the waves loomed larger, no longer colored with any green, just white foam laced grey.

Radhya said, "We should go find Padr. If the waves get too high, they could flip the hover."

They found Padr at the landside of the complex staring at the completely barren hills.

"What do you want me to do about the rest of the island?" he asked.

"Do whatever you think best. The contrast is nice, but so would a splendid view be nice. It's all in your hands. Unfortunately, you'll have to work it out later. The waves are getting higher, and I think perhaps we should go."

They hurried back through the spa to the beached hover. Strapping in, Padr wasted no time getting them underway. He sent the little vehicle zipping along the shoreline to the harbor's mouth. Rounding the point, the nose of the craft rose up to its full height, straight up, then crashed down.

Six-meter waves were pounding the coast in a fury, and the wind was doing its best to strip the leaves from the trees. Padr wrestled with the controls. He maintained just enough speed to keep the hover stationary in the wind and waves. They were crashing from trough to trough. Padr timed the waves. In the dip, he flipped the vessel sideways and around before the next wave could smash it to bits. He cut in some more speed and retreated into the harbor.

"Look out!" yelled Will pointing out the back window.

A rogue wave had rounded the headland. It picked up the small craft and hurled it onto the steep rocks of the island's face. Waves sucked them back and hurled them forward again; the hover leaking in many places.

"Hang on," thundered Padr.

A third time the waves crunched them to the cliff. This time the hover shattered like an egg on marble.

Radhya flew through the air into the water, tossed and twirled. She could not breathe. Thrust into the sky, she gulped foam and air, and then plunged into the dark roiling water again. She smashed into a rock and grasped it with all her might, only to be torn away from it and smashed into another rock and another. An arm snaked out and caught her by the tunic pulling her forward. Her salt stinging eyes caught a glimpse of Will as he pushed her leeward of himself. A large hand reached down and seized her shoulder. Padr hauled her panting onto the small ledge of rock at the base of the cliff. He reached down again and fished Will from the frothing water. Radhya had barely enough strength left to cling to the rock face.

"We have to work our way along the rock to the beach," yelled Padr over the banshee wail of the wind.

"Can't," gasped Radhya "no strength left."

"Have to. No choice," yelled Padr back.

He inched cautiously forward on the cliff. Will nudged her to follow. Stubbornly she shook her head. Will nudged her again. The sky opened up and wept stinging tears of rain.

"Come on," bellowed Padr, "I'll help you."

He held out his hand which she clung to as she inched her way forward. Will followed supporting her from the other side. Centimeter by painful centimeter they crept along the cliff climbing higher to avoid the waves that threatened to suck them back to a watery grave. The cliff above them lowered as they climbed. Finally, a subjective eternity later, they crawled over the lip of rock and were on top.

Now the wind smote them full force as if determined to force them back into the sea. The rain pelted down so hard visibility was arm's length. The trio staggered downslope, the only method they had of telling direction.

Eons later, a white building in front of his outstretched hand halted Padr. They worked their way to the left, trying to find a door. Padr yanked at something and vanished into the dark. Radhya fell in behind him, and Will tripped on top of her. The cessation of pounding was like sudden sensory deprivation, only the loud rasping of their lungs echoed through the space.

Will crawled to the door and sealed it shut. Radhya stumbled to her feet and hit a switch. Nothing happened.

"Power plant's shut down. No light, no heat, no messages, no food," she gasped.

Padr rose and prowled the room.

"What is this building?" he asked.

Radhya looked around.

"Massage therapy I think," she coughed.

Will checked her pulse. "I think we need to get out of these wet clothes," he stated.

Radhya tottered to the wall, barely visible in the gloom. Pulling out drawers, she finally found some sheets. Handing a couple to each man, she began to strip. Then she wrapped herself in sheets and spread her wet things to dry. She found a dry corner and curled up to sleep. The men followed her lead and soon joined her, one on either side.

Chapter 15

Padr was sound asleep on his back when they found them; Radhya snuggled to his side. Will cupped her back, his arm around her. The sharp intake of breath from 72 awakened Will. He rolled over with a loud groan.

"Well, sleeping beauties, care to tell us what happened?" Rory drawled. "We have been frantic looking for you. See Geo has been pried from his den and Noel insisted on sending 72."

Will sat up stiffly, feeling every bruise and pulled muscle. He slapped Padr on the back of the hand. Padr opened one swollen eye, but it drooped shut again. Radhya slept on.

"We were sure you were dead when we saw the hover wreckage on the beach," said Geo.

"We should be," answered Will. "Padr was amazing!"

Max, Rory, Geo and 72 looked dubiously at the battered hero.

Will babbled, "No really, I never saw anyone control a machine like that. We would have been safely back at the beach if that one giant wave hadn't come into the harbor. It smashed the hover. Padr found the ledge and got Radhya and me up onto it. Then he led us over the cliff and here. I'm amazed we survived."

He looked at Padr with great respect.

"It's all a big load of horse droppings," Padr murmured throwing a hand over his eyes.

"I doubt that. Radhya's an excellent judge of character. None of the rest of us could see anything in you, but she did," said Geo with a grunt. "We are a little bruised. However, I don't think any serious damage is done," Will continued.

Padr, moving gingerly, rolled into a sitting position.

"Why doesn't Radhya wake up?" asked Max.

"She's probably exhausted. It wasn't easy getting back here. She was thrown outside of the rocks that line the cliff. Padr and I were thrown to the inside, so she had it a little harder than us. Give her a minute," said Will.

"Have you got any food? I'm perishing," groaned Padr.

Max rummaged through the emergency pack he wore and came up with three energy bars. He gave Will and Padr each one. He knelt by Radhya and looked at her closely. Lifting her gently in his arms, he revealed a large purple swelling on the other side of her head.

"Will?" he questioned.

Dropping his food, Will examined her immediately.

"Does anyone have a portable scanner? I lost mine in the accident."

Rory dashed out the door to the waiting heliplane, returning swiftly and handing the device to Will. The doctor ran it over Radhya.

"Sprained wrist, again, torn ligaments right knee, multiple contusions, cracked rib, a large blood clot in the brain and a fracture of the skull."

Will became very still and white. Driving his fist into the floor, he jumped to his feet.

"I should have checked her when we got here, but I just let her go to sleep. She obviously had a rougher time than we did. I didn't realize it. I thought she couldn't keep up because she's a woman. This is all my fault."

"She's still alive isn't she?" asked Geo soberly.

"Yes, but she is unconscious, I don't know if her life signs are going up or down. She could spiral into deeper unconsciousness and die, or end up brain damaged and wake up a vegetable. A brain bleed is no joke."

Geo exchanged glances with Rory. Both looked over at 72. Geo raised a gnarled little finger.

Then the pilot nodded, and he said, "Bring her."

Will and Padr scrambled into their battered but dry clothes. They wrapped Radhya more tightly in the sheets. Carrying her as if she were about to break, Max followed Geo to the heliplane. Rory took off, taking everyone on a swift and wild ride. Shortly, they entered a deep inlet of the ocean, framed by steep cliffs on either side. The land was heavily forested with only a narrow margin of white sand beach. Numerous caves pocked the rock. Rory feathered the heliplane down on a slightly wider patch of sand and rubble. Geo snapped a dismemorizor capsule under 72's nose. The rest exited the vehicle.

The old man brushed the hair back from her forehead, placed a kiss there and murmured, "Take her to the Chandrans. They will know what to do."

Max, carrying Radhya, followed the sand around the back curve of the inlet. Will and Padr trailed after him. Geo and Rory said they would not be welcome, so they stayed with the heliplane. Max's arms were going numb when a large, not quite human shape beckoned from behind a tree. He headed doggedly in that direction.

Once among the big trees, Max was relieved of Radhya's weight by a huge black alien. The men followed him blindly, struggling through the thick underbrush that fought to impede their progress. Fortunately, the distance was short. The alien disappeared into a dark hole with Radhya. Padr lunged after her. Will grabbed his arm.

"I think they're going to help her," he whispered.

"Who are they?" demanded Padr.

"Ocean Chandrans, friends of Radhya," answered Max.

Max plunged into the dark cavity followed by Will and Padr. Feeling his way through the snaking corridor, he came to a warm, dimly lit cavern. Small red glowing spots, two meters from the floor, gave a feeble light. The rocky floor was lapped softly by waves. A row of large alien bodies lined the outside walls, shifting and moving restlessly in the warm, wet air. The alien carrying Radhya walked towards them. Three Chandrans stepped forward and enfolded the men in their arms.

"Seliflacn of the recreator, our friend, how may we serve you?" came the thought quietly into their brains.

Will spoke up, "Our machine overturned in the storm last night and broke. We got out, but Radhya is hurt. I can't fix her. Her old, uh, friend Geo, brought us here to you. I don't exactly know why."

"Is it her mind that suffers?" came the question.

"In a manner of speaking, she has a blood clot in her brain."

"Do you wish the lameeno, the bonding at this time?"

"Whatever will help her," replied Will and Max together.

"You must all go to the mother then."

The alien carrying Radhya went to the water and entered it. When it reached waist deep on him, a whale shape, perhaps ten meters long came to meet him. It extended arms and took Radhya's limp body. Padr lunged from the enfolding arms of his alien and dashed into the water. The big one there grasped and enfolded him. Max and Will followed more slowly.

"We understand your concern for your mate. Follow," the quiet voice encouraged.

Max and Will joined Padr and Radhya in the arms of the mother. The men felt their minds flying across the space to the whale mind. Their consciousness somehow guided into the deep, peaceful presence. It was female, ageless and unknowable, encompassing wisdom on a level different from humans, ancient and alien. She welcomed them and showed them somehow, Radhya's unconscious mind. They followed their guide.

It was an endless black ocean, no light, no stars, cold and forlorn. A wind moaned over the surface.

"Help me find her," came the thought.

The men felt themselves unite in purpose, Max, faithful, with a pure golden light, Padr, strong and determined, a glowing emerald green, and Will, confident, sure and stable, a pillar of violet purity, unshakable in his hope; together they dove into the dark sea.

Beneath the dark, roiling events tossed them about. Images of Barone, Geo, themselves, her brother and sister, Singha, so many images leaping and gibbering at them. Max was flipping Radhya, Padr hit her, Will was being sick, and Kung was leaping on Barone. Princess Felina was pushing her to contract with Barone, a black impenetrable sickness of evil and pain hurting her, images upon images pushing and shoving for their attention. A blackness padded around the edges, slipping sideways from view if they turned to stare, yet pacing their every move. Progress faltered. Then Padr took the lead forging ahead and down through the turmoil, pushing the images back, settling them into their places.

It lessened as they came to a shadowed place of feelings. Dark secrets lurked here, guilt and shame and fear. The terror of failure was overwhelming. Then there was a hunger to be loved, to be understood; yet it clouded with the terror of being unlovable. Padr's face laced through it all. He faltered unable to look at it. It called so clearly to his own insecurities and failures that he drew back. Faithful Max forged ahead, calming the attacking fear with warm golden light, pouring love in to fill the need, putting guilt and shame to flight.

They plunged down a third time. Here was a physical plane; a face turned away with the ills of the body. Will stepped forward here. He healed the cracked rib, sprained wrist, the torn ligament. He dissolved the blood clot and plastered the fracture closed. Will looked inward and entered himself with the power of the bond; healing his own ills, and then he entered Padr and cured his body. The bruises and sore muscles dissolved into wellness.

Down they plunged again into a white world. Everything was glowing sparkling white, brilliant and facetted and beautiful. They heard the guide's voice again.

"This is the center of her soul. Call her to you. Call with your love."

The three men tried calling with their voices. Nothing happened except the light sparkled brightly.

"Call with your love," came the thought again.

Max remembered the feelings he had for Radhya, her smile, her kindnesses, her humor, and her care for everyone. A faint blue flicker sparkled in one corner. Will followed his example pouring his entire mind into remembering her lightness and her laughter, her cutting intelligence. The electric radiance grew brighter. Slowly it began to fade again.

"You will lose her if you cannot call her back. The body will die without the mind," came their instructor.

Padr lowered his impregnable walls. A torrent of emotion flowed from his green light. The same fear of failure, the same fear of being unlovable as she carried. Padr sent his feelings for her through, admiring, sexual, fear of not being adequate to her need, desire for love, her love.

An electric blue beam fountained up around them. Love enveloped and soothed them. Care and fondness mixed with confusion about what was happening, loving them all deeply. The colors twined together and joined to make a multihued rainbow. Up they went, through the body, the dark world, sleeping now, through the images, reflecting the faces of the three men like mirrors, into the distance, bursting through the surface of the dark sea. The sea was brilliant with colors of the sunrise, the light striking from a rising orb. The rainbow rose to the guiding mind. There it split apart. The blue returned to Radhya. The golden beam retreated to Max and the violet to Will. The green lingered a moment, then returned to Padr, floating in the blood warm water.

The midday sun shone straight down into their eyes. The four woke within seconds of each other. Radhya smiled the largest smile of her life. She stretched and yawned.

"I feel wonderful," she glowed. "But how come I'm on a beach, naked with you three well clothed?"

"I'm sorry," replied Max turning away, "you had a sheet, but we lost it somewhere."

"You're so beautiful to look at. I'd give you my tunic, but then I couldn't look anymore," smiled Padr. "I'm not sure where the heliplane is anyway," he continued looking around.

"How did we get here? I thought we were at the spa?" Radhya asked.

"Do you remember the accident?" asked Will over his shoulder.

"Certainly, but obviously danger agrees with me. I feel great," she said pirouetting on her toes, arms raised high above her head.

"You look great," replied Padr feasting his eyes.

Radhya smiled at him, her brow furrowed.

"Last night we just collapsed," explained Will, "and you bashed into the rocks more than we did. Padr dragged me out, but then I had to go back in to get you."

"Yes, I remember Padr hauling both of us out."

"But I never checked you when we got to the spa, and you had a brain bleed." The guilt was loud in his voice.

Radhya looked at his back, and her brows furrowed more.

"Am I dead?" she asked. "Is this all in my head? Is that why Padr's looking at me like that?"

"No, no. Geo, Max, and Rory came to rescue us this morning. Max actually was the one to discover that you were hurt. Geo brought us to the Chandrans. The fathers asked if we wanted the lameeno. It was the only way we could save you. The fathers took us to a mother, and she helped us to call you, we also healed each other somehow, and that's it. Here we are."

Radhya fell to the sand. Shock and fear communicated itself in every line of her face and body.

"Do you mean to tell me they did the bonding, with all of us?" she asked softly.

"I don't know what you mean by the bonding, but it would be a good description of what happened," Max answered.

"But don't you see; now we're bound, forever. I never heard about anything able to reverse it. You, all of you are bound to me and to each other. We all belong to each other," she exclaimed in distress.

"Don't worry about it. No one forced us. We each chose to participate in this bonding," Padr said. "What was done, was done of our free will. It was wonderful. I'd do it again in a minute."

Radhya huddled on the sand arms tightly crossed in front of her. She looked at him in disbelief, murmuring, "But you don't even like me."

Padr drew off his tunic and handed it to her. She slipped quickly into it.

"I do like you. I always did. I just didn't feel safe enough to tell you. I… I had a hard time to trust that you could ever love me, after what I've been and am," he told her honestly gazing into her eyes.

"It was the only way to save your life," put in Max softly turning around again.

Radhya drew the men to her and hugged them all at once.

"Do you realize we have been more intimate than any other humans in history? We can learn to do it again, at will or need."

The men looked at her in silence until a whistling disturbed their contemplation. Rory came sauntering down the beach.

"Well, anyone interested in going home?" he asked.

He removed his jacket and handed it to Padr. He slipped it on but could not do it up. They followed Rory pensively down the sand. The heliplane was not far, and soon they were winging home.

As the vehicle landed, Radhya turned to Geo and asked, "How could you? You knew what would happen. I didn't want anyone coerced," Geo said, "I would do anything to save your life, including sacrificing the lives of your three friends. When you were eighteen, who held you from the fire while his legs burnt. When you were sixteen who almost died of poison meant for you and when you were fourteen who took the dagger meant for your heart. I love you as my daughter, and I would do anything to save your life. I think you would know that by now."

Radhya's face softened. She unbuckled and hugged the old man.

"I'm sorry," she said. "I owe you so much, and I should never complain about what you do to help me."

She leapt from the heliplane and dashed to her room in the house.

"Your legs burnt?" inquired Will looking at Geo's obvious legs.

"She fixed them for me. It was her first practical application of her formulas," he replied gruffly. "Likewise a new liver, and new kidneys, and a new heart."

The trio stared at him in amazement.

"A lot of people want Radhya dead. So please guard her well." Geo left them.

Chapter 16

The next morning, Radhya sent a smiling Amlina to the kitchen to start training with Aninya. Barone sent her a message saying that he expected her to join him for breakfast, so only slightly passed the prescribed hour she entered the dining room. She gave Noel a brilliant smile as she took her seat. Will and Padr were standing behind her chair. She could feel their presences in her mind; she kept probing at the spot. Max was also present in a strange not-here-feeling. She greeted 72 and another slave behind Barone's chair.

"My, we are in a good mood today," Noel stated sourly.

"My spa should be a wonderful success," she grinned at him.

72 leaned forward and whispered in Barone's ear. He frowned at her.

"I thought it wasn't yet operating?" he questioned.

"The facilities are all in place. I only need the staffing," she replied. "I leave tonight for Jabin's World. I assume you are leaving as well?"

"I am still very sore," he complained, "but perhaps I can hitch a ride with you. It seems the other royal I was traveling with has abandoned me."

"Why don't you just hire your own spaceship?" Radhya retorted, the smile fading from her face.

"Ah, well then, my dearest, I am forced to remain here as your guest," returned Noel with a sly grin of his own.

"If that is the case, by all means, accompany me to Jabin's World. You will have to bunk with the slaves for I have only one cabin and it is mine."

Radhya patted her lips and left for her business meeting with Geo. At the conclusion of the meeting, she rose to go.

"Assign D'Bara to Li. She can work in the stables while I'm gone. Keep her out of the house," suggested Radhya hand on the doorknob.

"Be extraordinarily careful, my little Radhya," warned Geo. "I have a very bad feeling about this trip."

"Never fear, old friend, Noel will be locked from my cabin. Once I drop him off, I won't need to see him again for two years. That's my hope anyway."

Geo shook his head as she went to pack her things. They walked into the westering sun that evening as they headed down the fungi path. Radhya, Max, Will, and Padr led the troupe. Aninya trailed behind with Barone's slaves, and he limped behind everyone. Dave met them at the bottom of the path with a large hovervan. When they all piled in, Dave drove them to the spaceport. Arrow was waiting for them, gangplank down. They trouped aboard and strapped down for liftoff. As soon as they were in overlight drive, Radhya headed for her cabin.

"How long until we reach Jabin's World?" Lord Barone asked Max.

"Three days milord," he answered.

"Am I to spend three days in this chair?" he inquired.

"There is only a small galley and head aft, this space, Lady Kirbyson's cabin and the bridge on this deck," replied Max. "And below are the holds that are not heated. So I presume this is where you will have to stay."

"We'll see about that." Lord Barone rose and marched to

Radhya's cabin. He pounded on the door. When there was no answer, he tried forcing the door, bashing his shoulder against it when it proved to be locked.

"72 get a toolkit and come here," he demanded.

Max, Will, Padr, and Dave moved forward at that and forced Lord Barone from the door.

"I'm sorry milord. Lady Kirbyson told you how it would be and you insisted on accompanying her," growled Dave. "You have no right to disturb her at her business, and I cannot let you break into her room."

Lord Barone turned away, disgust on his face. Then he whipped back facing Will.

"You are her personal physician?"

"Yes milord," answered Will.

"Should a man who has just undergone what I have, have to sit in a chair for three days and nights? She practically threw me out from sick bed."

"I'm sorry milord; I know nothing of genetic reconstruction. I am simply a doctor," replied Will noticing for the first time the fine lacy white foam in Lord Barone's irises. The women slaves they received had much more pronounced rings. Radhya did fine quality work, even for an enemy. Will snapped his attention back to Lord Barone.

"I said," he repeated raising his voice several decibels, "that I must lie down when it becomes too painful and how is that to be accomplished?"

Padr fielded this question, saying, "Milord can either lie on the floor, like slaves do, or he can recline the seat to one hundred and twenty degrees and sleep partially lying down."

Lord Barone paced back and forth in front of the quartet. He muttered and grumbled to himself.

Finally, he turned to them and said, "I want to talk to her. She has cheated me for the last time, and I want to talk to her. My lawyers will take care of it if she doesn't speak to me."

Will left to go to the bridge. He spoke to Stane who passed

the message to Radhya in her cabin. Will returned to stand in front of her door again. The door opened, and she called Max into the room. She shut the door in Barone's face.

"I need your skills," she began. "The way Barone is acting means trouble for me when we get there. Geo felt trouble, and I trust his instincts totally. I had installed a small shop in the hold by the engines. Stane put the heat on in there for you. I need weapons, mainly defensive, but also make a few offensive ones just in case. I need you to protect us. I have a few biological defenses, the specs are in the comp, but I would feel more secure if I knew you were working on it."

"Yes, Radhya. I'll help in any way I can," he smiled eagerly.

She handed him a powerful X10 comp. She touched his cheek gently and opened the door. Max left. She shut the door in Noel's face. An hour later, she opened the door again.

"Noel?"

Lord Barone rose gracelessly from his chair and entered her cabin, rudely pushing the bodyguards out of the way. The first thing he noticed was the oppressive blackness. Walls, ceiling, and floor were all matt black. A desk and chair were against one wall, and a tiny bunk was on the opposite wall. Through an open door, Noel could see a tiny bathroom. There were bare shelves over the bunk and over the desk was a screen. The screen was alight with a two-dimensional image of a man. He was in his seventies with wavy silver hair and a narrow oval face. His nose was large and bony, his mouth wide and generous. He had the distinguished look of an aristocrat.

Radhya seated herself on the chair and motioned Lord Barone to the narrow bunk. It was hard and even more uncomfortable than it looked. He shifted about in a vain attempt at easing his distress.

"Lord Noel Barone makes complaint," began Radhya. "He threatens legal action against me, claiming I cheated him. I have this on tape, recorded on this ship just hours ago."

The man on the screen said, "Lord Barone, please state the nature of this dishonesty against you."

Noel gulped and looked at Radhya's stony face. "I have just had a painful procedure, and now I am forced to endure three days and nights sitting in a chair."

"Who supplied the procedure and please describe it."

"I would rather not."

"Your wishes do not enter in. You have a complaint. This young lady's reputation is in question. You will divulge or do not trouble us ever again, or slander Lady Kirbyson."

Noel stared, recognizing, at last, the magisterial branch of the proctors.

"I, uh, I had a genetic alteration," he stammered.

"Describe the alteration, who provided it, the cost, and the result."

"I had a penis enlargement. Lady Radhya Kirbyson created it for me. It, uh, had no cost, it was a gift, and the result was a lot of pain."

"Was the genetic procedure a gift Lady Kirbyson?"

"It was," Radhya answered.

"The result was pain; I take it there was no enlargement then?"

"No," replied Noel. "I mean yes, I grew two and a half times larger, but still there was so much pain and there still is that I don't find any use for the procedure."

"How long ago was the procedure done?"

"About a week."

"How long does the discomfort usually last Lady Kirbyson?"

"For between two weeks and a month at the outside," she replied.

"Did you inform Lord Barone that there would be pain associated with the procedure?"

"Yes, many times before he took it."

"Did she so inform you, Lord Barone?"

"Yes, she did."

"What is your complaint? You received a free procedure that normally costs what Lady Kirbyson?"

Radhya replied, "The only other one I did cost seven million macros."

Noel started on the hard bunk, and then winced.

"Did she receive anything in return for this gift?"

"I gave her three female slaves fully trained," replied Noel.

"Estimated cost of three female slaves, with the most expensive training is two hundred and twenty-five minas, correct?"

"Yes," confirmed Noel. "But she offered me a ride home, and while I am still tender, she gives me only a chair to sleep in, beside the slaves."

"So your complaint is not the procedure you had done but a transportation contract unfulfilled?"

"It's not a contract," put in Barone.

"Is it a verbal contract?"

"Not exactly."

"Then what is it exactly?"

"I asked to accompany her to Jabin's World where I live."

"Did she tell you what the accommodations would be?"

"No, of course not."

"Did you tell him what the accommodations would be Lady Kirbyson?"

Radhya replied, "Yes, I did. I told him there was only one small cabin and it was mine."

Barone flushed red. "I expected her to share the cabin. We are engaged," he snarled at Radhya.

"Are you engaged to Lord Barone, Lady Kirbyson?"

"We have a contract to contract that I was forced into by threat of removing my status as a member of the aristocracy."

The face on the screen raised one grizzled eyebrow.

"Tell me about that."

Radhya explained, "At a banquet, I held to celebrate my racetrack's opening, I was approached by Lord Barone who asked me to contract with him. I refused. He danced with

Princess Felina, status five. When they returned, Princess Felina asked me to contract with Lord Barone the next day. I again refused. Princess Felina threatened to remove my status and have me sold as a slave if I did not enter into a contract with him. We negotiated a contract to contract the day after the status review. This was against my stated will. I insisted that a clause be inserted that provides that I contract only if I do not exceed his status by my own merits at that time."

"Your status?"

"676"

"Lord Barone your status?"

"498"

"Does your contract to contract allow you use of her property?"

"No," replied Noel.

"Are you paying for your ride, food, anything?"

"No," he again replied.

"So you, at no cost are given transportation to your home world, with slaves?"

"Yes."

"And you are registering a complaint about your accommodations?"

"Yes."

"Complaint dismissed. Grow up Lord Barone."

"Lady Kirbyson, can you supply proof that you were coerced into this contract to contract?"

"Yes. It is written right into the contract. There were several witnesses to my refusal as well as to the threat."

"Send a contract copy. Names of witnesses?"

"Lady Koom, Lady Amelia, Lord Pehelalatin, and Lord Desmoinnis."

"Postponed until verification."

The screen went to static, then dark.

"Care to threaten me some more milord?" asked Radhya in a hard voice.

Lord Barone was brick red, sputtering with rage.

"You won't live to break my contract. Proctors take years to settle these things. We'll be long contracted before there is anything done."

"Maybe, but you don't own me. Moreover, if you think to inherit, check my will. It's on public file. Now get out of my room."

"You'll be sorry you little slave loving tramp. You'll be sorry you treated me like this."

Noel stamped through the door. Radhya locked it behind him. Throwing herself on the bunk, she tried to recall the glorious peace of the day before. The emotions of three other people were in her mind, coming and going, a spot that two days before she didn't even know was there, now it nagged at her. She tried in vain to master her control of it, but it was elusive.

Time dragged on the little ship. Radhya tried to work but found concentration difficult, the new place in her mind intruding at odd moments pulling her into the emotions of one of the other three. Padr's frustration was the biggest distraction. Radhya knew how badly he wanted to dispose of Lord Barone. Will was very controlled, but the effort of such patience was a drain on Radhya. Max, on the other hand, was elated, working feverishly in the hold by himself. His sharp bursts of triumph were punctuated by waves of sheer delight at doing what he did best. He seemed to deal with the multiple emotions the best, Padr the worst. Once when Lord Barone raised his hand to hit Aninya, Radhya was sure Padr was going to strike the obnoxious Lord.

As the time approached for free-fall, preparatory to landing, Radhya emerged from her sanctuary; sleepless and haggard. She smiled at her slaves as she strapped in between Will and Padr. Max returned and strapped in behind her. Barone glared at all of them.

Arrow feathered her way down and landed with a gentle

bump. Lord Barone barged off the little ship without even a thank you. 72 bowed his head to Radhya and scurried after his master like a rat, the rest of Barone's slaves following, dragging his luggage with them. Radhya heaved a huge sigh of relief.

"Max, stay here with Stane. The two of you continue working on your projects. Padr, Will, come with me to Seellia's auction. Rory, Dave, and Aninya go to Jabin's auction. Rory, you have the numbers I want on your wrist comp, and you have my seal. Make sure you clean, feed and clothe them before you bring them here."

Radhya left, followed by her two faithful guards. She could feel the uncontrollable spurt of fear from the two of them as their feet touched the burning asphalt of the starport. The heat lay on the land, breathless and heavy; the stench in the streets overwhelming. Radhya veiled herself in a vain attempt to keep some of the odor out. The heat was radiating from every surface as she attended the sunset auction.

The pitiable merchandise, exhausted and beaten by the sun staggered out one by one. Radhya made her purchases in the state of helpless anger that always possessed her on this planet, confused with the fear, resentment, and anger of her two body-guards. The sky was black with stars shining cleanly when the ordeal was over.

"Will, can you take care of this lot, feed, wash, dress, you know the drill. I don't want to take any more of this. I'm going back to the Arrow."

"Yes, milady," Will replied. "Will you be all right with just one bodyguard?"

"We are going straight back to the ship. You'll know if anything happens, but I used to walk these streets all the time with just Rory. We'll be fine."

Padr and Radhya threaded their way through the twisting narrow streets. It was still hard to breathe in the airless heat. The street before the entry to the starport they heard loud yells behind them. Radhya turned. Padr pushed her. They raced for the starport gates with seven of Jabin's planetary guards pounding after them. She ran at her top speed, Padr at her side, but the guards caught up to them and surrounded them. They grabbed for Radhya. Padr blocked them with his arm. Grinning like gargoyles, the seven circled them. One lunged again at the Lady. Padr seized his arm and twisted it until they heard the bone snap. He hurled him to the ground. He kicked and struck at the remaining six, using his body as a weapon. He smashed one guard in the throat. Jabin's minion dropped like a stone.

Padr snapped another arm in two. The attackers brought out tazers. Padr kicked one in the groin but was tazed in return. They kept hitting him repeatedly with tazers ignoring Radhya for the moment. Ganging up on Padr, they tazed him into submission. He fell unconscious in the hot dirt of the street. Radhya felt a searing pain as the emerald light went out in her mind. She hurled herself at the attackers screaming and kicking. One guard flipped her onto her back, and another threatened to taze Padr some more if she did not stop. Radhya glared up at them, panting. One attacker on each side hauled her to her feet. The other two guards did the same with a limp Padr. He slumped bonelessly between the two beefy bullies. Two of the guards lay in the dust of the street; one was moaning softly, the other lay ominously still.

The guards pulled Padr and Radhya through street after street, turn, and twist. They came to a broad avenue cooled by fountains and shaded by a row of flat-topped trees. Turning right, Radhya recognized Jabin's palace from the holos she had seen.

It was enormous, barbarically decorated in gold, silver and precious stones, a garish and obscene exhibition of wealth. Radhya and an unconscious Padr were dragged through a side door and down a long corridor sloping into the earth. At a dimly lit guard station, she was stripped to her underwear; even her wrist comp was taken. She was shoved into a small cell with bare stone walls, floor, and ceiling. It was dim and windowless.

Seconds later Padr, relieved of his protecting uniform was tossed in behind her. The door slammed shut. Padr lay still where he had fallen.

Radhya paced the dimensions, five paces square. She returned to where Padr lay and straightened his limbs into a more comfortable position.

"Oh Padr," she whispered to him, "I'm such a fool. Geo warned me, Will warned me. Why didn't I count on Barone moving this fast? He was so angry when he left. Maybe I was a fool to call his bluff on the Arrow. Wake up Padr. I'm scared. Wake up, please. Don't you dare leave me. I just found you. Don't leave me now. You fought for me like Geo. He is the only other person who ever fought for me like that. You have given your life for me. Please Padr, wake up. I need you. If I wasn't locked in here, I could fix you, but I'm locked up. I don't even have my wrist comp. Padr, Padr wake up, please, please wake up. I've never heard of anyone ever taking as much electricity as you did, but you're strong, you can do it, wake up, please. This is all my fault."

Weary and worn, filled with self-loathing and worry Radhya fell asleep, Padr's head cradled on her lap.

Chapter 17

C old shivers ran down her spine, awakening Radhya. The cramps in her back and legs made her groan. She felt a pang of alarm when she saw Padr unmoved. His chest was still rising and falling, and she could feel a heartbeat when she placed a cold hand on it. Shifting her position a little to ease the cramps, she allowed her mind to wander back to the wakening on the beach; to when she felt such well-being. She sat up with a start.

The Chandrans had told her of the bond years ago, how one partner could help another in physical distress. She plumbed the depths of her mind to remember every detail. Feeling Will and Max as distant splashes of color, she knew she could call on them for strength should she be able to achieve a connection with Padr.

She recalled the warm water, the smell of wet stone and sand, the susurration of the lapping waves and the brilliant electric blue of her soul's color. With her glowing color, she tried to reach out to Padr. Repeatedly she tried. Sweat slicked her skin and puddled on the rock beneath her. She moved, laying down and clasping Padr in her arms as if he were a sick child. She leaned her head against his. Summoning a last desperate attempt she tried emotion, pouring all her desire and longing into the cerulean light. Feeling as though her mind would burst with the effort, the shaft or blue moved slowly, then faster piercing into his mind.

Radhya dove into the dark sea. It was familiar, yet not. She saw his memories, Debra and his slaughtered child radiating permanent pain, herself a balm and healing, Max and Will like longed for brothers, so many other memories all tangling and jibbering at her. She sank to the plain of fear where her fears and his met and reinforced each other. Will and Max poured strength into her here. Forging downward, she dealt with his guilt at failing to protect her and get to the Arrow. She soothed that with her pride at how well he fought.

Diving further, she found the internal burns and short circuits of his body. With her knowledge of anatomy, she healed them using the energy of her own body. Further, down to the center, the white light, no one was home. She called, lowering all barriers, baring her soul. Then bubbling up, the green responded, called to it's partner. The colors merged, became turquoise, enveloping Radhya, removing her stiffness, healing her bruises. Rising up through the body, the fears, and the memories, to the sea, green and blue and so beautiful. Small shreds of gold and violet stained the surface of the water. There was one last burst of teal, and then they separated each to their own body.

Padr opened his eyes. A tinge of emerald darkened their blue depths.

"I didn't know we could do that ourselves," he said, smiling.

"Shhh. We don't want to give away any secrets in case there are listeners. There could be watchers too," she whispered.

Padr sat up, drawing her tenderly into his arms. He slowly lowered his mouth to kiss her, while his hands caressed her body. The lingering effects of the bonding were powerful, drawing them close, but Radhya pushed him firmly away.

"No Padr, we can't," her voice was heavy with regret. "I was careless once this trip and I let my emotions get the better of me. That's why we're here. I can't make another mistake."

"After that closeness, you think our bodies coming together would be a mistake?" asked Padr puzzled.

"Yes, Padr. I have to for at least three reasons."

"I can't think of any," he said nibbling on her neck.

Radhya pulled away from him fully and stood as far away as the room permitted.

"Padr, I know you know how I feel. There is no way to keep that from you. But right now, we have to use our heads. If we come together here, they will record it and use it against me. We are arrested; at least I think we are."

"So give them something to watch. Aristocrats sleep with their slaves all the time."

"The men do, not the women! You are still a slave. If I became pregnant, my child would be a slave too. So no."

Wounded, Padr replied, "A feeble excuse. The most fertile of women try for ten years to get pregnant and count themselves lucky if it's not fifteen or twenty."

Radhya felt his hurt sear through her mind.

"Not me, Padr. Remember what I told you the night we cured Amlina. Well, that was fixed for both of us. Therefore, you see together...Well, women in my family are reflex ovulators. If I have sex with you, or anyone, I will get pregnant unless I use the utmost precautions. There is no mistake about it."

"What about your sister?"

"She was sterilized several years ago. She got pregnant so often it was becoming a health problem to have all those abortions. She had them all aborted, you know. Therefore, they froze a dozen good eggs from her for when she wants children, if ever, and they sterilized her. I'm not going through that."

Padr sat pensively in the corner.

After a long interval, he asked, "What is the third reason?"

"I have to know you really love me, that this isn't being

forced on you from circumstances or because you were coerced or tricked into the bonding."

"I thought you could feel my love through the bond?"

"Oh I can, I truly can. It's just that, well I don't deserve it. I bought you against your will. I did many things to you, the guard's training, everything against your will. You had no say. I even tried to control your attraction to D'Bara. Therefore, you can see I don't deserve anything but resentment from you. I...I can't believe you could love me because I ...I'm so confused. I really need to be sure."

"I can understand that," Padr responded softly, "I felt that way myself, I can't believe you could care for me after all I've been, but one thing the bonding has taught me is that if you open up and trust others, the love comes in. You'll learn it too, but I'll give you the time you need."

Padr was silent. The time seemed agonizingly long. Max and Will lay in each prisoner's mind growing more frantic with every minute. They finally resorted to playing children's memory games to pass the time, with the growling of their bellies the only way to tell that much time had passed.

When they figured they were immured in the dungeon forever, the door creaked open, and a guard threw in their clothes and Radhya's wrist comp. Grabbing that first and putting it on, Radhya dressed as quickly as possible in the dim light. The door complained again, only this time it opened wide. Radhya and Padr ducked through. Guards seized them by the arms and hustled them around a corner and up steep and narrow stairs. The lights grew brighter, hurting Radhya's eyes. When they were pushed before a large wooden desk on a platform, hot stinging light flooded their faces, veiling the someone behind the light.

"Well, well! The reclusive Lady Death before my planetary court. How does miss high and mighty feel now?" whined a voice, femininely high pitched and yet masculine at the same time.

Radhya bowed, "My Lord Jabin, may I know what charges I answer?"

"In due time," shrilled the voice. "I must say I like your handsome bodyguard. Shall we see what the two of you were up to in the holding cell?"

A life-sized screen descended from the ceiling to Radhya's right. Jabin hit play. The scene from the cell appeared silently on the screen. Radhya was pushing Padr away. Jabin fast-forwarded and finally stopped at the picture of Radhya and Padr playing children's games.

"So, you didn't. I thought I left you long enough."

"Long enough to grow faint with hunger Lord Jabin," Radhya complained.

"Don't you at all, or don't you with slaves, or don't you with men. You don't seem to be attracted to any of the aristocracy."

"My private life is private milord. Is my love life on trial here?" questioned Radhya with dignity.

A red stain appeared behind Jabin and whispered in his ear.

"Ah yes," he uttered. "A large, serious matter concerns me. You sent three slaves to purchase certain other slaves for you at the sunset auction?"

"Yes, milord."

"They did that and made me a teensy bit richer, but when your man Rory, foolish habit naming slaves, took the slaves away, it seems that a man named Kline was purchasing a small girl child, about five for his ah, amusement. Cute thing, the little girl, I should have had her myself, anyway, she was his by right of purchase, and he was describing to the vendor his use for her, asking how much could he get when he returned her tomorrow, when your slave, a cook, I believe, snatched the child from him and ran away with her and your big bodyguard to your ship. They are hidden there and won't come out. Therefore, we seize you as owner of the miscreant slave. You bear the responsibility."

"What does Kline want?" asked Radhya.

"He wished the cook flogged publicly, and the girl returned to him, in ah, virgin condition," Jabin giggled.

"Milord, I promised the cook a child, for the kitchen, to train, and for menial chores. Perhaps she doesn't understand how matters are conducted publicly."

"The wife of my former accountant understands, Lady Death."

"Then I counter offer four times the purchase price of the child for Kline and the purchase price on top of the court's costs for you."

Jabin held a quick whispered conference.

"Unacceptable. The slave must be flogged. The child may be kept by you for the agreed price."

"Lord Jabin, I appreciate your mercy, but the cook is an excellent one, and I prefer not to be without her if there is any way to avoid it."

Jabin laughed, his huge belly jouncing in the blinding light.

"No one enjoys good food more than I do," he announced. "It's good to know you have some fleshly vices. However, I cannot have a mere slave snatch chattels from paying customers and disappear with them. I must publicly show the slave punished. I can call the proctors, if you refuse to punish such an errant possession."

Radhya tasted bitter gall, Padr flinching from the pain of her emotions.

"So be it Lord, but I request the minimum strokes, for my palate's sake."

Jabin thought a moment, "I had planned on fifty, but in deference to your stomach, I will reduce it to ten, conditional on your attending my, ah, entertainments tonight."

"Yes Lord Jabin," Radhya answered meekly.

The tormenting lights faded to mere annoyance and Lord Jabin was revealed in all his greasy splendor. Slimy bangs framed his florid countenance, and a small black goatee punctuated his fat face. Greedy, little pig eyes roved possessively up and down Radhya. The great thick hand waved her to the accountant. Behind Jabin's chair, slender and red, stood Lord Barone, a superior smile on his thin lips.

Radhya checked her wrist comp. Obviously, someone had tried to tamper with it, but Geo had programmed it, and he was the best in the galaxy. Radhya ran a diagnostic on it. Virus clear, it informed her someone had tried to break into it. She hit reset and paid her bills. One of Jabin's slaves escorted her to another room. This room was laid for a banquet. Lord Jabin, of course, sat at the head of the table, with Radhya seated to his right. To his left sat a voluptuous blonde, and Lord Barone beside her. Padr stood behind Radhya's chair, straight and tall.

The Lord waddled to his seat and plumped down. He clapped his hands, and the feast appeared immediately.

"How long were we down there, Lord Jabin?" inquired Radhya drinking water thirstily.

"Only three days. Unfortunately, several official inquiries made me hurry your case. I once kept Lord Sutherland a full week. But I had to give him water of course," he laughed foolishly.

Radhya had Padr taste each dish.

"Are we distrustful?" asked Jabin.

Radhya nodded across the table, "An old friend taught me caution, at all times, even when dining with friends."

Barone smiled sourly at her as Padr leaned forward and whispered in her ear. Radhya nodded and did not touch the food. She did, however, drink a great deal of water. The water pitcher was refilled. With her first sip, a warm tingling flowed from her lips down her throat, through her belly, creating a powerful arousal. She glanced at Jabin, who was watching her with narrowed eyes. She set the water down and watched the other revelers without partaking of food or drink.

Couples were beginning to slip from their chairs to the floor, engaging in orgies of passion. Averting her eyes, she called heavily on her spiritual bonding. Making a pillar of peace amid the prurient lewdness, Padr was there, as were Will and Max in a distant sense. Jabin rose and seized her hand in his sweaty paw.

He led the way from the banquet room to his Coliseum. Radhya felt her heart sink. To one side, Padr stood staunchly loyal and supportive, his hand occasionally brushing hers. The gross Jabin, kept leaning over, his hot stinking breath blasting into her face. He signaled his guards to begin.

His lions tore several slaves apart, and three men were torn in half by tying them between two untamed stallions. From there the entertainment deteriorated into even more depraved bloodlusts. Radhya sent her mind elsewhere, to Max's golden light while Will's violet glow enveloped Padr.

Jabin kept peering at her in more and more of a drunken stupor, becoming more aggressive, slobbering on her, until, finally he pinched her nipple hard. Radhya shot to her feet.

"Lord Jabin, your advances are not welcome. I will leave now!" she snapped at him.

He leered at her drunkenly.

"Ah, but our agreement, you mush shtay for the enertainmen. Or you can come back t'marra" he said slyly.

"I kept my part of the bargain. I came to your banquet and your entertainment. That is all I agreed to."

She gazed at him coldly for a minute then commanded one of his slaves to lead them from the maze of Jabin's palace. They returned unmolested to the Arrow.

Chapter 18

Aninya met her at the door.

"Milady, I am so sorry, milady forgive me, I can explain, I am so sorry..."

Radhya waved her silence.

"In the morning guards will come and take you to the public square. You will be flogged ten times. I could only get it reduced that much."

Aninya raised hands to her horrified face.

"Milady, you can't permit..."

Radhya whirled on her angrily, sparks flashing like lightning in her eyes.

"My whole plan is in jeopardy because of your rash action. Jabin could legally have me drummed from the aristocracy because I have allowed you to run wild. Technically, he could require your death. That fat slug reduced your punishment from fifty lashes to ten because he thought to copulate with me tonight. You do not realize what your life costs me Aninya. I had to sit through his 'entertainments.' Watch out Aninya."

Aninya backed away from the fire in Radhya's eyes.

She continued, "Padr and I haven't eaten in three and a half days, and I want to eat. Then I'm going to sleep, and you can explain yourself in the morning."

Radhya stormed to her room.

"The name Lady Death suits her when she's like this," Padr smiled to Aninya.

Stricken, Aninya stood.

"Try to understand how much she's been through these last three or four days. She hated the incident with Barone on the ship. She hates this place and buying slaves. We were imprisoned together in our skivvies and believe me, that wasn't easy. Then she spent all night watching an orgy, starving with food in front of her and fending off Lord Jabin while people were dying in front of us. I think her nerves are shredded. Fetch a meal; I'll take it in to her."

Radhya answered the tap on her door ready to storm at Aninya again. When she saw Padr, she opened the door wider and let him in. Sitting at the desk, she gestured him to the bunk.

"She just forgets you know," he spoke to her softly.

"I know, but the horrors of Jabin's entertainments, and the feel of his slimy hands, oh Padr, I can't even endure the memory of it."

Radhya burst into uncontrollable tears, sobbing into her arms on the desk. Padr rose and put his arms around her. He could feel the black horror and terror rise up in her.

"Yes, you can and you will," he stated emphatically. "You won't let people like that get the better of you. You're stronger than that. Trust me I know. If you need anything, I can give you I'm here."

Turning, she burrowed into his strong shoulder. He sent her a flash of emerald presence. She returned a wash of clear blue gratitude and love. Smiling gratefully at him, she wiped the tears from her dirt-streaked face. Padr left her, went to the tiny washroom and returned with a damp cloth. He wiped her dusty face and hands gently. She sent him a giddy burst of lust, and giggled.

"You'd best be careful. I said I'd give you time, but I'm only human," he warned with a smile.

They demolished the long-delayed meal. Padr left with the tray, and Radhya rolled into her bunk. She wrapped mental tendrils of green, gold and violet around herself and was thus able to sleep soundly without nightmares.

Radhya was already in the shower scrubbing until her skin was raw, when the banging came at her door. Slipping on a robe, but still dripping she answered, opening the door as Max raised his fist to pound again.

"Radhya, the guards come in an hour. If you wish to talk with Aninya..." he trailed off.

"Be right there," she answered him.

Max gazed at her with a sharply furrowed brow. She could feel his anxiety.

Patting him on the hand, she said, "Don't worry. I think I have this figured out. Just be ready with your projects."

Max nodded and left. Radhya came behind him, dressed and fortified for the day. In the foremost seat, Aninya shook and trembled, her eyes red and swollen.

"Tell me," commanded Radhya.

"We went to the auction," began Aninya in a tremulous voice, "and we did what you asked, bought all the slaves you had designated. Then Rory was paying for them, and Dave was herding them to get something to eat, and there was a man, a reeking filthy man, holding this little girl by the hair. And she looked just like my daughter. She had the biggest, saddest, brown eyes, and he said as how she was a virgin, and he was asking the vendor how much she would be worth tomorrow when she was not a virgin. I lost my mind. I just grabbed her, and I ran all the way to the Arrow. The guards chased me, but they couldn't catch me. I've never run so fast in all my life, but I just had to save her. Stane turned the turret guns on them to keep them away. He did not fire, just threatened. They let Rory and Dave and your new slaves in to talk sense to me, but I wouldn't listen. I know you, Lady, you love children. You wouldn't let that happen to an innocent child. Please, Lady, you can't give her back!"

"No Aninya," sighed Radhya wearily, "she won't go back, I've already paid five times her asking price for her, but now that man has the means to buy four little girls instead of one, and Jabin has profited as well."

"Oh my Lady," cried Aninya stricken. "We were so worried when you didn't come. It was all my fault."

"Yes," interrupted Radhya, "it was. Now I'm going to put this on you."

She showed Aninya a large bottle of brown liquid.

"This will raise welts lasting about twelve hours. That is, so they think that I beat you. It is to save my life; yours and I can't count how many other slaves in the future. It will hurt, but that cannot be helped now. So strip."

Radhya applied the liquid in streaks across Aninya's face and brow. She made long weals across her breasts down her side to the hips. She crisscrossed her legs with stripes, but her upper back and arms were untouched. When she was finished the cook looked like raw meat.

Troopers hammered on the hatch. Radhya threw a sheet to Aninya to cover herself. Clothes would have been far too painful. The troopers took her and marched her away. Radhya followed with Padr, Max, Will, and Rory in tow. The early morning sun had scarcely peeked above the horizon when they arrived at the public square of the largest sunrise auction. The morning was a bearable temperature.

Jabin squatted on his throne, a raised platform, high above the crowd. He wore a jeweled robe of silver and royal purple. Like a red crow, Barone perched at his shoulder, looking shocked to see Radhya there, though he nodded to her graciously.

At Jabin's signal, the guards took Aninya to two poles stationed before the platform. Tying her to the uprights, they stripped off her sheet. The gathering crowds gasped in horror at the sight of Aninya's tortured flesh, even as accustomed to Lord Jabin's taste as they were. Crowing and smiling in delighted surprise, he clapped his hands and bowed his head toward Radhya. He signaled to begin. The heavy leather lash, braided with pieces of sharp bone, whistled down and tore into Aninya's back. The heart-stopping wet rip of tearing flesh contended with her screams in the heating morning air. Again and again, it struck. Radhya stood impassive, eyes fixed on the grisly scene, face still. Finally, after an eternity, the tenth and last time struck. Aninya hung limply from the posts; the whipper lowered his arm. The guards who brought Aninya regrouped around Jabin's platform.

Radhya nodded to Will and Rory, and they cut Aninya down and laid her bleeding body on the sheet. Not a centimeter of skin remained that was unabraded on her body. They carried her back to the Arrow face down. Radhya turned to follow when a slave from Jabin restrained her with a hand on her arm. She stiffened and turned on him furiously. He instantly removed his hand.

"My Lord Jabin requires a word with you," he stammered.

Turning, Radhya glared at the obese sadist on the throne. Then she marched to his platform and up the steps to stand right in front of him.

"You require more milord?"

"Oh no, my small requirements are satisfied. I just have a few unanswered questions."

"Which are milord?"

"Last night you seemed to have no appetite for the entertainment, yet you come to watch your own slave beaten? Then, too, obviously, your cook received some attention from you, judging by the marks, probably last night?"

"What is your question milord?"

"Do you or do you not enjoy watching the pain of others? I hear that you positively gloated over our friend Barone's pain and yet last night I could have sworn you were as disgusted as the others of your unique genetic heritage."

"Well milord, I don't know about what heritage you speak, but it, first of all, depends on whose pain. Some are more enjoyable than others are, then I am surprised that you can't tell boredom from disgust. I personally prefer a more hands-on approach. As for my cook, I prefer to do my own disciplining when necessary. I know certain people accuse me of being soft, but they do not know me. Now is that it? I have business to attend to," Radhya said turning to go.

"Wait!" Jabin grunted, one fat finger slid beside his nose. "I have heard this claimed of you before, but I am confused about you; I'm not sure what I believe. Perhaps you can give me one of these fine slaves to entertain us tonight. You might be more interested."

"Certainly," replied Radhya turning back to Jabin. "I will sell you one for one million macros."

"Surely you jest. If you enjoy, why not contribute, and that price is outrageous for a slave."

"I wish to return to work. I only went to your pitiful entertainments at your insistence. That being the case, I feel no obligation to supply fodder for it. As to the price, you're right. I think a million five far more reasonable considering the costs I have accumulated training them. This dark one has proven his value by almost defeating seven of your guards all by himself. He would have prevailed had it not been for their tazers, which we are prohibited to carry on your planet. That ability increases his value to me. The other is an engineer of some considerable skill. It cost me to finish his training."

Radhya waited, looking at the would-be Caesar.

"I am almost tempted to meet your price," Jabin smiled.

"Fine, let's go to the accountants. Do you want the dark haired one or the brown haired one? I won't sell both and have to return to Arrow unprotected."

Radhya moved several steps towards the accounting booth.

"None, I want none of your merchandise, not at your exorbitant price. I didn't realize how much you are like your brother. You, however," he continued in a hard voice, "will eat and drink tonight to the full."

"Milord, my obligation was last night alone."

"I decided to change that since you neither ate nor drank, nor anything else."

Jabin put a greasy paw on Radhya's arm, caressing her shoulder. She pulled away and clattered down the steps. The trio was out of the square and heading for Arrow as quickly as allowed for any shred of dignity.

At the Arrow, Radhya hissed and spat like an angry cat. Most of the slaves ducked from her presence, but Padr grabbed her by the shoulders and spoke in an anguished voice.

"Radhya what are you going to do? If you go tonight and you eat and drink I don't think even the bond will be able to resist those aphrodisiacs. Jabin means to ravish you tonight."

Radhya quieted in his hands. Deep in thought, her face puzzled, her selifla felt a deep calm come over her.

"Contact Rory. Tell him to request permission from the tower to leave immediately."

Rory called right back. "Permission is refused. Lord Jabin expects you tonight. What are your orders milady?"

"We run!" she said.

She spoke to her wrist comp, telling the slaves below to prepare for a hard ride. Rory and Stane prepared the ship to run for home while Radhya told Dave to supervise the slaves below in the hold.

"Will," she called, "how is Aninya? We need to go. Can she travel yet?"

"Another five minutes," called Will from Radhya's cabin.

"Max get below; get ready to use your projects. We'll probably escape or not based on your work. I hope you've been very inventive."

"Radhya," questioned Max, "Jabin has a lot of firepower on his two moons, but if we escape that, what is to stop Jabin from setting the proctors on you?"

"The proctors won't hear his complaint. I'm being held by force, and they frown on such things. What else could he say, that I turned down his invitation to his orgy? I wouldn't stay for his blood show? I had no agreement to have sex with him. Yeeelk! And my faithful Max, I have full confidence in your ability to blow his ships away."

Max hastened below to his workroom as Aninya emerged from Radhya's cabin whole and smiling bemusedly. She strapped down. Will and Padr strapped in on either side of Radhya. Dave gave the 'all secure' from the hold.

"Rory, burn plutonium," Radhya commanded over the intercom.

The little ship leapt skyward, blasting past the tower without warning. A large ship preparing to lift flashed warning lights at them. Rory piped the swearing from the large ship into the passenger compartment. While the tower repeatedly demanded they return Arrow hurtled on in silence. They shot out of the stratosphere into true space, and Rory oriented the vessel toward their objective.

The nearer moon spewed six small, fast, patrol craft. On the screen, they could see another six blips blasting from the further moon.

"Evasion!" snapped Radhya.

Arrow bucked and twisted, slipping this way and that, fully making use of all three dimensions, evading the patrol craft. Rory made her dance like a ballerina, but they were unable to clear the solar system's gravity well. She slipped around the planet in a polar orbit. Repeatedly, they approached the launch window for their own system, and were herded back to Jabin's World. The patrol craft shot lasers across their bow, blinding them temporarily. They jumped, danced, and hid behind the planets and satellites. There was no way to break from the orbit without sailing off into uncharted space. Radhya decided.

"There are too many to evade. Attack!" she instructed.

Arrow pivoted away from two pursuers. She ducked behind the nearer moon. Max released the bio-organisms of one of Radhya's defenses. Repelled by their own ship, the microbes swarmed the two patrol vessels, up the exhaust ports to the engines. The ships lost power, sailing straight ahead, unable to turn or stop.

Swinging around, using the gravity of the moon, Max lay a line of leach mines down in the path of their escape. Four patrol craft cut them off, and again they dove back around the planet. Four enormous explosions were disappearing on their next orbit. One ship came close enough to grapple. Bending orbit to the further moon, Max brought out his enhanced lasers. He shot out the navigation array and comm systems.

Two more patrols tried a kamikaze attack. They did not know of the Arrow's special alloy grown solely on Sparky's World. The first hit a wing, and it sheared off the cockpit and bridge spilling crew into the void. The second tried to duck underneath and failed, crumpling the nose into the tail of the ship, and then exploding away to crash on the planet.

Max pulled out one of his electronic inventions. The Arrow now pursued two ships around the further moon. They fled at their best speed, firing shots behind them. The Arrow accelerated and shot past them, beaming an EM pulse at the enemy. Instantly all their electronic systems became scrap metal. With the controls fried, they sailed straight on unable to change trajectories.

Arrow dashed for clear space, sweeping a laser ahead in case any more mines remained. They had to detonate one. Suddenly their forward momentum abruptly halted. The little ship jerked backward in the grip of a tractor beam.

The patrol vessel was hiding behind the nearer moon. Bracing with the mass of the moon, the attacking ship hauled Arrow back. Rory backed off the engines, then hit them full speed, with no effect. The Arrow began to whine. Max did some quick maneuvering on his X10. A powerful ray of light rode back down the tractor beam, and the patrol craft exploded into billions of tiny shards of metal.

"Incoming!" called Stane.

The screen showed several heavy cruisers heaving themselves from scattered positions on the surface. Telemetry read that they were large, slow, but extremely well armed. Against six or seven the Arrow did not have a chance. Rory kicked in more speed and made for the launch window.

"Punch it!" yelled Radhya.

The Arrow took off, racing for the edge of the gravity well. She reached it ahead of the cruisers who were just clearing the atmosphere. The rebels disappeared into the overlight space. Arrow made her best speed through the void and slipped into Pleasant's orbit three days later.

Chapter 19

Radhya stared wearily at the fungi path leading home.
"You know, for the first time in my life," she
sighed, "I regret our rules that we must walk everywhere we possibly can. I'm not sure I can make it."

The last week had been exhausting. They arrived home,
deposited the slaves at the Spa Island, trained them, took care
of track business and now, finally, they were returning home.
Radhya ruffled the hair of Deena, Aninya's new daughter as she
leaned against Will.

"I'll help you," he said taking her arm.

Radhya nodded slowly, and they commenced the trek.
Weary step plodded after weary step and got them home. She
detoured to the stables to see Li, who was grooming the bay
stallion.

"Milady Kirbyson, I am glad you are back," he began.

A string of curses erupted along with a loud clanging and
banging of equipment.

Ignoring the commotion, he continued, "You offered a
reward on your first race day?"

Radhya nodded.

"I felt it was not right to accept. It was only my job, but now I would like a reward. This slave you gave me takes all my time to watch. I must use the prod all the time. I feel I would like the reward for having her here."

"Yes Li," responded Radhya, "You deserve better, but I truly have no where else to send her. Name your reward."

"My wife Sumi wants another baby," Li bowed low.

"Anything Sumi wants she can have. If you want another child, by all means, go ahead."

"She wants you to help. She has tried, and nothing happens."

"Of course Li. Tell her to come, not tomorrow, but the day after, Okay?"

D'Bara limped around the side of the stall, her eyes shooting sparks of hate. Hair disheveled, and her hands calloused with broken nails, she smelled distinctly of horse manure.

"I'll get you for this you slut, you bitch!"

A scream tore from her cracked lips as Li hit her with the prod.

"Get back to work. You should have had those last three boxes done an hour ago."

Glaring, D'Bara sullenly staggered back to work.

"I need Tan to ride at the other tracks Li. I have a trainer for the road. His name is Forg. You, however, are the ultimate authority for all things related to the race. He works under you. You choose the races, and specify the training and Forg takes them out. Tan will ride for me still."

"Yes milady," replied Li. "Singha came in heat milady, but Sumi took care of it."

"Bless you Li. You may have ten children if you want them. I don't think I could take the yowling right now."

Li bowed. Radhya and her men continued through the yard and up the trail to the house. Geo met them at the door.

"You are in big trouble, young one. Stephan is looking for

you, and the proctors have complaints sworn against you from Jabin's World."

Radhya sighed deeply and almost fell over the last step. Padr and Will grabbed her and carried her to Geo's workroom. Max handed her the flight recorder.

"Call them up Geo," said Radhya seating herself in his big chair. It dwarfed her drooping figure.

Seconds later the big screen lit up. Faced with three proctors, the situation looked grim. She took a deep breath, then another, putting on her most imperious manner and squaring her shoulders.

A small, almost effeminate black man spoke first.

"Complaint against Lady Radhya Kirbyson by Lord Nile Jabin status 202. On Jabin's World, you did illegally leave the spaceport and then proceeded to destroy twelve patrol ships that attempted to fine you."

Radhya produced the flight recorder and plugged it into the terminal. She sent a microburst to the proctors.

"I admit guilt in leaving without clearance, and I stand ready to pay a fine. There were extenuating circumstances. We were refused permission to depart as well."

The man scanned the information from the recorder.

"Several unregistered weapons appear to have been used."

"They were experimental prototypes that would never have been used if we had not been attacked without provocation. You will notice all we tried to do at first was leave Lord Jabin's airspace. They fired upon us first, without warning or communication of intent. We only defended ourselves. The prototypes were duly registered and patented as soon as we made planetfall."

"I levy a fine of one hundred minas for unauthorized departure."

The black man disappeared from the screen. A tall, thin Caucasian with sandy hair and moustache took center screen.

"I have a complaint against Lady Radhya Kirbyson from

Lord Nile Jabin status 202, that you had contracted to attend Lord Nile Jabin's banquet and subsequent entertainments for considerations unspecified and left the planet rather than fulfill your obligations."

"While on Lord Jabin's World, my slave stole a child. I recompensed the owner four times over, and to Lord Jabin, I gave the child's cost above the court costs. My slave was flogged publicly. Lord Jabin reduced the flogging from fifty strokes to ten, upon my agreement to attend a banquet and entertainment. The banquet food was heavily laced with an aphrodisiac, and so was the water when I refused to eat. Most couples were copulating on the floor after the second course. The entertainment consisted of torture in various forms. After two hours I left, being repelled by several unwelcome sexual advances from Lord Jabin. Because I had not stayed until dawn, he insisted I owed him another night. I did disagree. Then I did not answer. Previous to this, my bodyguard slave and I were incarcerated in underclothes for three days in an unsuccessful attempt to have us copulate. I protest his treatment of aristocratic visitors."

"Was there evidence the banquet you did not attend would be the same?"

"Yes. In the morning, after the flogging, Lord Jabin said, 'You, however, will eat and drink to the full.' He also requested one of my slaves to torture, saying their pain would be more enjoyable to me if I knew them. When I offered to sell him one he claimed the price exorbitant and declined."

"Did a trained bodyguard taste the food?"

"Yes."

"Put him forward."

Radhya gestured Padr forward. He looked straight at the inquisitor.

"Was the food tainted?"

"Yes, it was heavily laced with vitaximetaprene."

"How do you know?"

"I was trained at Lord Barone's facility with the super deluxe training. It includes recognition of a wide variety of poisons or other substances that might be hidden in food or drink."

"Case dismissed. We will look into your complaint against Lord Jabin."

The sandy-haired man vanished from the screen. A large jowly oriental man remained. He gazed at her inscrutably.

"I bring no complaint. This is a request for information initiated by Lord Stephan Kirbyson, status 670, concerning his sister, Lady Petra Kirbyson, status 675. He claims Lord Noel Barone, status 498, is now administering her assets."

Radhya closed her eyes. Her bond mates poured strength into her.

"Lord Barone gave me a gift of three genetically altered female slaves. I believe this is already on record."

"Yes. Continue."

"On examination of the genetic prints of one, I noticed a striking similarity between her and my family. On closer examination, it appeared to be my sister, genetically altered. She tried to kill me. My guards restrained her. I know only my brother, my sister, or I have the training to do such alterations. I knew I had not, so I called my brother, who also said he had not. My only conclusion is she did it to herself in order to destroy me. Lord Barone hinted at such an outcome while in my presence."

"Do you know her whereabouts?"

"Yes. She is working under my trainer in the stables."

"Thank you for your co-operation," said the proctor.

The screen went to static. Radhya slumped back into the chair.

"Well done," congratulated Geo. "I'm sorry, but the proctors had to be faced the minute you came in. They placed a watcher."

The small red light in the corner continued to flash. Radhya pointed to it. Geo made the adjustment, and Stephan's face graced the screen.

"So, little sister, I traced Petra's path to Barone. I have the

proctors on it. If there is a chance of getting any of her property back to the family, they will see to it. I thought you would
want to know."

"Thank you, Steph. I just finished talking to the proctors. I
gave them all the information I had."

"I'll keep in touch then. Take care little sister and thank you
for the tip."

The small red flashing light was still now. The Lady waved a
hand, too tired even to speak.

"Everyone back to your old rooms tonight," she whispered.

Sensing her total enervation, Padr gathered her up out of
the chair. He lifted her into his arms and carried her up two
flights of stairs to the third floor. Will and Max followed. Max
opened the door, and Will folded down the fur flap on her living
bed. Padr lay her gently down. Will pulled up the fur.

"See you in the morning Radhya," Padr whispered to her.

The three men left the room. They did not see their lady the
next morning. She slept the night, the entire next day and night
as well. The following morning she awoke, lethargic and dopey,
but some vigorous exercise revived her.

Radhya was having breakfast in the slave's galley when Sumi
arrived. Full of energy again she led the way upstairs to the med
lab. Giving Sumi a bottle of brown liquid, she carefully
explaining its use. Sumi smiled broadly.

"Milady," she asked, "with so many women unable to
conceive these days why is it you do not market it and become
very wealthy?"

"In most cases, it is a problem with the fathers as much as
the mothers. They are more reluctant to be treated, besides
Sumi, I'm already wealthy. Years back, every time I invented
something my mother and father got angry with me because
Petra and Steph couldn't keep up with me. Some weeks I would
have six or seven new products. Anyway, I got in the habit of
squirreling them away, not putting them into production. I just

never got around to changing my habits. I still just hide things away."

"Wealth is one of the main markers of status is it not? And do you not want to move up in status review to avoid Lord Barone?"

"Yes, wealth first, then contract spouse, and social and birth standing," recited Radhya.

A brilliant smile lit up her face. "Sumi, I could kiss you."

She clattered down the stairs to Geo's office.

"Geo, I want all my patents put into production and I want them on the market yesterday. I'm going to get richer, so rich Lord Noel Barone hasn't a hope in heaven of catching me."

Her interplanetary team moved into action. Radhya's wealth doubled, then tripled, and finally almost two years later it had quintupled.

Chapter 20

A frica was a huge hunting preserve covering an entire continent. The plains Chandrans had devastated it in their lifetime, leaving only soil and sand and barren rock. After Padr had mapped the ten climatic zones, he designed ecosystems for each area. It was left to run riot and be as wild as it could grow. Each of the ten areas had its own base camp, which would later become local lodges for that section of the continent.

On the southeast coast was the main hunting lodge, the stepping off place for the hunting preserve, the only landscaped area of the continent, and it was as spectacular as the rest of Padr's work. Buildings of rustic red logs and grey local stone could accommodate about two hundred aristocratic visitors and their slaves while catering to them in its bucolic restaurant. Aninya trained the cooks, and the housekeepers who cared for the needs of the visitors and Radhya created separate log quarters for all the slaves who worked for her at the lodge, and who would eventually be the guides.

Max was in charge of hollowing out part of a mountain for

use as a hanger. The fleet of heliplanes was to bring the hunters to their specific targets when they were finished being used for the construction. Max was melting the rock and foaming it back on the walls of the outside to provide the appearance of untouched stone.

Supervising the entire operation, Radhya was eager to release the reconstructed animals to populate the continent. Will learned many of her genetic manipulations while he assisted. Waiting in the med lab until she finished her daily morning business meeting on the holophone with Geo, he could just hear her voice speaking.

"So my Tango Dancer and Son-O-War are great successes?" she asked.

"Oh yes," the old man laughed. "You've really set the racing community on its ear. All those people affiliated with Barone and Jabin especially. There are a number who scratch their horses as soon as they hear Tango or Son is entered. They keep trying to say you engineered them, but all the evidence says otherwise. Clever of you to make sure they were bred on Kentucky. It does my old heart good."

"Well you know, genetics originally started in breeding the best to the best. I don't know why it should be so surprising that I can say which stallion should cover which mare and have good results with the offspring."

"Ah well, they have been trying it for years without your kind of success. What about your breeding program down there?"

"All the small herbivores have been released. I'm losing the bigger herbivores today. Deer, moose, zebras, a whole bunch of different kinds of antelope, chechuns, bison, camels, sharpias, gorillas, elephants, rhino, hippo, mosletalons, and skeens..."

"Enough, enough. I don't have time for your entire inventory."

"It's going to seem very empty around here with most of the pens cleared out. I'll only have the carnivores left. But all the females are pregnant, and I want them to settle in and have their babies in the wild."

"Be careful, my dear, I know you always are, but be careful anyway. I'll speak to you tomorrow."

"Take care as well, Geo," she returned softly.

She was rubbing her hands together as she met up with Will outside the office door.

"Ready to ship them out partner?" she asked him.

"You bet," he answered.

The pair left the lodge and crossed a hanging bridge over a deep chasm. It looked rickety and old, but Max had woven monofilament into the frayed rope holding the structure aloft, so it was actually stronger than steel. Radhya bounced the bridge causing Will to grab the side ropes and hang on. Laughing, she ran across to the other side. Will followed more slowly and cautiously.

Once they passed through the screening pines, the smells and sounds of the critter camp smote them. Pens, fences, and people were everywhere. In a broad clearing for the heliplane at the far end, one of them was descending out of the sun, adding its mechanical noise to the squeals, whinnies, and trumpeting of the crated, confined herbivores. Many crates were shrouded with blankets in a vain attempt to keep the inmates quiet.

"Sounds like everyone is unhappy this morning doesn't it?" she yelled at Will.

"I would be too, locked up in a crate since before dawn."

Making their way to the settled heliplane, Will and Radhya saw Padr leap from the cockpit.

"There you are," he said giving her a quick smile of greeting. "All the vegetation in every zone is more than capable of supporting at least double the numbers you're going to release."

"Good. We have most of them crated and ready to go," she replied. "Let's get started."

They worked steadily, making sure the large loaders were

gentle with their cargo, loading vehicle after vehicle. Each would lift to its zone as soon as it was filled and another heliplane would spiral down to take its place. Padr tapped Radhya on the shoulder.

"I'm going to get something to eat and go to bed. I've been up since last evening surveying the vegetation."

"Go ahead. Sleep well," Radhya ran a hand down his arm in farewell.

"Four more loads, I think," spoke Will.

"Looks about right. Four more loads and we'll be done. It's just the last of the savannah animals," answered Radhya, backing away as the heliplane lifted from the circle of dust.

Dust billowed everywhere, whirling in miniature tornados from the downwash of the blades. The ten rhinos waiting their turn at departure in their separate crates took exception to the noise and bashed into the sides of their container. One loosened a plank and began to hit repeatedly on the weak spot.

"Look out!" yelled Radhya.

Will dashed to get a nail gun to repair the crate. The rhino hit again. The box quivered, and the front gave way. Two tons of angry, horned mammal was loose with fifty people in the yard. Most of the slaves scattered.

"She's coming for you," yelled Radhya at a small female slave standing frozen amid the confusion.

The furious beast charged. Radhya ran, but it was too late. The girl was flung high over the creature's back, landing in the dust, her head at an unnatural angle.

Radhya sped to a crate, snatching the blanket off. The cheechuns inside erupted into a cacophony of noise. The loose rhino turned to see what the commotion was.

"Get a tranquilizer gun. Shoot her and hurry!" Radhya yelled at the top of her lungs. "Hurry!"

The great beast charged straight at her. Radhya flapped the blanket. The animal made for it, picking up speed with every stride. At the last second, Radhya flipped the blanket up and twirled away.

"No!" screamed Will. "Get out of there!"

"There's no place to go!" she yelled back.

He raced towards her. The rhino stopped itself and spun for another charge. Head lowered, it snorted several times, throwing plumes of dust backward with its churning feet. Looking at Will, then Radhya, then Will again, it charged the running man. Radhya flapped the blanket frantically, but the behemoth was immune to the disturbance. She screamed, jumping up and down, but it ignored her. With a sickening thud, it impacted Will, throwing him sideways, seven meters from its horn. He landed on his side; a pool of blood spreading from a wound in his abdomen, staining the dust of the ground. The violet light in Radhya's mind flickered.

She tried to go to him, but a loud snort brought her to a standstill. Turning, she saw to see the rhino charging her again. She held out the blanket and flapped it wildly, moving as quickly as was safe away from Will. It raced towards her, catching the blanket on its horn and ripping it from her grasp.

Radhya stood defenseless. She knew it could sprint thirty-five klicks an hour, far faster than she could ever run. There was no way she could climb out of its reach. She mentally sent a farewell of blue emotion to Padr, Max, and Will's flickering presence, feeling his life force weakening. He needed her. His desperate need flowed to her down the bond. No one else could help him, and she would not do without his warm companionship. The beast snorted again, finally rid of the blanket, and began its charge. Radhya remembered a faint scrap of very ancient history, the Minotaur, and bull-leaping. It might work; better than letting Will bleed to death in front of her. Radhya ran towards the rhino as it was charging. Sudden gold and green strength flooded into her. The horn lowered to pierce her body and throw her. They came together. Radhya leapt as never before clearing the head. Her hands hit the rhino's back, and she was over, as if vaulting a giant pommel horse.

She landed on her feet running. A double thwak thwak sounded behind her. Storn, the slave in charge of the animal compound, was facing the rhino with a gun still pointed at it. The animal crumpled its nose into the dust at his feet. Radhya raised an arm in salute and thanks. Max and Padr raced towards Will from the path to the bridge. Radhya sprinted as well, reaching him first.

She was on her knees examining him as they dashed up, panting. Together the three poured strength and healing down the bond to him. Radhya tore Max's tunic from him and folded it to make a pressure bandage to reduce the bleeding. Padr removed his tunic and tore it into strips to bind the pad to the wound. Together they poured their essences into the flickering violet presence.

"It's no good," despaired Max. "He's bleeding too much. We can't hold him."

"Get him to the med lab at the lodge. I can fix this if we can get him there alive." Radhya raced ahead as fast as she could.

Padr and Max lifted Will and carried him ever so gently between them to the hanging bridge and across to the lodge. Guided by the sparkling blue presence, they carried him to the med lab and lay him on a table. The streetlights were already on. Radhya was dressed in surgical green, masked, with gloves already on. In a tub of clear liquid beside the table, electrodes were bubbling the fluid. Radhya attached the waiting IV to attempt to stabilize his blood pressure.

"Padr, Max stay with him. Don't let him go. I only need an hour. I'll give what I can, but I need to concentrate, and I need him to stay alive for an hour."

"Don't worry Radhya; we'll keep him with us," Max assured her.

Radhya inserted a long needle and drew out some of Will's liver cells, which she could tell through the bond and by the scanner was damaged beyond repair. Using the hypospray to create a local condition in his blood that prevented him from bleeding to death, she dropped the liver cells into the tub. A new liver began to grow at a highly accelerated pace. She shot him with another compound designed to increase his red cell production. Radhya then put Will under anesthetic and opened him up at the site of the wound.

Although there was very little bleeding because of her treatment, Will's liver was shredded. Slowly and carefully, she removed the fragments of it. By then the new one had grown, and she inserted it and hooked up the vital blood supply. Giving the local antidote to the clotting substance in order for the blood to flow, she checked for further damage, but the rest of Will's insides seemed to be fine. She applied the healing bacteria layer by layer. The incision closed and the final drops of clean blood were wiped from the last layer of fresh skin. She put on a new saline IV and switched off the sterilight.

"Thank you," she told Padr and Max with tears in her voice. "Thank you. You saved him. You saved his life."

"No Radhya. You saved him," Padr replied softly, wiping her tears with the back of his hand.

"No, if you two hadn't come to keep him alive, through the bond, I couldn't have saved him."

"But if you couldn't grow a new liver, the bond wouldn't have been able to keep him alive," he retorted.

They laughed in relief.

"Sometimes, I feel like I have three extra limbs or something," laughed Max. "And I have to take care of all of you all and keep you out of trouble. One of these days I'm going to get mixed up and make one of you do something I want to do."

"Oh, I think we all have pretty distinct personalities," Radhya argued.

"I know, and it's hard for a private person like me to share so many emotions, so widely," Padr retorted.

"Oh, and wasn't it you, a while ago, who told me I wouldn't

know an honest emotion if it bit me or something," she returned sweetly.

"Would you really like to be all alone again?" queried Max.

"No," Padr replied, "I need you all to keep me crazy."

They all dissolved into helpless laughter. Leaving, Radhya told Storn to supervise the rest of the loading and releases. Her group was off duty for a day or two.

Chapter 21

The next morning Will was pale but hale and healthy.

"I could think only of losing you," he gave Radhya as his excuse.

"You think I would be better off losing you, than you losing me?" she queried.

"I don't think any of us needs to be lost," Max finished the argument. "But where in the creator's ideas did you think to vault over that beast?"

"It was something I once read about the Minotaur, like a half man and half bull creature. I think that was how they defeated him. I don't exactly remember it now. It's very vague."

"Well, it worked. Although I thought my heart would stop when I saw you running towards it," Padr said. "I thought you were going to bulldog it or something."

"I would never have made it without your help. Thank you for that. But I'm late to talk to Geo now."

She left the men together reliving the event, and made her way to the office. The holophone was barely on when Geo's angry face appeared.

"How dare you take chances like that. Do you know how

important you are? You can't go around jumping over wildlife young lady."

"But Geo, if I hadn't jumped I would be dead now, and so would Will. If Max and Padr hadn't given me their strength, I wouldn't have made it either. I wasn't doing it for fun."

"No, I suppose not, and I apologize, but I was so frightened when I heard what happened. Is Will all right?"

"Yes. I had to use 'the Geo process' on him, but he's perfectly fine, just a little weak from blood loss."

"You performed the surgery?"

"Yes, I had to. There was no one else. It's funny, like he was helping me himself, putting skill into my hands. I don't know. It's hard to describe."

"Well done, my dear, well done. How would you like another half planet?"

"What?"

"Lady Kemmira is having a plague on her planet. She's willing to offer you either half of her land or half of her income for ten years to fix it."

"Will I have time? I still planned on the Animal Island complex. I have that to do with Padr before the review committee visits."

"Why don't you leave Padr here? He could be in charge of it. It's only the architecture and landscaping; all the animals are already there."

"I guess it would help my chances to stay away from Barone if I had another half-world. It should increase my status quite a bit although I think maybe the income might be better. Check and see which is greater then set up the contracts. I'll be home as soon as Will feels able to travel."

Radhya signed off. Will was dressed and on his feet when she returned to the infirmary. Throwing his arms around her neck, he drew her close, his lips descending and kissing her slowly. Violet shimmering light enveloped her, an upwelling of respect, gratitude, and love. Max and Padr joined in the emotions, but Radhya pulled away embarrassed.

"I needed to thank you," Will explained.

Radhya laughed. "Embarrassing me to death is a great thank you. You know I don't like hands on me."

"Tit for tat," he responded. "You had your hands inside me yesterday."

"Okay, I'll give you that. You are forgiven. Now look, we have work to do."

"Oh no more rhinos, please. They give me a pain," moaned Will, doubled over in mock pain.

"Ha ha. Padr, how would you feel about staying behind and overseeing the Animal Island complex? I have been offered half a planet to stop a problem and get an economy functioning again.

A pang shivered down the emerald strand in her mind.

"If I have to, I suppose I can," he replied, "However, I don't feel right about being that far apart from you and the others."

Radhya thought for a moment. Leaving Padr behind created uneasiness situated somewhere in the vicinity of her stomach, but she dismissed it.

"So the rest of you get packed. We're going to Kemmira's World."

Radhya, Max and Will took a heliplane to the starport, meeting Rory and Stane at the Arrow. Brief preparations over, they were off planet and headed for the stars. A restless discomfort bloomed in them. Will and Max grew uneasy while Radhya developed a splitting headache, the first since the bonding.

"Radhya, we have to go back," begged Max. "This isn't right; we have to go back for Padr."

Radhya looked at him in too much pain to think, the echoing drumbeat of agony drowned out her friend's words, destroying her ability to understand. It increased with every kilometer. Will lapsed into unconsciousness. Radhya crumpled into her seat in pain.

"Rory," yelled Max at the intercom, "turn around and go back."

"What does milady say?" came the voice on the intercom.

Radhya writhed in her seat making little-grunting noises in the back of her throat.

"Rory go back to Pleasant right now," Max commanded in a tone that brooked no opposition.

"Yes milord," Rory answered.

Rory spun the Arrow around on its trajectory and retraced their way to the planet. Radhya's pain leaked from her body the closer they drew to Pleasant. Waking, Will rose and cursed his blood loss as the problem.

Padr, pale and disheveled, with Kung, was waiting with his luggage as they landed. His hands were shaking, and his legs didn't work especially well.

"I've decided I can plan the Animal Island complex just as well with the three of you as I can alone at home. This way I can use Max's expertise, and I can make it just like you want Radhya," he said with an unconvincing smile.

"Why not just admit, Padr, that we are going to have to stick together from now on. We can be a planetary diameter apart, but no further."

Perplexed, Padr struggled for something to say. Radhya pulled him down to her, resting her forehead on his. The bond flowed, blue and green joining to made a turquoise fountain. The relief at being in each other's mind washed back and forth. Max and Will joined in the consolation that flowed between them like a brilliant rainbow.

"I'm relieved we are back together," she told him.

Trying again, the Arrow traveled to Kemmira's World without further incident. The starport was fancy. Radhya departed with her usual trio and Kung, leaving Stane and Rory to guard the ship. An escort with a horse-drawn conveyance waited at the gates of the port to bring them to the palace. Radhya exchanged glances with Padr. He nodded at her. The carriage took them down elegant tree-lined streets, broken at regular intervals by soaring gothic arches. It was a large city.

"I'm not particularly well traveled, is this usual?" she whispered to Padr seated opposite her.

He smiled back at her. "Yes, this is quite the usual for aristocratic visitors. Don't forget her income depends on pleasing enough of the royals with clothing and baubles that they keep coming back. I've been here myself a time or two."

They rolled the rest of the way in silence, marveling at the architecture by sending their feeling back and forth through the bond. Numerous other carriages bearing guests shared the road making Kung restless on the way, fidgeting his considerable weight from Padr to Radhya to the floor and around again. After a few klicks, they turned into an enormous circular driveway paved with cobblestones. The horses' hooves rang hollow echoing back from the high, bordering hedges that obscured their view until they rounded the curve. A complete reproduction of the Palace of Versailles was revealed.

The conveyance halted before a flagstone walkway. Two men in blue, white and gold livery opened the door and placed a footstool for them. One held out his hand to her. Gesturing to Max, Radhya took his hand when he preceded her down the steps and held his hand toward her. The others followed. Falling into their usual formation, Will on the right, Max on the left and Padr behind, Kung padded behind Padr and Radhya was just slightly in the lead. The two footmen led the way. Inside, the vaulted ceiling drew their eyes upward. Making a conscious effort to keep her eyes focused ahead, Radhya was led through gracious halls and spacious rooms filled with light, airy furniture. The footmen left them in what Radhya took to be a library or study for the walls were lined with old-fashioned antique books from floor to ceiling on two walls. The third wall had floor to ceiling windows divided into many tiny panes behind a large, real oak desk and five red, leather chairs. Radhya seated herself in the middle chair, and the men stood in a semicircle around her.

The door opened, and a woman entered. She was small, although still six centimeters taller than Radhya, impeccably groomed with gold fingernails and perfect makeup. Her hair was done pulled to the top of her head and tumbled down in streaks of gold, platinum, and bronze. She wore a red and gold dress of elegant styling and a female bodyguard in-house livery followed her.

"Lady Kirbyson?" she inquired in a soprano voice, feminine and clear.

Radhya rose and faced her.

"Please do sit down again. I am surprised. Most visitors are far too intimidated to be seated, especially on their first visit." Lady Kemmira smile was cold and somehow feral.

Moving behind the large desk, she seated herself. She looked straight at Radhya.

"I suppose they do not call you Lady Death for nothing."

Saying nothing in reply to the jibe, Radhya bowed her head. Lady Kemmira's eyes roved over her bodyguards.

"My Lord Kent, I didn't invite you, did I?" she spoke in surprise.

"No, Lady Kemmira you did not," answered Padr for himself, "I am no longer Lord Kent. I'm merely Padr, slave, and bodyguard to Lady Kirbyson."

"No!" The blonde exclaimed in shock. "I've been trying to get a contract with you for the past two years. It was almost concluded just before your parents died, but your brother has put me off ever since. Why wouldn't he tell me?"

"I don't know Lady Kemmira."

"Lady Kirbyson, you must sell him to me, at once," Kemmira demanded. "It is unthinkable a man like Lord Kent be a bodyguard to Lady Death."

"I'm sorry," Radhya replied coldly, with sparks flashing in her eyes, "my bodyguard is not for sale."

"Oh, but you must. I insist. I'll meet any price."

"Padr is not for sale." The men recognized the warning tones in Radhya's voice.

"I'll get you one way or another Lord Kent," Lady Kemmira promised him.

"No Lady Kemmira. If I were free, I would not contract with you, and I am now more than happy in the position that I hold with Lady Kirbyson," Padr told her plainly.

"Kent, you couldn't be," she contradicted wringing her hands in distress.

"But I am, please, leave me alone."

"If you only lured me here to buy my slave, then I'll be leaving," snarled Radhya rising to her feet.

"No, please, sit back down. I've just grown so used to thinking of Lord Kent as my spouse, that the shock got to me. If he is happier as your slave than my concubine, so be it. I asked you here on the recommendation of Lord Kirbyson. He said he could help me, but it would take, probably, five years. I'll be out of business by then. My problem, you see, is this insect that came out of nowhere and has ravaged both my silk crops in its adult form and my shocotton, in its larval form. And the eggs, that are laid in sticky cells in their wool, plague the sheep. Without high-quality material, it is impossible to have a fashion industry. We are working from the warehouse now; we have been for two years, but this year's failure is really going to hurt."

"Do you have a lab and samples of the pest?" Radhya queried.

"Yes, my scientists have been working, but neither insecticides nor organic spray will repel them or kill them."

"Okay," smiled Radhya, "if you can keep your hands off my bodyguard, let's get to work."

Lady Kemmira led them down a long hallway and then a lift took them to a deep basement compound. Kung complained mightily on the lift. Radhya was shown a series of well-equipped labs with workers busy with their labors.

"I want an X10 comp and a lab of my own, fully equipped. I want at least two or three hundred specimens of this insect in its various stages. I want a room nearby, for my slaves, Kung and I. I need a litter box and two kilos of meat every day for my lynxcat. I need an exercise room, well equipped next to my sleeping quarters. I won't work with your scientists, my techniques are private, and I work with my own. I also want good meals brought to us. The men get the same food as I do."

Lady Kemmira nodded. "I'll get my staff to make the arrangements."

The Lady left, and Radhya got right to work. As in her usual pattern, she worked late, rose early and worked; forgetting to eat half the time. Kung was their guardian, making sure no one spied on them and warning them of visitors. Will, Padr, and Max worked alongside, doing the mindless tasks or repetition so necessary for progress. Because they were a well-oiled team, a week later she had a servant call Lady Kemmira.

The Lady of the Palace appeared dressed in gold and silver, looking flustered and annoyed.

"Is there something you need? You could have just asked one of the servants," she said with irritation.

"I have finished. I have two products for you," replied Radhya triumphantly.

"You couldn't possibly be finished. Lord Kirbyson said five years!" Kemmira exclaimed.

"Well, Steph has always been a little slow at getting things done. Besides I thought he recommended me because he said I was faster?"

"Do you mean to tell me I am giving up half my planet's income for ten years for a week's worth of work?" she replied indignantly.

"Lady Kemmira," Radhya sighed, "Isn't it the quality of the work that counts, not the time taken to produce it? If you don't want these things, I'll take them home with me along with all the evidence that you've been sabotaged."

"What?" exclaimed Lady Kemmira.

"I found evidence that these bugs were genetically created from earwigs and tailored especially to ruin your crops," Radhya called a genetic print to the screen. "See this here and here; those squiggles mean these things were altered from another insect form."

"You did it. You did it so I would hire you and give you all my money."

Radhya threw her hands in the air.

"Why in all the creator's wisdom would I tell you about the sabotage if I had done it?" she snapped.

"Nobody else could have, and that's why you could cure it so fast!" stated Lady Kemmira emphatically.

"Call the proctors and make complaint. I dare you. At least two other people could have done it. One is my brother Stephan, and the other is the one who obviously did, my outlaw sister Petra. She has already made herself a slave."

"How do you know it was her?"

"One, she works for Lord Barone. He is administering her estate right now. It's a matter of record. Two, a similar, but not exact pest infected her world ten years ago, and I eradicated it for her. Three, you are in competition with her in the fabric and fashion industries, and Petra hates competition. Four, how can you tell a painting is by a certain artist without his signature? You tell by his composition and even his brush strokes. Believe me; these things have Petra written all over them. Now do you want the solution or not? It does come with a guarantee. No success, no payment."

Lady Kemmira nodded numbly in shock.

"First, I have five hundred thousand sterile males to be released."

"What! You're not going to spread more of those pests?"

"Yes, you are. These males are improved to give out hundred times more powerful pheromones. That will attract the females to mate with them alone. They will lay no eggs. Racial suicide. The second is a spray for your silkworms' food. It is totally harmless to them, but it creates a biological reaction which makes the cocoons smell very repugnant to the insects so the adults will avoid the silkworms. This year's crop will be saved."

"Will the silk smell bad to us as well?"

Radhya held a cocoon out to Lady Kemmira.

"Sniff," she commanded.

Lady Kemmira drew in a deep breath. "That's heavenly, how beautiful."

She sniffed again and again.

"Will it wash out?"

"I don't know. You'll have to experiment with that."

"I don't know how to thank you."

"Just pay the bill."

Radhya packed up her tools and followed by her men and Kung, trailed after the Lady to the part of the palace exposed to the world.

"Why don't you stay tonight? I'm having a small dinner party, and I want you for my guest of honor. I had planned already to ask the servants to tender you an invitation."

Radhya replied, "I thank you, but I brought only working clothes."

Kemmira laughed. "This is the fashion capital of the Commonwealth. I think I can give you something. Consider it a bonus for such speedy work."

Unsure, Radhya nodded her head. Lady Kemmira showed them to a large sumptuous bedroom with a dark walnut, four poster bed in the middle of the floor, matching the chests and bureaus around the perimeter of the room. The hangings, curtains, and bedspread were white lace in addition to the white lace topping the four easy chairs scattered around the room. Kung sniffed and prowled around the premises.

Max opened the door when a tap sounded at it and it a large

woman slave with an armful of clothing entered. A man stood behind her.

"Lady Kemmira requests that your slave Padr be your escort tonight and balance the party," the man requested.

Radhya exchanged glances with him.

"Care to play dress up Padr?" she asked

He grinned and replied, "It might be fun, for old time's sake."

"Very well, tell Lady Kemmira that Lord Kent will escort me."

The man bowed and left. The woman held out black, male evening wear to Padr, high collared with a bow tie that would completely hide his slave collar.

"Max can be my slave and Will can be yours," Radhya suggested.

They grinned. The woman slave hauled Radhya off to one of the washrooms. Two torturous hours later she was ready. Kemmira had dressed her in pale grey silk, the color of her eyes. Stones of shell pink circled her throat and fell between her breasts in the low cut, floor length gown. Radhya looked belligerently at the men. Makeup made her radiant even in her pique.

"Outstanding!" said Max.

"As usual she cleans up well," commented Will.

Radhya stared at Padr as if she had never seen him before, looking almost frightened. Padr returned the look, and they gazed into each other's eyes a long moment.

"If only she would just smile, she would outshine anyone there," quipped Padr holding out his arm to her as he felt her uncertainty.

The slave led them through the elegantly appointed hallways to a banquet room almost as large as the one at Radhya's visitor's center. A hundred or more people lined the room setting Radhya's alarm bells off immediately. She sent 'warning' down the bond. The men sent back 'relax and enjoy.' Radhya sent 'danger' again.

Noticing Padr and herself were the only ones without color, she remarked that everyone was brilliantly dressed in a rainbow of colors. The women were looking at the pair of them and tittering behind their hands, while the men, who were fashion plates of sartorial splendor, observed them superciliously. Radhya overheard a comment about last year's fashion. Lady Kemmira came sparkling up in a dress that appeared to be diamonds. The refracted light was eye-achingly bright.

Lady Kemmira grasped Padr by the arm and led him to a seat beside herself. Will followed to stand behind his chair. Radhya was seated by one of Kemmira's slaves on the opposite side of the table from Padr, more than halfway down. About twenty-five people were between them.

The meal was long and boring as only those functions could be, without anything that Radhya cared to eat. The elderly aristocrat on Radhya's right kept falling asleep, and the young one on her left was interested only in the young lady on the other side of the table. Radhya spent two and half-hours in splendid isolation. Without the bond with her friends, she would have run screaming from the room.

The interminable dinner drew to a close as slaves began clearing the cutlery. Lady Kemmira rose to her feet and tapped on a crystal glass. The delicate chime rang throughout the room halting conversation.

"Thank you all for coming. It is good to celebrate again. Now my material problems will soon be solved thanks to Lady Kirbyson," Polite applause greeted her remark, "I also want to take the opportunity to announce my agreement to contract with Lord Kent."

She pulled Padr to his feet amid much more vigorous applause. She snuggled to his side. Radhya leapt to her feet.

"I beg your pardon?" she snapped.

"Lord Kent and I are contracting tomorrow. This is our engagement party."

"The former Lord Kent is a slave, stripped of status, and wealth and owned by me. It is not legal for you to contract to him."

"I can get the King to pardon him. He promised me anything I wanted as a reward for the last special outfit I created for him. So I plan to ask him for this."

Radhya sat down. If Padr could be set free, she had no right to hold him to her. She clamped firmly down on the bond so he could not sense her sense of betrayal, confusion, and pain.

Padr pushed Lady Kemmira away from him. Disgust was written large on his face as the petite blonde hung on to his arm.

"I will not contract with you, not for my freedom, nor all the money in the Commonwealth. I would rather be Radhya's slave than your free mate. I despise your trickery and deceit. You told us this banquet was to honor Radhya for her exceptional work on your behalf. She is a woman of honor, she saved your planet and your income; and you try to trick her and steal me from her. You are totally despicable."

He tore his arm away from Lady Kemmira and marched to Radhya's seat. He offered Lady Kirbyson his arm as Lady Kemmira fled the room in tears. As Radhya and her men left the banquet room, a slave appeared to escort them back to their room.

A riled Radhya was still pacing in fury an hour later, disturbing the slaves who were trying to pack, when a timid tap came at the door. Ignoring safety, Radhya whipped it open. Lady Kemmira stood there, alone.

"I'm sorry. I didn't realize Lord Kent was in love with you. I've always been told you didn't have those sorts of feelings for men. I certainly didn't expect either of you to deny me in front of the aristocracy. That just isn't done. Now I will be the laughing stock of the royalty for years. I don't know what to do anymore. Lady Kirbyson, Radhya, help me please." She held out an imploring hand.

Radhya snapped back, "I did help you, and you helped yourself, to my bodyguard."

"I'm sorry. I am just so desperate. I need an heir. A legal heir. I knew about Padr becoming a slave, everyone does, but I thought, for his freedom.....I'm thirty-seven. I'll never have a child without a mate, and I can't get one of those. Please help me. Do you think your brother?"

"Ask anyone but me to help you there. Try if you want, but he's as selfish as the sun is hot. Come in."

Radhya closed the door, Kung prowling restlessly, growling at the newcomer. She pulled a tiny comp from her packed luggage. Typing a few commands, patterns began to flow across the screen stopping five minutes later.

"Your two best matches for children are already contracted. The third is Lord Sutherland. If you and he had children the odds are in the ninetieth percentile that they would be defect free and relatively intelligent."

"Lord Sutherland is terribly old and grey. Where is Padr in relation to me? "

"Nine hundred and seventy-five. A very poor match for you indeed."

"Oh, I guess we weren't meant for each other."

"No," interrupted Padr, "Radhya and I are a perfect match. In more ways than just genetically too."

"Lord Jambawe is also a good match for you," continued Radhya. "Eighty-seven percent probability of excellent offspring."

"Well, he at least is young, if a long way from my status. Oh, what's the use? I probably can't even get pregnant now."

"I can help you with that, for a price. But your infertility problems are very common in the aristocracy and growing with every generation. We are really getting into trouble. Birth rates have fallen drastically. Our women are unable to conceive. Our men are unable to impregnate. More and more the children that are born have defects, mental or physical. Our little boys are born with small penises. Do you know the average royal's penis is only one quarter the size of a freedman's? That is always the first indicator of trouble in any population. And there are more heart and kidney defects in our children every year."

"Do you know why?"

"Yes of course. It's hundreds of years of inbreeding. Everyone wants to keep their status, so they only contract with those nearest them in status. The best are dropped out the bottom. Like Lord Kent, sold as slaves and the gene pool gets narrower and narrower. We've got to smarten up. We are destroying ourselves as a group of people."

"So if I contract with Lord Jambawe and have trouble, you can help me to conceive?"

"Yes. Contact my majordomo, Geo. He'll make all the arrangements."

"Thank you, and I'm sorry," Lady Kemmira said softly. "And I do envy you your perfect match."

She left.

"Is all that you told her true?" questioned Padr.

"Yes. It's another reason we have to free the slaves."

"But am I really your best match?"

Radhya tapped the comp again. The charts came up.

"I told you before I was made for you, look, and the top is mine. Yours is next, then Will's, then Max's. Do you see the correspondences? Padr and I are ninety-nine point nine percentile, Will and I are ninety-eight point nine percentile and Max, and I are ninety-eight point eight percentile."

"So I'm your worst match?" asked Max stricken.

Radhya laughed, "Max, most matches are in the thirtieth percentile. You would be an excellent father for any children I may have. Anything over seventy-five is very good. So, you can see how good you really all are. But grandpa made me to go with Padr."

"You knew all this when you bought us, didn't you?" asked Will.

"Absolutely. My grandfather ran experiments. We are the result of his attempt to manipulate human genes inside the parent's bodies. There were just nine of us altogether. I can't tell you who the last one is, but there were four others he manipulated in vitro. They are all dead," she answered.

"So do you know who our fathers are?" asked Max.

"I don't need grandpa's notes for that. I know. You were raised by a stepfather but your mother got you from an important, high-status Lord, Max."

"Can you tell me his name?"

"Do you really want to know?"

Padr looked at Radhya, nostrils flared, eyes wide. He looked at Will and back at Radhya.

"Yes Padr, the genes show don't they. I am surprised no one ever guessed before. Max is also the picture of his genetic father."

"Lord Grant?" asked Padr aghast.

"Got it in one," replied Radhya.

"Lord Grant is my father?" queried Max.

Radhya nodded her head.

"He is rather elderly now, but he was a good friend of my grandfather."

"Who is Will's father?" Max continued.

"I don't want to know!" exclaimed Will. "He abandoned my mother to raise me alone. He's never even seen me. I don't want to even know who he is. My mother died alone in agony, and no one came to care for her except me, so he means nothing to me."

"Fair enough," said Radhya, "We are your family now, and you never have to be alone again."

Love and support poured down the bond to Will easing his distress.

Radhya finally settled to sleep in the big bed with Kung at her back while the men distributed themselves on the floor. Early in the morning, they left for home.

Chapter 22

T he selection committee consisted of five people. Two were men, and three were women. Radhya rather hoped for the reverse, as she found it easier to use logic to influence men.

One of the men, Lord Grant, was very elderly. He was stooped over, and his hair was snow white; his large, velvet brown, long-lashed eyes, however, were shrewd and missed nothing. Tall, lean and athletic looking, Lord Kimber's dark hair and blue eyes reminded her somewhat of Padr, but the pug nose made his profile radically different. Radhya gave him an especially brilliant smile. Lady Clarke was a petite blonde, shorter even than Radhya. Her oval face was graced with large hazel eyes, slender lips, but a large curving nose. With quick and lively movements, and her reputation as an excellent horsewoman preceded her. Lady Bezalel was plain, with mousy brown hair and nondescript features, holding herself prim and aloof. Radhya's alarm bells rang at the sight of her. The last judge was Princess Felina's best friend, Lady Simms, a huge raw-boned woman, taller than Padr. With a short and turned up nose and a wide, full-lipped mouth, she had small sea-green eyes and exceptionally curly, fiery red hair. Her grin was infectious.

"Sky's afire, Lady Kirbyson; I didn't expect you to meet us at the spaceport," boomed Lady Simms.

"You seem over eager," mentioned Lord Grant.

"I am eager," replied Radhya, "and I freely admit I am anxious for you to choose Pleasant for the review. Then everyone can see what a wonderful place my pleasure planet is."

"Refreshing honesty," snorted Lord Grant.

Radhya escorted the committee, with their guards, to the waiting hovervan, acting as a tour guide to point out the Ocean of Delight on the right and the Mountains of Mist which were living up to their name.

"In the other direction from that in which we are traveling, are facilities for the endurance riding competition. I'm also nearing completion on a show jumping complex at the same location."

"When will they be complete?" questioned Lady Clarke.

"The endurance complex will be finished before the end of this week. I planned a tour for you. The jumping complex will be finished in about two more months."

"What else, besides horses, do you have to offer?" asked Lord Grant.

"I have the best spa in the Commonwealth on Spa Island, just offshore. In the south, I have a small continent that is a hunting park. It is stocked with every form of big game and predator in the Commonwealth. Many extinct species have been recreated. I have parks and the most incredible gardens you have ever seen. I also have, just off-shore again, my species zoo, on Animal Island. It is an amazingly landscaped zoo that gives you the feeling of walking among the animals. However, they are safely confined. I also have hiking trails to beautiful natural scenery, and there is a gambling casino on another of my offshore islands. Over on Sport Island, you may enjoy snow sports or water sports in the same day. There are many other attractions as well."

"Do you own the entire planet?" asked Lord Kimber.

"Yes milord, I do," Radhya replied.

"Employees or slaves?" he further inquired.

"Slaves milord."

"Everywhere?"

"Yes everywhere."

"A tidy profit for you then."

"Yes indeed, milord Kimber. A substantial outlay, but a good profit. On the left, you see the track. It has become quite popular in the last two years. There is even talk by the Racing Committee to create a new Triple Crown, with my Double Helix race as one of the legs. On the right is the visitor's center. There are more than enough rooms to accommodate all the aristocrats in the Commonwealth.

The hover stopped. Radhya escorted the committee from the vehicle, pausing as they stopped to admire the scenery, pivoting to take in the track.

"If this is a sample, this has to be the most beautiful planet in the galaxy," said Lady Clarke.

Radhya led them to the hotel. To show the range of her hospitality, she placed each delegate on a separate floor. The committee settled in for the remainder of the afternoon. In the evening they toured the track and the stables, everywhere exclaiming about the beauty and variety of the terrain. That evening they had a small banquet in the private dining hall.

"So far," said Lady Simms, "I'm impressed. You are one of the three last candidates, but I can't see the others even coming close. Felina also wishes for the review to be held here."

"We still have one more to see," put in Lord Grant testily.

"These facilities are first-rate," stated Lady Clarke. "I am very impressed. Aren't you the owner of Tango Dancer and Son-O-War?"

"Yes, milady."

"Since both are unbeaten in their racing careers, are you going to race them against each other?"

"I don't know. If I have the review here, I might be tempted to arrange such a match race. It would only be myself beating myself in any event."

"But a good draw," commented Lord Kimber.

The banquet continued long into the night. Radhya drew strength and patience as well as alertness from Will, Max, and Padr, who took shifts in being stationed behind her chair. When the long meal was over, and the men and women of the status review venue selection committee retired, Radhya confirmed the next day's arrangements.

After breakfast, the next morning, they flew to Animal Island. Here they spent an entire day wandering among gorgeous scenery, looking at rare, exotic birds, animals, reptiles and creatures more alien still.

That evening, at dark, they flew to Island Monte Vegas, where the delegates got to gamble on the house. In the early morning hours, they flew back to the visitor's center for a half-day of rest. The afternoon passed touring Sports Island.

The following day was restful as they visited Spa Island and were treated to all the pampering anyone could possibly want. After that, they flew south to Africa.

As they did not hunt, Lady Kirbyson and Lady Bezalel remained in the lodge while the other four royals and their entourages hunted the savannah and jungles. Many trophy animals were tranquilized and holos taken. Lord Grant returned positively glowing, and very reluctant to leave. However, after a night at the lodge, they began the long trip back, to visit the endurance facility.

Lady Clarke and Lady Simms were very taken with the new idea, and both vowed to enter horses when the competitions began.

Before the aristocrats were willing to return home, however, they insisted on seeing where Radhya's home was. Reluctantly she agreed.

On the fifth day of the visit, Radhya led the visitors up the fungus path to her home.

"It feels unusual to be walking again," commented Lord Grant. "It is so easy to get used to riding everywhere."

"Yes milord," replied Radhya, "walking is an excellent custom, one I truly support. I only supplied transportation in the interests of time, knowing how valuable it is to you."

"Yes, yes," the old man grunted. "We all understand that. Still one misses the full impact of one's environment with all that zipping about."

The others murmured in agreement as Lord Grant stopped to smell the row of moonglows planted on either side of the path. Continuing slowly, at the gate they met Radhya's skunks.

"Don't tell me you have animals running loose around here?" shrieked Lady Bezalel.

"Yes milady. They don't stray far from the path, and they make an excellent line of defense," explained Radhya.

Lady Bezalel edged past, keeping the others between her and the animals. Lady Simms was laughing at her as she strode after, the rest of the entourage following. At Lady Clarke's request, Radhya led them down the path to visit the stable before they moved on to the house. The broodmares, grazing peacefully in the fields were striking against the background of the dense, lush forest. Little foals frolicked beside their dams. The troupe stopped to watch for a few minutes, to bask in the serenity.

The scenario changed abruptly in the stable yard. D'Bara flung shovels, pails, mops, brushes, and currycombs at Li who was attempting to avoid her barrage and use the prod on her. The obscenities pouring from her mouth made Lord Kimber blush, and Lady Bezalel looked ready to faint.

Radhya whispered to Will. He took a hypospray from his belt kit and snuck up behind D'Bara, shooting her in the back of the neck. She whirled, eyes insane, foam on the corners of her mouth. A flying hand caught Will on the side of the head stunning him. She caught sight of Radhya and charged her.

"I'll kill you," she screamed. "You think you've got me, but I'll kill you with my own hands."

The drug kicked in and D'Bara fell on her face in the dirt, six meters from Radhya's feet.

"How appalling! Why would you keep such a creature?" gasped Lady Clarke.

Lord Grant grunted, "You should flog this to death, Lady Kirbyson."

"I wouldn't have a mouth like that anywhere in my service or employ," spat Lady Bezalel.

"You really should dispose of it," advised Lord Kimber.

Lady Simms asked, "Why?"

Radhya smiled gratefully at her. "It's a long story. I'll tell you sometime."

Li and another stable hand grabbed the unconscious woman and dragged her to a pile of used hay, where they carelessly tossed her. Padr put a hand on Radhya's shoulder.

"I can't believe I once thought I preferred her to you. I must have been out of my mind," he whispered.

"See, you should be grateful I saved you from a life devoted to D'Bara," Radhya teased back in a low murmur.

Padr squeezed her shoulder, and they both smiled. Radhya continued with the tour as Sumi waved from the deck of her house. Her newborn nursed as a toddler played at her feet.

"That's my vet, but she just had a child, so we won't meet her today, if you don't mind," explained Radhya.

The group nodded, and they continued on their way to the mansion, leaving Will to inspect the newborn. Geo greeted them at the door. As he led the aristocrats away to freshen up before dinner, Radhya hurried to the kitchen to check with Aninya. The meal was gourmet, of the highest quality. Aninya exceeded her own high standards.

"I don't care how great the last planet is," Lady Simms told Radhya at the meal; "I am giving you my vote."

"Thank you very much milady."

"And I," broke in Lord Kimber; "I am much taken with the variety of everything. Why did no one ever think of a pleasure planet before?"

"Thank you, milord Kimber," returned Radhya. "I don't know why it's never been done before; it seems an obvious idea."

"Yes, yes a very fine facility," grunted Lord Grant, "definitely the best we've seen so far, but I reserve my vote until we've seen the last place."

"I, too, am strongly inclined to place the review here. However, in all fairness, there is one more planet to check out," added Lady Clarke.

"I for one, shall never vote for this place," hissed Lady Bezalel.

Lady Simms boomed, "Why ever not?"

"Those horrible little animals are running loose everywhere. Besides, that is the problem; that there is too much to do. We should be here to concentrate on our status, not....not play. Status review is serious business," Lady Bezalel snapped back.

Lord Grant chuckled. "My dear Sonya, the master comps determine status. The proctors program the comps. Once you hand in your information, there is absolutely nothing to do at these things except make rude comments about what the other royals are wearing."

"I happen to think the banquets and dances and all the exchanges of information are very important," Lady Bezalel responded.

"Oh, posh. You can talk business or contracting better over a kill or a card table than on the dance floor," Lord Grant huffed.

"Just the same, I'll never vote for you," snarled Lady Bezalel at Radhya. "You strutting around, showing off your body to try to turn men's heads. Dazzling them with your oh, so superior intellect. You don't get my vote, ever."

She threw her napkin to the floor and left the room trailed by her slave. The other royals looked at each other in embarrassed silence.

"I am sorry," apologized Lord Kimber, "I cannot excuse such appalling behavior towards a hostess."

Lord Grant waved a withered hand in dismissal.

"Don't distress yourselves, Lord, Ladies. She is entitled to her own opinion."

The meal fizzled into silence, and the remaining royals excused themselves to the den for a private discussion.

Radhya went to Geo's office with Max and Padr.

"Well old friend," she began, "it appears that I have possibly four out of five convinced this is the best place."

"And be assured that it is. You've seen to that my dear," Geo replied.

"Padr and Max designed most of it. The credit should go to them," insisted Radhya.

"Yes but…"

The door to Geo's office burst open. D'Bara reeled in, a hoof pick in one hand and a tine from a manure fork in the other.

"You slut, I told you I'd kill you. Die, die, die!" she shrieked.

Padr and Max leapt across the room as D'Bara dove towards Radhya, spit flying, eyes wild. The distance prevented their interception, but Geo was close. He stepped between the two women, using his unprotected body as a shield for Radhya. The manure tine ripped into his lungs as the hoof pick tore open his carotid artery. He collapsed to the floor. Padr and Max snatched D'Bara and heaved her from Geo's bleeding body. Radhya fell down beside the old man.

She screamed into her wrist comp, "Will, Will I need you, Geo's study, full medical kit!"

She held Geo's spurting neck together with her hands,

unable to stem the fountaining blood which forced between her fingers.

"Let me go," the old man whispered. "It's time."

"No!" she cried in anguish, her tears falling on the wrinkled black cheek. "No old friend, don't leave me. I love you, and I need you!"

Wheezing, he raised a hand and caressed her tear stained face.

"You've been my daughter. Always know how proud I was of you. I always knew I'd die protecting you. I, I...."

His eyes rolled up, and his last breath rattled out.

"NO!" Radhya's howl ascended to heaven.

Will dashed in with full kit breathless in his run from Sumi's house.

"Will, get him back, save him, you have to save him!"

He fell to his knees and went to work on Geo as Radhya rose and faced D'Bara. The murderess stood proudly in the firm grip of Padr and Max. She had a triumphant sneer on her once beautiful face.

"I know you Petra," said Radhya quietly.

The blonde's dark eyes widened.

"You revealed yourself the first day here. I put you at the stable to safeguard you from doing anything foolish until Steph, and I could find a way to return you to the aristocracy and get your property back. I even paid him to try to reinstate you. You repay me by trying to kill me, and by killing my oldest friend."

Petra tossed her head. "You took everything I had, you slut. You took my planet; even Noel is supposed to contract to you. I'm just sorry I missed you. It would do me good to see you lying there bleeding."

"I took nothing. Everything I have, I worked for, I developed. While you were teasing boys and playing, I was working. Stephan inherited father's estate, and you inherited mother's. Geo was all I was ever given from our parents, and now you've destroyed him."

"I'm glad. It's so good to hurt you," Petra hissed.

"I can't get him back," declared Will.

"Keep trying please!" pleaded Radhya. "Now dear sister, it's at an end with us."

"You wouldn't dare you spineless wonder," her sister snarled.

Radhya walked up to her taller sister. She reached up, grabbed the sneering head and twisted. The neck broke with an audible snap, and the corpse slumped between the bodyguard's hands.

"Throw it in the forest for the wolves," Radhya commanded in a voice of ice.

She turned to Will and Geo. Will was dripping sweat as he repeatedly tried to bring Geo back.

"It's been fifteen minutes," he gasped.

She stopped him with her hand.

"You're right, by now there's nothing left to come back." She looked at him with tears streaming, "But how will I ever live without him."

She collapsed across the old man's bloody chest and sobbed until she was sick. When Max and Padr returned, breathless, Will, sitting on the floor, his arm around Radhya, looked helplessly at them.

"Harrummph, what's all this commotion," Lord Grant and the other members of the selection committee were in the doorway.

"Milord Grant," Padr bowed low. "That stable slave attempted to kill R… Lady Kirbyson, and Geo prevented it at the cost of his life."

"Well good man, good man. What's wrong with your Lady?"

Padr hesitated in answering.

"Well answer the question boy."

"She was very close to the old man. I believe he was her childhood protector."

"Ah well, she is distraught. Perhaps adding the status review to that will be too much for her."

"Oh no, milord. Lady Kirbyson loves working. It would be the best thing possible for her at this time."

"But she is so emotional," said Lord Kimber with distaste.

"Excuse me, milord, what you see now is not at all how she was through all this," Padr explained. "She first tried to save Geo, when he died in her arms; she killed the slave herself, with her bare hands. I shouldn't wonder that this isn't a reaction to executing the murdering wench."

"Ah," replied Lord Kimber "In that case I understand. Some women have great stress at killing things. Why I myself, as a boy of ten, cried like a baby when I killed my first stag. Is it her first kill?"

"I wouldn't know milord. I do know Lady Kirbyson doesn't hunt."

Lord Kimber nodded knowingly, and the committee left the room. Radhya was beyond awareness of anyone; her presence in the bond a frozen river of ice.

"Radhya," spoke Max softly, "Let us take him."

When she did not respond, they lifted her from the body. Max and Will took her to her room.

"We should put her to bed, but not with all that blood," said Will.

The men exchanged puzzled looks.

"I'll get Padr," proposed Max.

Will nodded and stayed with Radhya while Max fetched Padr.

Entering the room, Padr took Radhya from Will and carried her into the shower room, tossing out her black and bloody garments as he stripped them from her body. When she was clean, he toweled her dry and lay her in her bed.

"Now what?" he asked Will.

"I don't want to leave her alone like this. She is practically catatonic. We should stay with her," Will replied.

"What about Geo?" asked Max.

"I called Rory. He's on his way," Padr informed them.

The three pulled up chairs and sat around Radhya's bed. Padr held her hand and tried to reach her with the bond, sending warm and comforting verdant waves to her gelid mind. Golden light and violet shimmer poured solace and support into her. Of Radhya there was no feeling. Padr held her hand tight.

In the morning, a silent, dry-eyed Radhya escorted the Status Review Venue Selection Committee back to the spaceport, observing the formalities like an automaton.

Geo was buried that night, all the stars of the Milky Way his funeral candles. Every slave of Radhya's household was in attendance. Max said a prayer over him to the creator of all while Radhya planted a tree on the head of his grave, a tall sequoia sapling. It would live a thousand years or more.

Chapter 23

In the slave's galley, Max, Padr, Will, Rory, Dave, Stane, Sumi, Kaarl, Amlina, Aninya, and their son Dani met with Radhya. The slaves sat around the table while the lynxcats prowled among them, upset by the tension. Radhya stood with her back to the room, gazing out the window at the new sapling.

"I don't like it Padr. She's completely shut down. All I get is black. Have you felt her in the bond since Geo died?" whispered Max.

"No, but that was a terrible shock. You have to give her time and space," Padr whispered back.

"I think you're wrong," cut in Will, "I think she needs to be with us now, not to cut herself off. Remember, she's spent most of her life like that. It's how she copes, but she needs to trust us, and she needs our help. There's something very dark here."

Padr answered, "I still think she needs her space. You can't crowd people."

"We're not people; we're her bond mates. Haven't you felt it getting weaker?" asked Max.

Padr nodded thoughtfully, "We should go tonight and ask

the Chandrans."

The other two nodded.

Radhya turned from the window, cold and distant. Even Kung and Ringha wrestling could not bring a smile to her face.

"I have to continue the plan. Geo would have wanted that," she began. "I don't have confidence anymore I can succeed, but at least I will die trying."

"She's planning suicide," Will whispered.

"That's why she's shut us out," Max retorted.

Radhya continued, "Rory, you are past fifty and most pilots retire before your age. I hate to lose you as my primary pilot, but I need a majordomo more, and other than Geo, you are the only one who keeps up with everything. Will you take over Geo's position?"

"Milady I would be most honored. I was going to approach you about retiring after the status review because my reflexes are getting too slow."

Radhya nodded at him. "Stane, you are primary pilot now, and I would like you to train young Dani here as co. How old are you Dani?"

"Milady, I'm thirteen almost fourteen," he replied with his eyes wide with wonder.

"Are you willing to train as pilot?"

"Oh yes, my lady!" he responded eagerly. "I've always loved space, and I can't believe I'm to train for it. It's... it's I just don't know."

Dani was grinning from ear to ear. Radhya had a small smile at his delight.

"Aninya, Kaarl any objections?"

"No milady," murmured Kaarl.

"I thank you, milady. You'll make Dani very, very valuable and I thank you for that," Aninya babbled.

"Just train your new daughter to be as fine a chef as you are and both of your children will be more than common slaves. If I succeed, they will be successful freedmen in time as well."

Aninya bowed her head to hide the tears.

"Dave, how does the security shape up?"

"Very well milady. I have successfully duplicated Lord Barone's techniques for training, and I have five slaves in the training right now. All the other plans have been finalized."

"Good, Kaarl, prepare all my documents for the proctors to review. Even if they don't select Pleasant, I need them for the comps."

"Yes milady."

"Aninya, Amlina, if we get selected I need you to have menus prepared for me to choose from."

"Yes milady," the women responded.

"Sumi, is Singha due to kit soon? I can't split myself more once Pleasant is selected, if it is."

"She could go into labor at any hour now. I suspect Ringha will bear just at the time scheduled for the review."

"Can you keep a close eye on them for me?"

"Of course milady," Sumi bowed.

"Any other business?"

When there was no reply, Radhya dismissed them. She returned to the window. The selifla sent puzzlement around the bond, but from Radhya there was just blackness, only a frozen silent wall. Will rose and went to her. He put his hands on her shoulders.

"I know you loved Geo very much, but we love you, and we need you. Won't you let us help you?"

Radhya shook him off and turned away with a weary sigh.

"You don't understand. Geo was my father, my real father. The Great Lord Kirbyson, my supposed father, contributed only the genes that made me. I was an embarrassment to him. How many Lords have three children, two is a rarity, and three is unheard of. Geo fed my soul, made me grow, learn, and work. He made me a real person, and I owed him so much. I am nothing without him."

Walking over Max said, "I heard him say he was proud of

you. We all lose our fathers, and he was very old. He died the way he wanted to, protecting you."

Radhya's eyes blazed, "You don't understand. None of you understands. I was doing this for him. It was all for Geo. You wouldn't even be here except for him. He picked my co-conspirators for me. He picked you."

She dashed from the room, tears streaming from her eyes. Max tried to follow, but Padr restrained him.

"Let her go. She's in no mood to hear us."

"But I can't feel her anymore," Max argued, his voice laced with sorrow.

Padr looked at him, eyes pained.

"Come on," he said, "We'll see the Chandrans right now."

The three bodyguards slipped to the den and through the wall. Arming themselves with tazers, they traveled through the mountain passage to the forest. After a quiet trip, they reached the beach. A short way along, a grizzled grey alien waved to them from the woods. Reaching the Chandran, the three men were enfolded by him.

"You have great pain?" came the thought. "We felt you from a great distance. Tell me its source."

"Geo died," Will explained, "and Radhya has shut us out. We can't feel her in the bond."

The Chandran released them in its excess of horror and pulled away.

"Help us, please!" begged Max.

The alien gathered them again.

"You must restore the bond. The recreator is the nexus. Once formed it should never be broken. The recreator will die. All will sicken with great pain, but the nexus will die without the bond. Stay here."

The father released them and vanished behind the trees as the men milled about in confusion. Shortly, the Chandran returned with two others. One was a beautiful golden color, the other a rusty brown. Gesturing for the men to return home, they followed.

Although the aliens had great difficulty climbing the hillside, they managed to keep up. At the tunnel, they bent almost double to fit through. They gazed around curiously in the den, touching and examining the furnishings.

Embracing Will, the brown communicated, "Fetch the recreator here."

Will staggered from the den and trotted up the stairs. Radhya was not in lab one or two. Nor was she in the med lab, exercise room, storage room, or the washroom. He took a deep breath and returned to her room. He tapped on the door. When there was no answer, he opened the door and entered. He searched everywhere among the flowers and animals, but she was nowhere. He checked the dressing room and shower suits. Radhya was not there. Puzzled, Will tried to reach her through the bond. There were no feelings from Radhya, only Max and Padr patiently waiting, working to stave off waves of fear.

Will trotted downstairs checking the second floor, but she was not there. On the first floor, he surveyed the kitchen, parlor, Geo's den, slave's quarters, the washrooms, and the dining room which were likewise empty. Rory's office contained only Rory.

Returning upstairs he opened Max's door. Radhya was not there. The next room was Padr's, and Radhya was curled in a fetal position on the floor. Will entered and shook her. She moaned.

"I don't feel very good," she whispered.

"It's the bond. You've shut it down, and it's making you sick," Will replied.

He helped her up, but could barely walk. He tried to pick her up, but she refused. She tried to go to the med lab, but Will steered her down the stairs. Trembling and shaking, she stumbled several times descending. Will, half carrying her, brought her downstairs to the den.

Radhya gasped at the sight of the Chandrans. She staggered

and would have fallen but for Max's steadying hand. Will urged her to lie down on the carpet, which she did with Padr and Max on either side. Will sit at her head, half supporting her body. The Chandrans encircled them, touching them all.

"You must never close down the bond," floated the thought. "The bond is your life and your strength. You are no longer four, but one in four bodies. You must keep your strength flowing one to the other. That way it increases and your life increases. You gain many years with the bond. Radhya, recreator, you are the nexus, open your mind and let your bond mates in. They have each other. You are alone; if you do not, you will die."

"I can't!" wailed Radhya.

"You must," came the thought.

Radhya relaxed every muscle in her body, slowly, determinedly. She tried to call the electric blue light, but the dark was an impenetrable barrier. She struggled with her mind until sweat was pouring off her. She quit trying and felt herself start to sink into the black, dying.

"Radhya no. Try Radhya, come on."

She heard the voices faintly, from a great distance.

"We're losing her. Radhya stay with me, don't leave me."

"Is this what Geo felt?" she wondered.

"NO!" A loud yell penetrated to her.

"That's what I said when Geo died," she thought.

She managed to crack her eyes open a little. Padr's face was next to hers, panic in his eyes, and fear in every line.

"No, fight Radhya. I love you. Let me go instead of you. I've only made a mess of my life. Will and Max need you. Don't leave us alone."

"Padr's joined completely with the other two," she thought wonderingly. "The original rebel is part of the group, but he's wrong. My life is just as ruined as his ever was."

She knew their lives depended on her. She performed the mental equivalent of a strip, laying every part of her mind bare to her companions, without the strength to help herself, yet wanting to survive. The emerald arrowed in immediately, cradling her consciousness tenderly. The gold and violet right after, pouring strength and healing into her. The evil black still threatened, rising to conquer her.

"It's a volcano!" came the green thought.

"No," corrected the violet, "It's a boil, full of pus and infection."

The three colors sharpened into a lancet, piercing the black and red throbbing cancer that threatened Radhya. The pain burst over them, an outrushing tide of pure poison. Her deepest, most painful memories invaded their minds.

Radhya was a teenager and Geo a younger, more vigorous man. He was striding back and forth in a darkly paneled room. They heard his voice.

"No! I'm not letting you go."

Radhya replied, "I am going. You are not going to stop me."

"Radhya, be reasonable, you don't know the kind of men you are dealing with."

"I know they poisoned my Grandfather. I know they want to kill me. I know I will get revenge."

Geo continued, "It is a very bad idea, and I can't let you go into a situation that is that obviously dangerous. Your confidence is too high compared to your skill at survival."

"Geo, I am the master here, and you are the slave. I am going to get the information to bring these murderers down to slave status. I owe Grandpa that."

"Your Grandfather would not want you to jeopardize yourself to get revenge for him. You know that. I can't let you go."

"Geo, I beat the university aristocrats, didn't I?"

"Yes, little darlin', you did. Nevertheless, they were men and women with at least a few morals left. You have no idea of depravity of the men you want to get involved with now. They would dearly love to torture you and kill you very, very slowly. You can't do this."

"I can and I will." Radhya strode to the door.

Geo seized her by the arms. "I can't let you do this."

She tapped some codes into her wrist comp. Geo arched backward as a horrific scream burst from his throat. He fell to the floor in convulsions. Radhya stood looking down at him.

"I'm going," she said.

The shame in the memory took their breath away, curdling in their guts and tensing all muscles into a painful rictus. They struggled to pull air into their starving lungs, but the memory continued.

Radhya and a young Rory were in a tiny two-man ship about to land on a small dark planet. The craft was slipping planetward with skill and stealth. Landing behind a large snow covered hill, Rory cloaked the ship.

"Stay here," Radhya commanded. "I'll be back as soon as I gather the information. Have the ship ready to lift the second I get back."

Rory nodded as she slipped a hood over her head and popped the canopy. She was over the side and struggling up the hill in the blink of an eye. On the other side, a squat transport ship steamed in the freezing air. Radhya crouched on the hillside pointing a holomera at the scene as dozens of bewildered, naked people disembarked in the chill. One of the women, a tall, elegant brunette with a perfect oval face, fought with the guards. They tazed her into unconsciousness, then kicked her over the side of the gangplank. Radhya heard the crack of the woman's head hit the frozen ground from her perch on the hill. The woman lay moaning in the snow. Large hovers drove up, and the new slaves were herded into the back. The vehicles were open, so the cold was not relieved for the victims.

Keeping low, Radhya snuck around the ship and jogged after the retreating vehicle. A new one approached, and she buried herself in the snow. After it passed, she rose and contin-ued. A long, low, wide building hove up out of the blowing snow. It was enormous, but Radhya circled it, finding no entrance, except the one that the slaves were using. She waited until the door was clear, and then tried to slink inside.

"I was wondering when you were going to come in and join us," a voice spoke behind her. "If you wanted a tour, you should just have asked, Lady Kirbyson."

Radhya whirled. Lord Reman stood behind her, dressed in scarlet red, like blood to her eyes. He grabbed her arm and twisted up behind her back. He marched her into the room where dozens of slaves were being fitted with collars.

"Is this what you wanted to see? Or maybe you wanted a closer look."

Reman tore away her clothes, leaving her as naked as the slaves around them.

"Not bad. Not bad at all. Maybe we can have a little fun, after your re-education." He fondled her, and she came near to throwing up.

"You know former Lady Jamison didn't make it. I could just brand you with her number and sell you in her place. It would be very easy, and I already have a sale for her. Lord Jabin is always especially interested in ex-royals."

Lord Reman fitted a collar around her neck. "Barone would kill me if he knew you were here, so we will have to keep it quiet, but just to get you started, this is what the slave collar discipline is like."

Reman hit some buttons and pain shot through Radhya. Even the memory of that pain was heart stopping. The Chandrans added strength to the humans and encouraged them to continue.

The memory continued, Radhya lay on the wooden floor in a pool of her own vomit. Others lay around her, in their sickness, or having convulsions. Cries and moans rose about them. Reman was droning on and on about the horrors in store for her. From somewhere Radhya summoned the strength, rose from the floor and slapped him across the face. He grabbed her by the hair and pulled her head back. His hand was around her throat.

Another red-clad figure came into the room.

"Is there trouble Chet?"

"Noel? I, uh, need to discipline this slave. It's a little aggressive."

Lord Barone came around and looked at Radhya. "Where is the brand?"

"I'm not a slave. I'm Lady Kirbyson, and this filth has put a collar on me," she spat.

Lord Barone's eyes widened. "Kirbyson? What are you doing on my planet? I don't remember inviting you. Besides, young royals should always travel with bodyguards, big ones with wide shoulders and lots of muscle."

Radhya flushed scarlet. "I was spying, trying to discover who killed my grandfather."

She raised her chin in bravado.

"Noel, Lady Jamison suffered a fall from the ramp and died. This one could replace her," said Reman with a sly smile. "Jabin likes them young and pretty."

Barone nodded, his eyes roving up and down her naked body. "I wouldn't mind her myself. Let me check her connections before I make a decision." He marched from the room.

Lord Reman tied her wrists in front of her and fastened her to a stanchion on the floor. With a wink and a smirk, he left the room. Radhya stared at the writhing humanity on the floor, their smells and cries of pain soon to be her own and knew shame to the deepest core of her soul.

The door blew in with a tremendous crash. Geo stood there, three other men in familiar livery behind him. The back door swung open, and Reman dashed in followed by a dozen grey-clad guards. The Lord stood at the back directing his men against Radhya's rescuers. Geo fought like a maniac, throwing bodies left and right. He shrugged off the tazers and slapped the projectile weapons from the hands of the enemy before they could aim them. Reaching Radhya's side, he pulled a huge knife from his belt and slashed the bonds holding her.

He dashed across the room and grabbed Reman before he could escape to the back. Crushing his throat, he made him release the collar around Radhya's neck, and then he threw him to the floor like garbage.

Lord Barone entered the room caring a tank on his back with a long nozzle protruding from it.

"What are you doing to my training facility?" he demanded.

"I am retrieving, my Lady," snapped Geo.

A long tongue of flame shot out of the tube Barone carried.

"And I am protecting my property," snarled Barone.

"Run Radhya," yelled Geo.

He placed himself between Barone and Radhya. She dashed for the door. The three other slaves surrounded her and brought her to a waiting spaceship not far from the building. Radhya paused.

"Geo," she cried.

Rory raced down the ramp. "I'll get him. "

Two men returned with Rory. Radhya boarded the ship and sealed the doors. Throwing on a garment, she watched in anxious suspense.

Rory staggered through the snow, Geo in a fireman's carry over his shoulder, wind whipped stinging particles into his eyes. Radhya opened the door. He dumped Geo on the metal grating and leapt for the cockpit. The small ship lifted without waiting for the passengers to buckle in.

Radhya stared at Geo. He lay unmoving, barely breathing. From the knees down, his legs were gone. Smoking black stumps were all that was left of his thighs, and scorch marks criss-crossed the rest of his body. His eyes slitted open despite the pain. Radhya fell to her knees beside him.

"Are you okay? Did they hurt you?" he croaked.

"They put a slave collar on me and activated it. That's all they had time to do. Then you came."

"I'm sorry you were hurt."

Geo closed his eyes.

Radhya's shame rose and overwhelmed them. Padr accepted, swallowing all the recriminations, matching them with the feelings from his own past. The horror at her own actions still pulled her from life. Padr, Max, and Will poured love at her. Radhya struggled.

A faint blue spark kindled in her consciousness. She breathed upon it with her spirit. She superimposed their faces on the spark. It grew to a small flickering flame. A shuddering breath rushed into her dying body.

"Come on darling, you can do it," entreated Padr.

She could feel Will pounding on her chest, and her face was wet with Max's tears.

"Max should never cry," she thought. "His soul should see only beauty."

Clinging tenaciously to the thought of helping Max, Will, and Padr, she rose on the blue flame. The black was thick and heavy. She pounded on it from within. Their colors pummeled it from without. It cracked. Through the fractures, she could see the gold, green and violet. Her soul yearned as never before, and the dark gave way before it. The colors merged in a glorious kaleidoscope, healing, purging, cleaning, twirling around the bond mates, affirming and cementing the love. The rainbow colors swirled in an ecstasy of sharing. They settled exhausted into themselves. Padr held Radhya close.

The Chandrans surrounded them again. "We are sorry you did not understand, to isolate is death."

"Why weren't the men affected?" asked Radhya lying contented in Padr's arms.

"The fathers have the Talrie, the brotherhood of males. It is as strong as the Seliflarie, the bonding of genders. They did not shut themselves in, you did, you are the nexus, and therefore you were the one to suffer the most. They felt pain as well."

"Is there more we should know about the bonding?" she asked.

"Your lives will be long, be without disease, unless you neglect the bond. You neglected the bond. There is a way to have emotions to yourself. We show you. "

The Chandrans did something to each of the humans' brains. The colors of the selifla dimmed. A twist in the brain and they were back to full brilliance.

"If there arises a need for separateness that is how to obtain it. If there is a need for far voyaging apart, use the Kenrie we just showed you. But not for too long. The more you join, the better will your life be. The Mokdor is a way to see with another selifla's eyes."

Another part of the brain was accessed. Suddenly Radhya found herself staring down at her body. An eye blink and the perspective shifted, herself, Padr and Will. Again, this time she could see Max, Will, and herself. She did not want to leave Padr's mind. A gentle push and she was home in her own skull. Then the men each tried it. She could feel each presence as they shared her mind and looked with her eyes. Each returned home.

"Mokdor is useful, but again keep the time short. The body deteriorates without the mind."

"Thank you, thank you for coming here. I know how hard daylight is for you, and how difficult it is to leave your mother," Radhya uttered to the Chandrans.

"She insisted we try to save you. If the bonding failed, there would be no more we could do for your species. Now we go."

The Chandrans vanished into the hidden passage as Radhya gazed at the three men who again, had saved her life.

"I don't know what to say," she whispered.

Love and affection coursed down the bond.

"We're relieved to have you back. Do you know I felt worse at the thought of losing you than when my son and Debra died?" asked Padr.

"Yes I did know," said Radhya softly. "The same way I know

the pain of Max's father's death and his pony being sold, and I know how Will fears to be abandoned again after his mother died when he was seven. I feel all your pain, but it amounts to nothing next to your love and your acceptance of my pain. We heal each other. I must remember that."

As they were hugging, a tapping came at the door.

"Milady, are you there?" came an anxious voice.

Max rose and opened the door. Rory was fidgeting in the doorway. He looked at them curiously.

"Milady, Lord Grant wishes to speak to you, in the office."

Radhya rose gracefully. She shook her ebony hair into place and rearranged the folds of her robe. Then she strode across the dining room to Rory's office. At her nod, Rory put through the call.

"Yes, Lady Kirbyson, quite a wait you gave me," huffed Lord Grant.

"Forgive me, Lord Grant, I was elsewhere, and my comm was off. I apologize."

"Yes, of course, accepted," he continued. "Are you feeling better after the altercation?"

"Yes milord, very well. Thank you for asking," Radhya smiled broadly at the old man.

"Ah, good. That being the case, as chairman of the Status Review Location Selection Committee, I have the pleasure to inform you that your planet, Pleasant, has been selected to host the status review in exactly sixty-three days."

"Thank you, milord Grant. Thank you more than I can express," beamed Radhya.

"Quite all right my dear. Frankly, that last planet was a drag; dark, dreary and fishing was the only occupation for a gentleman. See you in two months."

The old man winked and signed off. Radhya stood in silence for a moment. She looked at Rory and grinned broadly.

"Tell everyone we're green for the status review. Plan countdown started at sixty-six. Go."

Chapter 24

Having heard of Radhya's pleasure world, many aristocrats arrived a week or more early to enjoy the many activities. Lady Clarke handily won the endurance race scheduled the week before the review, with Lady Simms a close second. Radhya herself placed fortieth in a field of one hundred.

Two days before the review, Princess Felina arrived with her father, mother and Prince Phlip. Prince Phlip was very fair skinned with golden blonde hair and light blue eyes with a downward slant. Two meters tall and slender, with long legs, long thin fingers, and toes, his face was not the usual aristocratic oval but round and childish looking. He had a short upturned nose, and full pouty lips, the exact image of his father but younger. King Smon added silver to the gold of his hair, while Queen Chas proved to be a platinum blonde with a kind, aging face. Smile lines bracketed her violet eyes, and her slender lips were hidden by the wrinkles wreathing her mouth. She was buxom and short, reaching to the king's shoulder. Prince Phlip and Padr disappeared together.

Felina immediately began decorating for Radhya's contract

day to Lord Barone. A decorated cake three meters high, thick with flowers, ribbons, birds, and stars was her centerpiece. Since Radhya's house color was forest green and Noel's red, it made a garish, highly visible clash. Felina was in her element decorating the banquet room and ballroom in green, red and white. Red flowers burgeoned on every table, and green ivy garlanded every door and opening. All the place settings were changed to red and green, on snowy cloths. Even the chairs wore verdant dresses with red ribbons.

Radhya tried to stay out of her way as much as possible, but finally, Felina cornered her.

"Radhya, my dear bride, I have been looking everywhere for you. I have a gift," cooed Felina.

She handed Radhya a box. Opening it, Radhya saw two slender gold bracelets, a wire fine golden hair band, and a golden choker the width of her little finger.

"Thank you, princess, a lovely gift but...."

"Radhya, put it on, right now," giggled the Princess.

Radhya donned the jewelry, one bracelet to each wrist as she was instructed, the choker and the hair band. Felina produced a tiny jeweled box and hit a green button. A holo dress flowed into being around Radhya. It billowed up her arms in full sleeves to the choker and clung to her body to the waist where it flared into a bell with a two-meter train behind. The hair band flowered into a sparkling headpiece with a long veil reaching to the floor. It was glistening white with rainbow shadows drifting through it, like a soap bubble.

"Felina, I am speechless. It is truly magnificent. I cannot accept such an extravagant gift."

"Oh poo, of course, you can. Besides, it's from Noel, not just me."

Felina pressed another button, and the dress disappeared. Radhya tried to remove the jewelry but it sealed itself around her neck as firmly as a slave's collar.

Felina produced a miniature key from the little box. She giggled.

"I'm going to give this to Noel. He'll remove it on your contract night. Oh, I need to warn you, he's moved the ceremony up to the third night, right after final business. I hope that will be all right."

A shadow of worry darkened the princess's face, and the effort to dismiss the concern caused a struggle with her lips. She smiled, and with a final giggle, the princess departed with the key. Radhya headed for Dave immediately.

"Check me out, I can't get this off, and it's from Barone. He's liable to blow my head off," Radhya told him.

Dave took her to the security room and ran her through the scanners, twice.

"No trace of explosives," Dave said. "It appears to be a lot of nano electrical equipment. Any idea as to what is its intended function?"

"It's supposed to be a contracting dress," Radhya snapped.

"Yes, I can see that it could be. There are a number of miniature holocams and quite a few unusual electrical circuits. It even has a minicomp."

"It had something like soap bubbles floating over the surface of it."

"Well, that would explain those connections. You might want to check this out with Max. He's our best engineer, but as far as I can tell, you're clean."

"Thanks, Dave," muttered Radhya grabbing the printout as she hurried from the room. Business pulled her from her straight line to Max and distracted her from the jewelry.

On the day of the review, Radhya was first in line; handing her documents to the proctors, who had their tables set up in the beautiful foyer of the visitor's center. She stepped back and watched the other aristocrats present their documents. Some were proud, strutting like pheasants; looking to see who noticed them; talking in loud voices.

Others were furtive, eyes downcast and timid; avoiding contact as much as possible. Radhya noticed Lord Barone in the latter category.

She returned to her room for breakfast to be greeted by Kung and Singha. Radhya had just sold the last of Singha's latest batch of kits the day before, and the big cat was heartbroken.

"Max, I want you to take Singha, leashed, everywhere with us, and Padr you take Kung, he likes you best. Next to me of course. I want all of you to stay close. There are usually more assassination attempts at these reviews than anywhere else," Radhya informed them.

"No wonder, when you have so many spoiled children in one place," retorted Will.

"Now, now," chided Radhya, "they are supposed to be your betters. Not that even one of them is fit to iron your tunic, or would know how, but they think they are your betters."

They were laughing as Aninya bustled into the room.

"I thought you had your hands full with all the banquet preparations?" Radhya queried.

"I came to help you dress milady."

"I'm sorry Aninya; I plan on my usual basic black robes for the next three days."

"But surely the dancing and all tonight and tomorrow, you can't show up in that."

Radhya sighed, "I don't know why not. I don't like dressing up. However, I suppose you're right. I want plain and simple, and only for the evening banquet and dancing. If someone is going to kill me, I want to be comfortable. Come back if you have time before the banquet starts."

"Yes, milady."

Aninya left as Radhya gathered up her guards, two and four footed, and left to do her duty socializing.

On day two, the grind was not as difficult. Many of the aristocracy, having presented their documents and fulfilled the required hobnobbing, were off to other locations enjoying their favorite activities. Dave reported only one attempted murder, and that appeared to have been a violent disagreement over a race finish. He had quietly begun moving his trained body-guards into the visitors' center a few at a time.

The third and final day dawned misty and still. The long, nerve-racking awarding ceremony began in the ballroom at nine in the morning. The proctors on the platform called each member of the aristocracy, starting with the lowest status, those who had the highest number. They worked their way up in status, counting down the numbers. Each royal was given a medallion with their status for the next ten years, and their wrist comp was adjusted. Then he or she returned to their seat, and the next royal was called up for the tedious and time-consuming activity. The faces of the recipients mirrored both pleasure and delight if they had risen, or shame and disgust for those going down in rank.

Radhya was startled when Lord Barone was called in the six hundreds. He had slipped over two hundred points from his previous place ten years ago. He looked furious, but she felt a shaft of triumph as she waited her turn. She waited anxiously through the five hundreds and four hundreds. When the two hundreds were finished, she was about to inquire if she had been forgotten or had put her information in too early and lost it. Padr reminded her of how much proctors like to be told they were wrong, so she sat back down in the restless sea of humanity.

The withered old woman on the platform finally called out, "Status 187: Lady Radhya Kirbyson."

Stunned, Radhya sat there, and the men prodded her to her feet. They escorted her to the base of the stage. She had to walk from there herself; only royals were allowed on the platform that day. She solemnly accepted her medallion and had her comp adjusted. With all the dignity she could muster, she returned to her guards, and went grinning to her seat.

"Amazing," whispered Will. "No one ever moved so far so fast."

"You did it. You deserve it," whispered Max.

Clasping her arm, Padr murmured, "You are an astonishing woman."

The ceremony ended with Princess Felina, Prince Phlip, Queen Chas and King Smon. The proctors left the stage and Lord Grant, the mediator, called any other business. Radhya shot to her feet pulse pounding.

"We recognize Lady Krin of Jabin's World," Lord Grant announced.

The delicate, red-haired Krin made her way forward to the platform. Radhya sank to her chair with a sick feeling in the pit of her stomach.

"I am gratified," began the tiny beauty, "to supervise the contracting this day, of my very good friend, Lord Barone, to a woman who had the most unbelievable rise in status we have ever seen in the aristocracy, Lady Kirbyson. Please, both of you come on up here."

Someone must have pushed the dress button, for suddenly Radhya was clothed in the holo gown. Fury pounded through every vein in her body. She stormed to the stage and fairly flew up the stairs. The bodyguards had to scramble to follow.

"Lady Krin, I had a contract to contract, but only if my status did not exceed his. I believe I now exceed him by over five hundred points."

Radhya's voice was picked up by the omni mikes on stage and broadcast to the entire room. The aristocrats tittered and murmured among themselves as Lord Barone slithered up beside her.

Noel held out his document for inspection. The proctors returned to the stage to inspect the record. The clause Radhya had insisted on was no longer there. "I have witnesses who saw the missing part and who heard from me that I would not sign without the status rider being present."

"It is not here now. And you will contract with me or lose all status and be reduced to slavery. A shame since you moved so far up the ranks," Barone sneered at her, all pretense of love forgotten.

"I will never contract with you. I will die first. You told me with your own mouth this contract was only to get my possessions and patents. I personally hate the sight of you."

"You will contract with me," Barone stated.

The royals in the audience were watching the altercation with rapt attention.

Nerves worn raw by the tension of the review and now abraded further by this odious Lord, Radhya screamed at the man in red, "I would rather be dead."

"I can arrange that," he snapped back.

Lord Barone gestured to the crowd of fascinated aristocrats. Jabin stood and aimed a device at the stage causing the holo dress to explode into a pyrotechnic lightening display. Radhya toppled backward. An ululating scream tore from her throat. Pinwheeling from the stage to the dance floor, her body arched into a convulsion as the horrified aristocrats retreated from her in revulsion.

Dave plowed through the fleeing crowds. Padr, Will, and Max stood at her side.

"Don't touch her!" yelled Max's arms spread wide, "you'll be caught in the electrical field too."

"She's dying!" shouted Will.

Padr grasped both of them by the shoulders.

"The bond," he insisted.

They joined in pouring strength and healing into Radhya's convulsing body. Dave reached her. He grabbed the ring about her throat. He let go with an epithet. Glancing at the blisters on his hand, he seized it again. Muscles bulging he tore the metal from her throat. The sparks lessened. He ripped the hair band away. His hands were scorching and blackening, the odor of burning flesh filled the ballroom. He extracted one wrist from its metal circle. His mangled hands could barely function, but he used what remained of his hands and his great strength and severed the final piece of metal.

Radhya lay panting on the floor. Her three guards collapsed back against the platform and slid slowly to the floor, exhausted. Kung and Singha, lips pulled back, stood guard over Radhya's prone body. Dave curled into a fetal position; the smoking charred stumps of his hands held gingerly before his chest. Soft moans of pain escaped his tightly clamped lips.

Lord Barone leapt lightly from the platform as Lord Jabin waddled his way through the stunned crowds to stand beside him.

"I claim Lady Kirbyson's lands and estates and assets by reason of the contract to contract as yet unfulfilled," Lord Barone spoke in a ringing voice, but the omni mike could not pick up his voice from the floor.

"I deny your right," Radhya hurled back. "I give complaint against you for attempted murder; mutilation and pain caused to my bodyguards and myself!"

She rose from the floor like a resurrection from the burning depths of hell, unsinged, her black robes falling in charred flakes from her body. Padr struggled weakly forward. He removed his tunic and draped it around her naked body. Her grey eyes sent a message into his blue ones, reinforced by the wash of gratitude down the bond. Jabin, gone shock white, backed against the stage, only the solid structure keeping him on his feet. Murmurs and exclamations rose from the crowd. Many pointed or moved closer to hear the action.

"Your brain at least must be fried. There is no way a human body can endure current like that," stated Noel unbelievingly.

"I wasn't alone. Distribute the current among four bodies and each individual carries only one-quarter of the load," she told him.

Turning to the crowd, she spoke, "I had a grand speech prepared, all about our declining birth rates, birth defects and the problems of our society. I think you can see by this what our moral standards have led us to. We are a bunch of selfish, spoiled, adult children. We use others as slaves. I feel this is morally wrong, but, further, we mistreat them when they are in that position. The only way we can dig ourselves from the morass of moral decay we are all in, is to make positive changes to our institutions, starting with that of slavery. I propose a bill of rights for slaves, requiring they be given sufficient food, clothing, and shelter. That it be illegal to discard or kill them when they become ill or old. That it be illegal to sell children away from their parents before the age of sixteen years. That they have the right to decent medical care. It needs to be illegal to torture people for amusement. I demand these rights as the first step to saving our society."

Rory, in his secret chamber, set the huge, hidden incarceration machine into action. The windows on the ocean darkened as the shield rose over them. Ventilators kicked in as the building sealed itself. The royals began to murmur and call out inquiries. Radhya ignored them for the minute. She looked at Jabin. There was a rictus of fear on his face as he tried moving sideways to avoid her. Radhya looked at Singha crouching on the floor beside her. She moved a little finger and indicated Jabin.

Singha crept around one side. Kung took the other. A thin warbling scream trembled from Jabin's throat. He attempted to run; exactly the wrong strategy. He made two steps before Kung hamstrung him. Singha leapt on his back, biting his neck. The blood fountained. She put a muscular paw around his throat and then she efficiently broke his neck.

"You all saw him push the button to kill me. Justice is done. Any complaint?" demanded Radhya.

Some of the royals were gathering their lynxcats, and others were talking to their bodyguards. The soft voices had grown to loud complaints. Radhya pointed to the walls, now lined with her trained guards, all armed with tazers, chemical sprays, billy sticks and less obvious weapons.

"What is going on here?"

"You killed Jabin; he deserved it, but let us go!"

"What are you going to do with us?"

"Why are we being held here?"

"Let us go!"

The crowd was becoming unruly, restive, and growing angry. Radhya gestured to Rory. A spray hissed down from the ceiling. The royals pushed and shoved to get away, but there was no longer any exit. Their bodyguards inhaled the vapor, which reacted with the chemicals from the food they had eaten and slowly slumped to the floor, fast asleep. Most of the aristocrats sat down on their chairs. Radhya climbed up to the platform where the mikes could distribute her voice to the entire audience.

As she gazed over the people, her eyes lit on a group at the front, her brother and Lady Kemmira with Lord Jambawe, Lady Simms and Lady Clarke. They were smiling and gesturing for her to continue. Heartened Radhya did so.

"For your information, I intend to hold you all hostages until these matters are resolved to my satisfaction," Radhya spoke loudly to the stunned people.

She jumped off the platform and went to Dave. Will was finished giving him first aid and painkillers. Radhya returned strength down the bond to all her men. Working together, they hauled Dave through the now quiet crowd, to the lift, taking him to Radhya's room. Will treated him with one of Radhya's special preparations and they watched as new skin covered the raw flesh of his stumps. Dave gazed despondently at where his hands used to be. Radhya put her hands on his shoulders and looked into his eyes.

"Milady," he began with tears in his voice.

"Don't worry Dave. I don't let a slave suffer for saving me, and you did. Our strength was almost exhausted. You saved everything."

She took a green paste from the bathroom. Donning gloves, she smeared it everywhere Dave had damage.

"This is going to itch like mad, but you mustn't touch or scratch," she told him.

"Unbelievable!" exclaimed Will as within minutes new fingers began to grow.

"It isn't an alteration of the genetic code," explained Radhya. "It merely stimulates the RNA to cause the flesh and bone to regrow, at an accelerated rate. You'll be absolutely starving very soon, so I'll send Jemelina up to spoon feed you. You can't touch anything until it's finished."

Radhya hugged each of her companions in turn. Then she quietly retired to the bathroom. A few hours later, dressed in a sea green gown, and accompanied by her bodyguards, she rejoined the churning caldron of aristocrats.

Her guards had circulated among the people and removed the sleeping bodyguards. They were laid out in a separate, locked room. The royals were once again talking themselves into a state of agitation.

The evening meal was simple; soup, bread, and fruit. The royals, for the most part, ate in stunned silence or sullen anger. The room was dark and enclosed. A few complained to their closest neighbors in hushed tones. Most of them kept glancing at Lady Death seated at the head table with the royal family. The king, queen, and prince were silent. Princess Felina bubbled on, happier than Radhya had ever seen her. Padr, Max, and Will sat at the table with them causing curious looks.

When the brief meal was over, Radhya led the way to the ballroom where she ascended the stage. Gradually the floor filled with aristocrats, a restless sea of faces.

Glancing behind her at her bond mates she began, "First, don't try to attack me with your lynxcats. Singha is their mother, and I am hers. I am sure you all know how firmly bonded these little darlings become." Radhya stroked Singha's head at her knee. "There is not one here who will disobey their mother." A few royals checked sheepishly around. "You had a simple meal. To a slave, a meal like that would be pure luxury. I spoke earlier about the bill of rights for slaves. I had circulated a rough draft copy asking for any suggestions. The only ones I received were all along the lines of burn it, or put it in a spot I won't mention. That being the case, I am going to ask the proctors to take a count now of in favor and opposed."

Radhya seated herself on a chair on the platform, between Will and Padr. She grasped Padr's hand and held on tightly. The proctors passed among the peers recording votes. In a surprisingly short time, the eldest brought Radhya a strip of paper, then left. She rose and went to the front.

"Apparently, you people don't get it. We have 42% for and 51% against, and 6% have no opinion," Taking a breath Radhya continued. "Empathy was once defined as your pain in my heart. It seems an emotion rarely practiced in this day and age. Many of you regard slaves as nonhuman, no more endowed with life than the robe you wear or a table you eat from. Empathy seems to be forgotten. Yet all of you complain at a simple meal, resent being enclosed, unable to go where you want, when you want. This metal enclosing us is special. There is no way to break in or out. Even an attack from space would destroy all of you in here before it would melt or cut the metal. So listen well to me, I have something important to get across to you. I was helped to form empathic bonds with three of my slaves. That bond helped me to survive the attack you witnessed earlier today. It ensures excellent health for my selifla and myself. We will live, barring murder and accident, about three hundred and fifty years. We never have to feel alone again. Don't you think empathy deserves a second look? So, for your edification, I am going to introduce the Chandran fathers. They are going to give you a small, very small taste of empathy."

A little servant's side door opened at her command. The lights dimmed. Ducking under the low opening, twenty-five Chandran fathers entered the ballroom. The crowds drew back in fear, gazing at the strangers with widened eyes as the aliens spread through the room. Behind them limped and tottered twenty-five, much-abused slaves Stane had flown in that morning from Jabin's amusement pits. One slave went with each Chandran. The slaves were pitiable wretches, starving, lame, covered with sores and fresh lash marks. The Chandrans enfolded an aristocrat in their arms along with one of the slaves.

Radhya retreated to her chair again as the fathers worked their way through the room. Squirming through the crowd, many royals tried to avoid the aliens. Those they took first. Others fought initially, but the superior strength prevailed. Some were released quickly; others took a long time. Radhya fell asleep, her head pillowed on Padr's shoulder. Will and Max, Kung and Singha kept watch. Well into the night, Will shook her gently.

"This part's over. Good luck," he whispered.

Radhya twisted her stiff neck and made her way to the front of the platform. She looked over the silent crowd of pampered people. Without exception, every face showed signs of shock. Some of them seemed barely able to stand upright.

"The proctors will pass and take a second vote," Radhya croaked.

Radhya returned to her seat. This vote was even swifter than the last. Radhya looked at the strip of paper. Her brows rose.

"We have among us, one dissenter. The rest, who now know, however briefly, what it is like to be a slave, feel the bill of rights should pass. I invite our dissenter, as per our constitution, to come forward and present his case."

Lord Barone rose to his feet and strode to the platform.

"I don't care for trickery," he exclaimed. Radhya gagged at his effrontery. "This is trickery; this meddling in our minds can't be real. It's a trick this evil woman, whom we all call Lady Death, set up so she can have her slaves in her bed. She's a slut, and you are all fools to listen to her. If we give rights to our slaves, think what it will cost. Do you really want all that extra expense? Think of your comfort, think of yourself. She has kidnapped us. Can you trust someone like that?"

Barone turned and sneered at Radhya, then walked to her chair and sat down.

"I assure you what you felt was not a trick. Ask yourself if thoughts like that ever existed anywhere within your mind? If the answer is no, then they must come from outside yourself. As for trickery, I would think a man planning to assassinate the woman he claims to love, and arranges to contract with, would be the epitome of trickery. As for comfort, better fed, clothed, healthier slaves give you a better return for you money than sick, weak ones."

"Don't trust that bitch!"

Four proctors closed in on Barone.

"We wanted to see where this whole kidnapping was headed," they told Radhya. "If violence were used, you would be liable. The vote was fairly conducted. The education was not illegal. However, we judge for your complaint against Lord Noel Barone, status 688, in that he did attempt to defraud you of property, patents, and wealth, in that he attempted to force you to uphold an illegal contract to contract, in that he used coercive force and threat to get the original contract to contract, in that he did attempt murder, in that he defrauded Lady Petra Kirbyson, deceased, of her holdings, and had her reduced illegally to a slave, who met her death as a result of said slavery. Barone, you are guilty and are henceforth reduced to the rank of a slave yourself. All remaining property and patents including the ones stolen from the late Lady Kirbyson are awarded to her sister Lady Radhya Kirbyson. As you are no longer a member of the aristocracy, the vote is unanimous. The bill of rights for slaves is hereby law. Break it at your peril."

The proctors led a screaming and ranting Barone away. The crowds were silent for a moment, then broke into loud cheering, backslapping, and congratulations. Lady Felina ascended the platform, and the crowd quieted.

"I am so proud," began the princess, "to call my friend this day, Lady Radhya Kirbyson, whose incredible rise in status is exceeded only by her determination to improve our society. She is an inspiration to us all. This lovely woman once asked me for a favor. Today I give that favor. Daddy..."

Princess Felina stepped aside, and her father took her place on the platform.

"My people, I have a great responsibility for governing the Commonwealth. Sometimes one becomes so involved in mundane affairs that the greater issues are overlooked. I originally was doing this to please my daughter; now, however, I feel it is only appropriate to give a reward to the Lady who has opened our eyes to a terrible injustice. To thank you for your work in this area, Lady Radhya Kirbyson I grant full royal pardon to your slaves named Geo, Rory, Padr, Max and Will."

Radhya's jaw dropped, and she gaped like a fish, at a total loss for words. The King produced a key, removing the collars from Max, Will, and Padr. Rory rushed from his hidden room and had his collar removed as well.

"Must I go to your home for this Geo then?" King Smon asked.

"I thank you for such generosity, your highness, but Geo was murdered and therefore is not available to be freed."

"Very well then, since former Lord Barone will not need his status, I confer it upon Padr Kent. You are once again Lord Padr Kent status 688."

The crowd burst into applause, cheering and stamping their feet for Padr, who was grinning fit to split his face. Radhya burst into tears, fell into Padr's arms and buried her face in his tunic.

The Chandrans slipped quietly away to their warm, dim caverns. Radhya had the aristocrats' bodyguards released, and the shield lowered, returning to her rooms laughing and crying at the same time.

Epilogue

William woke Radhya from sleep. The festive celebrations had run long, and she was still tired. Stumbling to the window, she looked longingly at the dark sea. The chime shivered in the air. Turning, she beheld Stephan.

"Well done, little sister. Well done indeed."

"Thank you Steph, but why are you in my room before dawn? I would have loved a few more hours of sleep."

"Since you received all the assets that Petra owned..."

"Now Steph, the proctors did that. I had nothing to do with it."

"No, no you misunderstand. I don't want Petra's stuff. I want what you have."

"Steph, you're not making any sense. I don't have anything you could want."

"I want your bonding thing. You see, I have a friend, actually three friends, and we want what you have with your bodyguards, never to be alone. Please Radhya, I have never asked anything from you. I always threaten and bribe, but I never ask. Now I am asking."

"Why not? We had always hoped that others would wish to join in a bonding, I just never expected you to be one of them. You do realize that you feel each bond mate's emotions, and it's best to stay at least on the same planet."

"Radhya, I want this, and so do the others."

"Very well, meet us downstairs in half an hour. Bring your friends."

Radhya pried herself from the windows dressed. Descending with Padr, Will, and Max, she met Stephan and his seliflacn; Lady Felina, her bodyguard Sen, and Lady Simms were waiting with her brother. All were dressed in plain white robes. Startled, Radhya paused.

"Felina and I have been having an affair for a number of years now," Stephan explained. "That is why I tried so hard to make money, so I could become closer to her in status and maybe become an acceptable contract spouse. It will never happen, so we want to be bonded and with our best friends."

Radhya nodded and led the way in the darkness. It was a long walk down the beach, the waves making a soft susurration beside them. The sun was sending pink and gold feelers into the sky, reflecting off the water in tartan patterns when Radhya slipped through a crack in the rock.

She slid to one side and conversed with one of the fathers a moment, moving with her companions to line the walls of the cave. Four fathers approached the seliflacn. They escorted them to the mother floating in the waist deep water. She enfolded the four of them in her arms and lifted the quartet to her bulky belly. The soft whispering music of the fathers filled the cavern, song of the lameeno, the bonding, then a new song, the lameeno-ka, the bonding of humans. The instruments were strange and totally nonhuman, but beautiful nevertheless.

Time ceased for an interval. Rainbow shadows danced on the walls. Slipping from the mother's embrace, Sen helped Felina, and Stephan helped Simms, and they waded back through the shimmering mini waves to Radhya, Padr, Will, and

Max. Felina hugged Radhya with all her might. Her eyes were shining like blue diamonds. Stephan tried to speak but failed, expressing his emotion with tears in his eyes.

Eight bonded humans returned to the visitor's center, and Radhya retired to her room for a few more hours of sleep. Again, Will woke her far too early.

"This is a habit you are going to have to break," she yawned at him.

Aninya entered crying, "Milady you must prepare."

"No Aninya, I must sleep. The job is done; the slaves have started on the road to freedom."

Aninya smiled at her. Pulling on Radhya's arm, she hauled her mistress out of bed and into the bathroom. When her hair and makeup were done, Aninya brought an elegant white dress to Radhya.

"This is Jemelina's latest creation," she smiled.

"Oh no!" exclaimed Radhya heading out the door.

Aninya seized her by the arm and brought her back. The dress was a perfect fit, clinging softly at the high-necked top and flowing gently to the floor.

"White just isn't my color," commented the Lady, "but at least this time she did the measurements correctly."

Aninya clapped her hands. "Milady you look wonderful."

Together they descended in the lift.

"Where are the guys?" asked Radhya peering around.

"Milady, they will meet you in the foyer," explained Aninya.

Max and Will waited for her and Max handed her a large arrangement of white lilies, moonglows, and orchids.

"You look spectacular," whispered Will, a gigantic grin on his face.

"Milady?" said Max holding out his arm.

As she put her hand on his arm, he led her to the ballroom. The decorations had changed, the red replaced with sky blue. The king waited by the dividing doors in solemn, royal splendor. Max handed Radhya to him. They entered the ballroom, filled with aristocracy from wall to wall, together. On the platform at the front, a lone royal waited, sporting a sky blue uniform. As Radhya paced slowly with the king, a tune from antiquity filled the air. King Smon walked her up the stairs, and handed her to the aristocrat waiting there, Padr. They turned and faced the crowd. Radhya could see the newly bonded four grinning as though their faces would split, Princess Felina clapping her pudgy hands.

King Smon spoke, "My people, I have the great honor today to present for contracting Lady Kirbyson and Lord Kent. May they have as much happiness as they bring to others."

The crowd went wild with applause as a servant in royal livery brought the document. Together, Radhya and Padr pressed their thumbs to the designated spots.

Radhya gazed up at him. The most incredible feelings of pleasure were coming to her down the bond. His deep blue eyes looked longingly into hers as his mouth descended ever so slowly for their first kiss.

Message to the reader

Sincere thank you to all my readers. I hope you enjoyed this book, my first baby as it were. I love to write, but that is all useless without out you. Please search out and enjoy my other creations. It is so much more fun to travel the roads together.

About the Author

Gail Gernat lives in Northern Ontario, in the country with her beloved husband, Norman, a crazy dog and two aging tom cats. While being involved in many projects, this award-winning author enjoys being very close to nature. Gail is also living with lymphoma and these factors inform much of her writing.

LERA'S SORROW - (Darkliete Book 1)

Lera and her cousin have completed their long childhood and their training as healers. Sent to their grandparents back in Madean, they must negotiate the strange new world, and attain their werwinstans. Fate intervenes in the shape of handsome young Ian, very human and very poisonous to the elven. Trying out her independence for the first time in her life, what will Lera decide? Where will she discover her loyalty to lay, with love or with duty?

ILLERA'S DARKLIETE - (Darkliete Book 2)

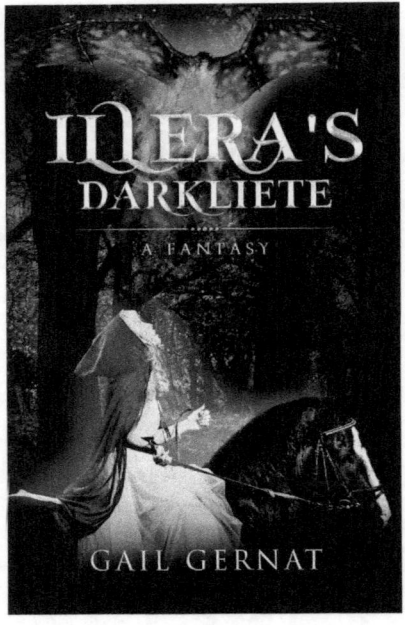

When the messengers from Frain arrive to secure the hand of
Princess Illera for their cruel, selfish heir to the throne, Torul,
she hides. Forced by circumstances and her own father, Illera
and her three companions journey to the cold, dark north.
Fighting against her fate, Illera plunges the quartet into danger.
But when she accedes to the demands of cruel destiny they must
fight against a ravening evil that knows no restraint. Using her
mixed blood heritage, can this innocent child learn and mature
fast enough to control both herself and the forces ripping her
world apart? Can she negotiate the political intrigues and defeat
the hordes of Shul, the pirates of Carnuvon and the hatreds
of Frain?

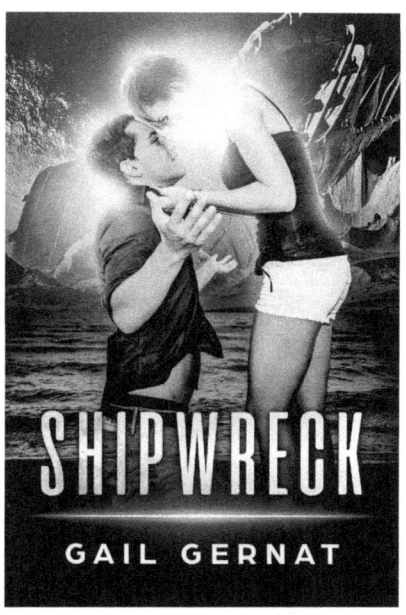

Fiery-haired Bridgit has a temper as hot as her hair, so when the colony transport gets into trouble in deep space she must work with the only other person awake; the man she most despises. Despite their best efforts, the ship crashes on an unknown planet. Bridgit is forced into impossible situations in order to survive and protect the remaining colonists.

www.ingramcontent.com/pod-product-compliance
Lightning Source LLC
Chambersburg PA
CBHW060543180626
46817CB00002B/710